Praise for

The EYE of ZEUS

"With twists, loyalty between friends, and its cast's cleverness, the middle grade fantasy *The Eye of Zeus* hits all the right notes."

—*Foreword Clarion Reviews*

"This charming and brilliant novel is superbly plotted and will win over readers . . . Phoebe's voice is dead on and authentic, as are those of her friends. The author's masterful prose and style serve the story instead of merely taking center stage . . . This author and novel are ready for prime time and the big time."

—*Publishers Weekly*, BookLife Prize Critic's Report

Praise for The Witches of Orkney series:

"An enchanting new book full of magical mischief and adventure, Alane Adams's *The Blue Witch* is guaranteed to please"

—*Foreword Clarion Reviews*

"Bright, brave characters star in this exhilarating tale of magic and mystical creatures."

—*Kirkus Reviews*

for everyone. Fantasy, mythology, a touch of romance, and enough sword fights and battles to appease even the most action-hungry make *Kalifus Rising* a well-rounded, solid choice for those craving a new type of adventure."

—*Foreword Clarion Reviews* FIVE STAR review

"Adams is a master of exposition, never letting it slow the narrative by immersing it in rapid-fire dialogue . . . Indelible characters, both good and evil, and a rescue storyline that refuses to dawdle."

—*Kirkus Reviews*

"This series will do well with the *Percy Jackson* crowd and fans of Norse mythology. **VERDICT:** A great choice for middle school collections."

—*School Library Journal*

"*The Red Sun: Legends of* Orkney by Alane Adams is a book that will take children on a roller coaster ride of adventure and fantasy where whimsical and menacing creatures and witches will enthrall readers."

—Readers' Favorite (5 stars out of 5)

"*The Red Sun* is a roller coaster ride of adventure, Norse mythology, magic and mayhem. Between Sam facing awesome villains in the magical realm of Orkney to teachers turning into lizards, I had the best time doing the voiceover for the audiobook. Don't miss out on this terrific story!"

—Karan Brar, actor on Disney's *Jessie* and *Bunk'd*

Published by SparkPress, a BookSparks imprint,
A division of SparkPoint Studio, LLC
Phoenix, Arizona, USA, 85007
www.gosparkpress.com

Published 2020
Printed in the United States of America
ISBN: 978-1-68463-028-8
ISBN: 978-1-68463-029-5
Library of Congress Control Number: 2019916095

Illustrations by Robin Thompson
Interior design by Tabitha Lahr

THE EYE of ZEUS

LEGENDS of
OLYMPUS: Book 1

The
EYE of ZEUS

ALANE ADAMS

spark press

To My #TeacherTwitter Posse

MT· OLYMPUS

ACHERON
RIVER

DELPHI

 THEBES

NEMEA

 CROMMYON

SWAMPS
OF LERNA

SPARTA

ANCIENT GREECE
LEGENDS of
OLYMPUS

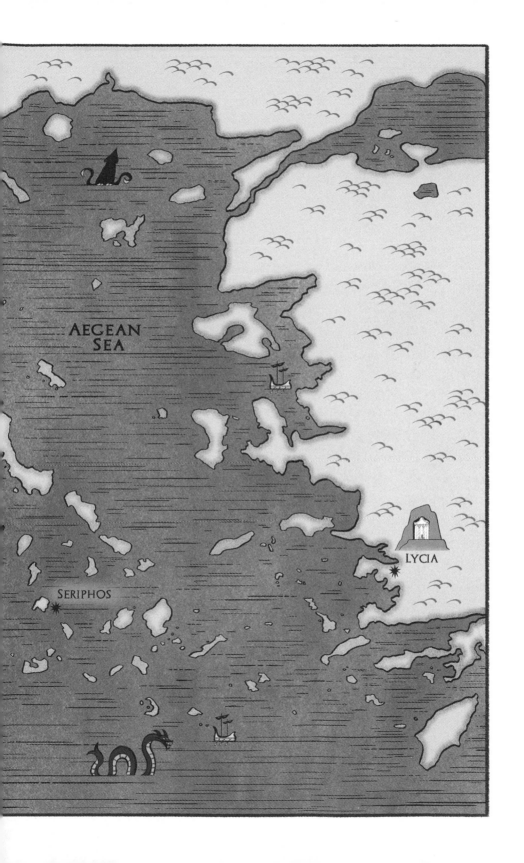

CHAPTER 1

If there's one thing a foster kid's not supposed to do, it's draw attention to herself. I should know, I've been in the system my entire life. I mean literally since the day I was born, and my parents left me at a bus stop on the Lower East Side of Manhattan. A bus stop!

Seriously, people, there are better places to leave a kid.

Maybe they were doing me a favor. They could be a pair of black-hat computer hackers living off the grid. Or maybe they were astronauts leaving on a trip to Mars and couldn't risk taking a child along.

I liked that one.

But let's face it—they probably took one look at my scrunched-up red face and decided I was going to be trouble with a capital *T*, and wisely skipped town without me.

I try to live up to their expectations.

Can you blame me? It's not like I've had good role models. My foster families have been a n*iiiii*ghtmare. I could tell stories. Like the time foster dad number five locked me in a closet because a sudden hailstorm put baseball-sized dents in his new Mustang. The one he bought with the money the state paid him for my braces. Was I mad? Yeah. But a hailstorm? Even I'm not that clever.

Or the time my foster sister said I tried to barbecue her cat up in a tree. The cat had a habit of peeing in my backpack. Let's just say I had a grudge. But it's not like I can send lightning into trees.

And they thought I was the crazy one.

I'm not *saying* things don't happen when I'm around. What I'm *saying* is they're not my fault.

I'm Phoebe, by the way. Phoebe Katz.

Carl says I should be more responsible.

Carl's my social worker. He's from Brooklyn. His head reminds me of a bowling ball with a mustache. Carl's the only one who cares if I'm breathing or not.

Of course, it's his job to care. But I don't hold that against him. See, Carl's the one who found me that day on the bench. I owe him.

If he had known how much trouble I was going to cause him, he probably would have left me there.

But that's jumping ahead of the story . . .

CHAPTER 2

It was Tuesday, which meant Lasagna Day in the cafeteria. Compared to Mystery Meat Monday it was
something to look forward to. There was a History
Fair at my latest attempt at staying in school, Dexter Academy, and I'd spent all night finishing my model of the
Acropolis, gluing row after row of sugar cubes in place.
It leaned to one side, but if you tilted your head, it wasn't
so bad.

Ordinarily, I didn't give two zots about school or
grades, but if my entry won an award, Carl had promised
to get me a new cell phone—one that didn't flip open—so
I had made an extra effort. I'd even tucked my uniform
shirt in and brushed the knots out of my hair.

The auditorium buzzed with activity as students set up
their displays. My friend Damian Rodina waved to an open
spot next to him. Damian was a braniac to the nth degree,
which would normally bore me, but he kind of grew on
you when he was rattling off useless facts. I angled my way
toward him, carefully balancing my model, and bumped
right into Dexter's resident queen of snobs, Julia Pillsbury.

Julia stood by her replica of a volcano labeled MT. ETNA. Gooey orange sludge oozed down the sides toward a neatly constructed village surrounded by plastic pine trees. No doubt her team of butlers and personal assistants had worked all night so as not to damage her perfect nails.

Julia glanced down at the model in my hands and laughed in that irritating way of hers. "You can't be serious, Phoebe—a trained squirrel could have glued straighter walls than that."

Ordinarily I would have found a way to insult her back, but I didn't want to drop my model, so I stepped aside and moved on.

I was the bigger person, got it?

Julia was the one who stuck her red-booted foot out and tripped me.

In slow motion, I sprawled forward, falling flat on my face. As my chin hit the linoleum floor, my project went flying, shattering into a bazillion pieces.

"Oops." Julia put a hand to her mouth, feigning shock.

A wave of rage and frustration washed over me as I eyed the broken mess. I had tried my best, for once. Really tried. And this was what I got for caring.

I pushed to my feet, ignoring my stinging chin and bruised knees. Little Miss Perfect was about to get a mouthful of my knuckles. My fingers curled into tight fists as a sudden clap of thunder outside made everyone in the room gasp. A bright bolt of lightning lit up the windows, and the air pressure in the room dropped, making my ears pop.

Damian appeared at my side. "Don't do it, Phoebes. There's a ninety-seven percent chance you'll be expelled."

I snorted. Being expelled would be worth it to wipe that superior look off her face.

A girl with black pigtails died pink at the ends stomped up on the other side of me, planted her Doc Marten boots, and smashed one fist into her open palm. "Want me to take care of her, Katzy?"

Angie Spaciacolli. The third member of our group. As usual, her school tie was pulled to the side, and her shirt flaps were untucked.

"No, I got this."

Julia laughed, tossing blond hair over one shoulder. "Oh, look, the loser brigade's in town. Nerd, thug, and charity case." She pointed in turn at Damian, Angie, and then me.

My rage boiled higher. Picking on me was one thing, but picking on my friends? Another boom of thunder rattled the windows as my fingernails dug into my palms.

Julia cast a glance at my fists, then gave a tiny shrug and folded her arms. "You wouldn't dare lay a finger on me."

Oh, I dared. Carl would just have to find me a new school. He'd done it before.

I raised my fist, but before I got a chance to ruin that perfect nose, her volcano burped. She turned toward it at the exact moment it erupted in a spray of fake lava.

Julia screamed as globs of rotten-smelling orange goop dripped from her eyelashes and hair. She pointed a shaking finger at me. "You. You did this."

I was too busy laughing along with Damian, who just snickered under his hand, and Angie, who was bent over double, to point out that was ridiculous.

"Hear, hear, what's the meaning of this?"

Mr. Arnold, the school principal, rushed to Julia's side. He reminded me of a walrus with legs. A long whiskered mustache drooped down over his chin, and his beetle brows were drawn into a frown.

"This clumsy goat dropped her project, and now she's ruined mine!" Julia shrieked. "I want her expelled. Wait till Daddy hears about this." She stomped her red boot and rushed out.

Principal Arnold turned to me, one thick brow raised in that accusing way I was used to seeing from every adult I met. "Well, Miss Katz? Anything to say?"

Loads.

"I didn't touch her stupid volcano! Julia's the one who tripped *me* and made me drop *my* project."

"Did anyone see her trip you?" He looked pointedly at Damian and Angie.

Damian flushed and shook his head. "Sorry, Phoebes, I wasn't looking."

"Me neither," Angie admitted.

Arnold harrumphed. "Then there's no proof you didn't trip over your own two feet. Miss Pillsbury has an impeccable reputation, whereas you . . ."

He didn't need to finish. I knew all about my reputation.

"See that you clean up this mess," he ordered.

I choked. That was so unfair! I opened my mouth to give him a piece of my mind, but Damian dragged me away.

"I see no way to avoid expulsion if you yell at the principal. I'll help."

The bell rang and Arnold clapped his hands, barking orders for students to go to class.

"That includes you, Mr. Rodina."

Damian grimaced, mouthing an apology to me, and followed the others out.

Angie made faces behind Arnold's back, making me smile, and then I was alone.

CHAPTER 3

T he morning thunderstorm continued to rock the building as I set about cleaning up. Whatever Julia had used to make the lava was quickly turning into orange cement. I grabbed a bucket of water from the janitor's closet and got down on my knees, scrubbing away my frustration.

Just when I was settling into a new place, something always happened, and it fell apart. *Kaboom.* A few tears of self-pity escaped before a slice of daylight brought my head up. The storm had blown open a side door, sending a gust of wind through the gym.

Great. If any more projects got damaged, Arnold would blame *me*.

Wiping my eyes, I dropped my brush, hurrying over to close the door. The auditorium had a raised stage along one end. The red velvet curtains were closed, but as I passed by, I could have sworn they swayed slightly, as if someone stood behind them.

A gust of wind slammed the metal door against the wall, drawing my attention back. I tugged it closed, making sure it latched.

That's when things got weird.

A growling noise had me whirling around.

"Who's there?"

The stage curtains fluttered. Something was definitely moving back there.

"If that's you, Julia, you're not scaring me." Which was a big fat lie. My heart pinged around in my chest like a pinball. I wanted to run for the safety of the hallways, but no way was I going to let on I was scared. Not until I found out who or what was behind that curtain.

Tiptoeing up the steps, I grabbed the heavy velvet and yanked the curtain aside, then sighed with relief.

It was only Weezer, a St. Bernard–sized stray that hung around the cafeteria bins for the scraps the lunch ladies tossed him. He must have run in when the door opened.

Weezer had thick black fur and a pair of canines that jutted up from his lower snout. His scarred ears had seen their share of fights. I grimaced as I caught a whiff of him. He smelled as if he'd been rolling around in a dumpster.

"Hey, Weezer." I reached my hand out slowly so as not to spook him. "Did the storm scare you?" I took a step closer, but the normally friendly mutt bared his teeth and growled at me.

I put my hands up. "Message received. I'll leave you alone." I started to back away when he began to shake himself from side to side, as if he were wet. When he stopped, he had another head.

That's right. Two slobbering heads. One dog.

I blinked to make sure my brain hadn't misfired.

The two heads snarled at me like a pair of chainsaws, and both sets of eyes glowed a freaky shade of red.

I backed away. "Nice doggo, I mean, doggos."

Weezer lowered his heads. One paw clawed at the wooden floor, scraping up splinters as his beefy shoulders hunched, ready to charge.

I screamed loud and long, then made a run for it. I leaped off the stage, hitting the ground hard, then tumbled to my feet and sprinted off.

Weezer's toenails scrabbled to find traction, and then he was after me. The mutant dog was like a wrecking ball, knocking tables over as he gave chase. A replica of Fort Knox went flying, exploding in a tumble of Lincoln Logs.

I headed for the exit to the main hallway, but Weezer skidded to a halt in front of me, lowering his heads to growl. Muttering an apology to Damian, I grabbed his toothpick Colosseum and threw it at the beast, then raced for the side door. Weezer yelped, then scrambled after me, skittering on the slippery linoleum.

My hands hit the exit bar. Freedom was so close, but I was jerked to a halt as one of Weezer's snouts snapped down on a mouthful of my sweater. I reached back and ripped the fabric loose, then raced out the door and streaked around the building. I probably would have run all the way to the Lincoln Tunnel, but I ran smack into someone.

The shocked eyes of Miss Carole, the school guidance counselor, looked down at me. She gripped my shoulders to steady me.

"Phoebe, are you all right? What on earth are you doing running down the middle of the sidewalk?"

Silver eyes looked curiously into mine. Miss Carole had always been nice to me, even let me feed crickets to Leonard, the basilisk lizard she kept in her office.

Turning, I searched for any sign of the mutant dog, but the street was empty. "I . . . I'm not sure."

Miss Carole put her arm around my shoulders and guided me up the stairs and back through the front door of the school. "There, there, dear, everything's going to be just fine."

Miss Carole was a great counselor, but a lousy predictor of my future.

I spent the rest of the morning sitting on a bench outside Principal Arnold's office waiting for Carl. It took forty minutes for him to get there with traffic. He barely looked at me before entering the principal's office and shutting the door in my face.

I slumped on the bench, flinching at the accusations that leaked through the walls. Destruction of school property. Vandalism. Gross misconduct.

Finally, the door jerked open and Carl beckoned me in. We sat on hard wooden chairs facing Arnold's desk. I glanced sideways at Carl. He had a blank look in his eyes that scared me. Like maybe he was getting tired of bailing me out.

"Phoebe, is there something you'd like to say to Mr. Arnold?" Carl prompted as I sat there like a lump.

I took a breath and turned on the Phoebe-charm, giving Mr. Arnold my brightest smile. "I'm sooo sorry all those projects got damaged, but it really wasn't my fault. The side door blew open and the wind knocked everything over. I tried to close it, but I wasn't fast enough."

Mr. Arnold steepled his fingers, resting his chin on the tips. "So you didn't destroy them deliberately?" He leaned forward, raising one beetle brow. "A little payback?"

I shook my head. "I would never." *Not unless a two-headed dog was about to take a bite out of me.*

"I'm concerned, Miss Katz." He slapped his hand on a thick folder. "I've read your file. You've had quite your share of escapades. Shoplifting. Skipping class. I hope you don't think that sort of behavior will be tolerated here."

My jaw clenched so hard I thought my teeth might break. The shoplifting had been a stupid package of Twinkies. Foster family number eight had kept padlocks on the refrigerator and pantry. A girl got hungry.

"No, sir. I was hoping for a fresh start."

He wavered, drumming his fingers on the file. "I will give you one last chance, Miss Katz, to prove you belong here. Detention, rest of the week."

I sagged with relief. *Not expelled.*

Out in the hallway, Carl ran a hand over his bald pate. "You promised you would make this work, Phoebe."

"It really wasn't my fault," I protested, but his face remained set.

"Course not, it never is," he said wearily. "You know, you got something big inside you, kid. It's called potential. But if you don't start using it, it just might dry up."

And then Carl, my Carl, walked away, not looking back even once.

CHAPTER 4

Most days after school, the three of us hung out at Vito's, the pizzeria owned by Angie's dad. Free slices and unlimited refills on soda while we did homework—not bad. Usually we walked over together, but thanks to my stupid detention, I was late. I hurried along Fifth Avenue, worried that Carl was never going to speak to me again, all because of a two-headed dog that I had probably imagined.

I'd be lost without Carl.

Maybe it was because he was the one who'd found me at that bus stop. He was the only link to the mystery of who I really was. We met for pancakes most Sundays, and I always ask him about that day.

"But I told you this story a hunnerd times, kid," he starts with a sigh.

"Just tell me again," I plead.

Carl sighs. "I was walking home, not my usual route, but something made me want to walk by Katz's Deli and pick up a sandwich."

"You named me after a deli," I say with an eye roll. "Not very original."

"Hey, they got the best pastrami in town. So I come out with my sandwich, and it starts to pour buckets. Like I never seen it rain that hard before. I run to the bus stop cuz it's the only place that's dry, and there you are, bundled in a blanket, screaming your head off. I look around, but I don't see a soul. When I picked you up, you smiled at me, and the rain stopped."

"That's when you found the note," I prompt.

"Yup, tucked inside your blanket with a little mirror."

"What did it say?"

He recites, "Her name is Phoebe. See that she is taken care of until it is time."

"Until it's time for what?"

He shrugs. "Beats me."

"But you think it means they're coming back, right?" I stare into his brown eyes.

"Sure, kid, whatever you say."

Every foster kid has the same stupid dream. That one day those parents who dumped them on the steps of a church or a fire station or, in my case, a bus stop on Second Avenue will come back for them, saying it had all been some kind of tragic mistake.

Stupid, right?

It'd been twelve years. It was probably time to forget them and get on with my life.

A strange voice brought me to a halt.

Phooooeeeebeee.

I turned around, scanning the afternoon crowds, wondering if Angie and Damian had waited for me. A man on his cell phone bumped into me.

"Watch it, kid."

I hurried on, determined to forget everything about this day, but two steps later, the voice came again, louder this time.

Be careful, Phoebe of Argos. Winds of trouble are blowing your way.

I spun in a circle, searching for the source of the voice.

The Rockefeller Center soared eighty stories above me. At its base sat the bronze statue of Atlas holding up the world. I took a step closer.

Was it . . . moving?

As I gawked, the giant bronze Greek Titan jumped down from his pedestal and marched over to where I stood frozen in place.

Atlas plonked the round globe onto the sidewalk, then stretched his arms wide and groaned.

"Ahhh—you've no idea how heavy the universe is."

I took a step back, looking around to see if anyone else was seeing what I was seeing, but it was like the world had been emptied of people. Where had the afternoon crowds gone? The taxis screaming by on Fifth Avenue?

"Princess of Argos, I bring a warning," he continued. "The doorway between our worlds has been opened. You are in danger."

"Nope. This can't be happening." I pinched myself on the arm. "You're not real."

"Don't I look real?" He leaned down, metallic eyes glaring at me from under thick brows.

I glared right back. "That's not the point. Statues can't talk. And dogs can't grow two heads, so I'm obviously dreaming this whole day."

Atlas blinked, his eyelids clinking together. "A two-headed dog? Hmm. It seems the magic of Olympus has leaked into your world." His bronze eyes narrowed.

"There can be only one reason the doorway reopened. The prophecy has begun."

"Prophecy? What prophecy?"

"It is not for me to say." Atlas straightened, lifted the globe back onto his shoulder, and climbed onto his platform. "Speak to Athena. She will explain everything." A ripple passed over him and he grew still.

A taxi blared its horn and I jumped. Crowds filled the sidewalk again, jostling me in the side.

I did the only logical thing.

I ran.

Chapter 5

I didn't stop running until I reached Vito's. Angie and Damian were in the back, a plate of gnawed crusts all that remained of a cheese pizza.

"Katzy, you look like you saw a ghost." Angie took a slurp from her soda.

Damian stood, taking my arm. "Everything all right, Phoebes?"

My legs gave way and I sank into a chair. "No. We need to talk."

I told them what really happened in the auditorium, including Weezer growing an extra head.

"Seriously, a two-headed dog?" Angie shook her head in disbelief. "You know I don't care you ruined my project along with practically everyone else's."

"I swear on my life, Weezer shook his head from side to side and *bam*, another head came out. Then he chased me through the auditorium." I pulled my sweater over my head and showed them the holes. "See? He tried to bite me."

Damian rubbed his chin. "There are many stories of two-headed dogs in Greek mythology. Hades had a three-headed dog named Cerberus that guarded the entrance to the underworld."

"See, they exist," I said, relieved.

"No, Phoebe—mythology isn't real," Damian said with a laugh. "They're ancient stories people made up to explain how the world was created. Fascinating, but not real."

"Well, Weezer and his two heads were real. And there's more. You know that statue of Atlas? The one at the Rockefeller Center?"

They both nodded.

"It came to life today. Jumped down from its stand and talked to me."

Angie's lips twitched. "Did he ask you out on a date?"

I wanted to scream. "This isn't a joke. He called me the princess of Argos and said something about winds of trouble and destroying Olympus."

"You're serious right now?"

"Cross my heart." I made an X across my chest.

"I can think of no logical explanation for a bronze statue to suddenly animate itself," Damian pronounced.

I folded my arms. "Well, it did. And it said I had to talk to Athena, whoever that is."

Angie put her hand on my arm. "Katzy, if something's wrong, you can tell us. You don't have to make up stories."

"I'm not making this up. Why would I?"

"Some people make up stories when they're experiencing trauma," Damian recited. "Scientific studies show—"

"I'm not a piece of stupid science! I'm your friend. Either you believe me, or we're done."

There was silence for a moment, and then Angie snorted.

"Oh, puh-lease." She twirled the pink ends of her pigtails. "You say that once a week. Look, Pops owns a pizza joint out in Queens. I go with him to pick up the money on weekends. When I was little, I used to play in this park nearby."

"Athens Square Park," Damian said, eyes lighting up. "I know it! It's filled with Greek statues."

"Exactly." Angie smiled smugly. "And if I'm not mistaken, one of them is Athena."

I blinked in shock. "So you believe me?"

"No. But it's better than doing homework. I'll get one of Pops's guys to give us a ride. We'll have a look-see and be home before dark."

"Thanks, Angie." Shame made me flush. "I don't deserve you guys. Sorry I threatened . . . you know . . . not to be friends."

She winked. "Can't get rid of us that easily, right, Big D?"

Damian launched into a long list of statistics on friendships until we both yelled at him to shut it. Angie led us around back, and we piled into a white van that smelled of flour and pepperoni. Thirty minutes later, we were dropped at the park.

I pushed open the wrought-iron gate. Some old men played chess at tables lined up along the fence. A playground and basketball courts took up one end. A few moms pushed their kids on the swings. At the other end, an octagonal plaza was paved with gray and white tiles. Three fluted columns held up a semicircular arch of stone. Bronzed statues were arranged along the edges of the plaza.

We walked up to the first figure. A balding man dressed in a toga rested his chin on his hand.

"Socrates," Angie read from the nameplate.

Damian opened his mouth but didn't speak.

"Oh, go ahead." I elbowed him in the side. "I can see you're dying to tell us everything you know."

His eyes lit up. "Socrates was a famous Greek philosopher who never wrote anything himself."

"Then how come he was so famous?" Angie asked.

"He had a student named Plato who wrote all his sayings down. My favorite is 'only the wise know they know nothing.'"

"Check out this one," Angie called. She stood by a tall statue of a man holding a grinning mask in one hand and a crying mask in the other. She jumped up on the pedestal and stuck her head under his arm.

"How do I look?"

"Like a giant dork. Who was Sophocles?" I asked, reading his name.

"Playwright," Damian answered. "He wrote about Greek tragedies like the Trojan War, but he also wrote comedies."

A gust of wind scattered leaves across the tiles. The sun was starting to go down. "Where's Athena?" I asked, and then my breath caught. A tall figure stood at the end of the plaza, facing toward the setting sun. It was her. Somehow I just knew it.

We walked in front of the statue, looking up in awe. Athena wore a plumed helmet and a long gown with a sash carved with snakes. Her face was serene and kind, one graceful arm extended in a greeting.

"She's beautiful," I whispered.

"Athena was the goddess of wisdom," Damian explained. "Favorite daughter of Zeus. She was very brave and fought in many battles."

Angie rapped on the bronze. "Seems pretty solid to me. How do we get her to speak?"

I bit my lip. "I don't know. Atlas started talking to me on his own."

"Try asking her a question," Damian said.

I couldn't think of anything clever, so I just said, "Hello, Athena, it's me, Phoebe."

A pigeon landed on her outstretched hand, eyeing us curiously before taking flight.

"This is dumb. We should just go," I muttered.

"Try saying it louder," Angie urged.

I sighed, then took a breath and shouted, "ATHENA, HELLO, ARE YOU THERE?"

The old men looked up from their chess game.

"It's not working." I turned to go, but Damian and Angie each grabbed an arm and spun me back around.

"Try again," Angie said.

"This time close your eyes and concentrate," Damian suggested.

Sometimes my friends really annoyed me. But they had come all this way just to help me, so I shut my eyes and took a deep breath, then let it out slowly.

At first I didn't feel anything. Then a faint tingling made my skin prickle. A breeze drifted across the park. It grew stronger, tumbling the air around us, growing louder and louder until my hair snapped in my face.

"What's happening?" Angie asked over the noise of the wind.

"Phoebe's happening," Damian answered in an awed voice.

CHAPTER 6

The winds swirled in a frenzy around us, but it was
eerily quiet inside the vortex. Athena's bronzed
hand slowly opened and closed, and then her face
softened into a smile as she tilted her head toward us.

"Hello, younglings. Who asks to speak to Athena?"

Angie nudged me.

"Uh, hi," I said. "I'm Phoebe."

Athena's eyes widened. "Phoebe, at last we meet. I
know your brother well."

I laughed. "You must have the wrong Phoebe. I don't
have a brother."

Athena stepped down from her pedestal and crossed
to my side. "Yes, you do. You feel him here when you're
alone." She put a hand over my heart.

Pain rippled through me. A faint memory of another
heartbeat echoed in my head, like a distant drumbeat.
"I . . . I remember feeling like there was someone else
before. Like there's this part of me that's always missing."
I squirmed a little. I had never told anyone that.

Athena smiled gently. "It is only natural. Perseus is
your twin. You spent nine months together."

"Uh, excuse me, but Perseus didn't have a twin," Damian said with that know-it-all voice of his. "According to mythology, Perseus was born to Danae, daughter of Acrisius, the king of Argos. The Oracle of Delphi gave the king a prophecy that Danae would one day give birth to a son that would kill him. He banished his daughter to an underground prison so she would never marry, but Zeus found her and fell in love with her."

"Yes, Father is ever the romantic," Athena said with a smile.

"But there was only Perseus," Damian said confidently.

"No. There was a twin," she corrected. "None knew there were two babes besides Danae and the oracle that attended the birth. The oracle hid the female child from sight when Acrisius stormed into the nursery, demanding to see the child of the prophecy. He drew his sword, prepared to kill the infant, but Danae begged him for mercy. He refused to listen until she reminded him who the father was. Fearing Zeus's wrath, he let the child live, but he banished Danae and Perseus that very night, setting them adrift in a boat, intending never to see them again."

Damian jumped in. "But years later, Perseus returned and by accident—"

Athena held a hand up in warning. "Say no more. The stories you have read about our world have not yet unfolded. It is dangerous for me to know the future."

"What do you mean, future?" I asked. "Didn't those things all happen thousands of years ago?"

"Yes and no. The immortal gods are not bound by the wheels of time. Our world turns on its own axis, separate from your own in a never-ending cycle. Right now, Perseus is still a boy, the same age as you."

Angie stepped forward. "Whoa, back the truck up. Are you saying Olympus is real?"

Athena gave her a curious look. "Of course the city of the gods exists. Why wouldn't it?"

"Because they were stories," Damian said, looking confused.

"True stories," Athena corrected. "The gods live on."

"Then how come we don't see you dropping by?" Angie asked.

"Mankind evolved," Athena explained. "Like children that grew up, they didn't need the gods interfering in their lives anymore. An agreement was made among the immortals to seal the passage between earth and Olympus and its ancient isles. Only once before has it been broken."

"When was that?" I asked.

"When the oracle brought you here."

"Hold on—why is all this happening now?" Angie asked. "It's been twelve years."

Athena turned to her. "Ares has broken the seal between our worlds."

"Ares, god of war, Ares?" Damian croaked, sounding utterly flabbergasted.

"Yes. Phoebe, listen carefully—Ares can be after only one thing."

"What's that?"

"You."

"Me?" I squeaked. "Why me?"

"Because you hold the fate of Olympus in your hands."

There was silence. I wanted to laugh in her face, but she looked so serious, I let her down gently. "Sorry to disappoint, but I'm a big nobody. My parents abandoned me at a bus stop."

Athena put one bronzed hand on my shoulder. "Phoebe, you were never abandoned. Our father sent you away to protect you from a terrible prophecy, one even worse than that of Perseus."

My mind was spinning so fast I could hardly take in her words. "Our father?"

"Zeus. Why else do you think you can change the weather?" She looked up at the swirl of wind that cocooned us. "He gifted the power to you before he sent you here. Have you never noticed when you are upset or angry, strange things happen?"

I nodded slowly. "Like causing a sudden hailstorm?" *Maybe I did owe my former foster dad an apology for denting his car.*

"Or a thunderstorm," Damian added. "Like this morning in the cafeteria. You were definitely mad."

Athena nodded. "One day, you will learn the language to call it at will. But be wary. Using your powers will draw Ares to you. He mustn't find you. We will be relocating you somewhere immediately."

"Wait—what? No! I like it here."

Athena shook her head. "It is too dangerous now. Events are in motion. You will be hidden again—perhaps Nebraska. I hear the cornfields are lovely."

She climbed back onto her pedestal. "Await the sign, Princess of Argos. Into hiding you must go. If Ares finds you, it will be the end of Olympus. Do you hear me? Olympus and everything around it will be destroyed."

Her body stiffened as she resumed her pose. The wind stilled, and Athena was a statue again.

"Holy pepperoni," Angie said. "Did that just happen?"

"I'm entirely uncertain how that was possible," Damian allowed.

"I have a brother." *One I will never get to see*, I realized with a sharp pain in my gut.

My friends looked at me with pity in their eyes.

Angie squeezed my shoulder. "We should go. Pops doesn't like it when I'm late."

We turned around—and found a beefy Dalmatian blocking our way. It started shaking just like Weezer. Before I could shout a warning to the others, another spotted head appeared next to the first. Its eyes glowed red, and its nails rasped on the concrete as it prowled closer.

"Is that what I think it is?" Damian asked as we backed away.

"Yup. Told you I wasn't lying."

Angie pulled a comb from her back pocket and flicked it open, revealing a flimsy switchblade.

My eyes popped. "Seriously, Angie? A knife?"

She waved it at the mutt. "Pops gave it to me for my birthday. Says a girl needs to know how to protect herself. What do either of you have?"

Damian shrugged, holding out empty hands.

A crazy idea popped into my head. "Athena said Zeus gifted me with the power to control the weather. Let's see what I can do." I linked my fingers together and pushed my palms out, cracking my knuckles.

Clenching my right hand into a tight fist, I imagined what I needed. Rain? No. Thunder? Not much help against a two-headed dog.

Then an image lit up the backs of my eyes. An image of a bright white lightning bolt.

That will do nicely.

Instantly, my hand tingled with electricity. I opened and closed my fist, feeling the energy build until the most incredible, no, *awesome* thing ever happened.

A sizzling bolt of pure energy the length of my forearm appeared in my hand. It jumped and pulsed, as if it couldn't wait to be unleashed.

I have the power to call lightning. Cool.

It was like holding a live wire. The hair on my arm stood up as white energy crackled and danced along the bolt. The two-headed Dalmatian howled, and then it charged us.

I didn't have time to think. I threw my arm forward

as it leaped, embedding the glowing bolt in its chest. It froze in midair, encased in a halo of searing electricity. It shook violently as glowing white fire quickly consumed it, incinerating it into a pile of ash.

We stood in shocked silence as the wind scattered the ashes across the plaza.

Angie was the first to speak.

"Did you really just cremate a two-headed dog with lightning?"

I couldn't answer her because I was too busy freaking out. My breath came in ragged gasps, leaving me light-headed and woozy.

"Come on," Damian said, tugging on my arm. "We better go before something worse shows up."

CHAPTER 7

After we exited the subway, Angie and Damian offered to walk me home, but I needed some time alone to clear my head. I shoved my hands in the pockets of my jacket and walked the six blocks to the home of my current foster family. The Harolds were nice enough people—they'd raised a few kids of their own, so they didn't blow up every time I left my cereal bowl in the sink. And Mrs. H was a decent cook.

But I still felt like a visitor every time I walked in the door. That's part of being in the system. You always have a go-bag packed in case things go south.

I let myself in, relieved to find the apartment empty. They'd left a note saying they were at their weekly ballroom dance class, and there were leftovers in the fridge. I had no appetite, so I headed straight for my room and flopped on my bed, staring at the ceiling. In one day, I'd been chased by two-headed dogs, talked to statues, wielded lightning bolts, and, yeah, found out my dad was Zeus.

I dug in the drawer of my nightstand and pulled out the small round mirror, the one Carl had said was tucked in my blanket when he found me. I hadn't looked at it in months. The front side was polished glass. I studied my blue-green eyes and freckles, wondering why Zeus would give me a useless mirror.

I sat up.

Zeus was some kind of all-powerful god. Why would he hand out a useless trinket?

Unless . . . it wasn't useless.

I turned the mirror over. The tarnished silver back had six indented shapes arranged in a circle. They were all different: an upside-down triangle, a horn, a crescent moon, a boomerang, an S shape, and a pointed oval that might be a feather.

I hadn't given it much thought before, but now I wondered if it was some kind of code. Maybe a secret message?

Next day at school, I cornered Damian by his locker.

"Look at this." I showed him the mirror.

"What is it?"

"Zeus gave it to me."

"Shh!" Damian put a finger over my lips, looking around nervously. "The walls have ears."

"That makes no sense. Walls don't have ears."

"It's a saying. Strange things have been happening. We have to be careful. Let me take a closer look." He turned it over in his hands. "What do these shapes mean?"

"No idea."

We were so busy staring at it we didn't see Julia Pillsbury swoop down on us.

"What have we here?" She snatched the mirror from Damian's hands. "That's mine. I've been looking everywhere for it."

"Knock it off, Julia. You know it's not yours. Give it back." I held out my hand.

"I lost this last week, didn't I, Mitzie?" she said to one of the sycophants that always trailed her around.

The girl bobbed her head obediently. "Your favorite."

Julia stroked the mirror as if it were a long-lost treasure. "Daddy bought it for me on his last trip to Europe. I should report you to Mr. Arnold for theft." She put a finger to her chin. "That would certainly get you expelled."

This girl really was the most infuriating thing. Maybe a lightning bolt to that perfect face would change her tune.

"Don't lose your temper," Damian said in my ear. "You heard Athena. You can't draw attention to yourself."

I hated when Damian was right. I pasted on a fake smile, trying to keep my temper in check. "Look, Julia, it's just some old mirror I found. It's not worth anything."

"Then you won't care if I keep it." With a satisfied smile, she tucked it in her bag and waltzed off with Mitzie in tow.

Angie walked up, chewing noisily on a wad of pink bubblegum. "What'd I miss?"

"Julia has something of mine," I said, seething. "But I've an idea how to get it back. Cover for me next period—I have to duck out. Won't take long. I'll see you at lunch."

"Sure, Katzy, whatever you say."

"Be careful," Damian warned, placing a hand on my arm.

"Relax, I'm not going to use my powers."

Angie waited for me in the lunch line, looking around anxiously. I slid in beside her and grabbed a tray.

"Where'd you go?" she asked as we inched our way forward. "Mrs. Heaton had a tiz-fit because you weren't there, but I told her you were distraught over your project getting ruined."

"Thanks, Angie." I spied Julia sitting at her usual table surrounded by her fan club.

Perfect.

The lunch ladies working the counter were a pair of unkempt sisters named Ilsa and Elsa. Ilsa glared at me as I held my tray out, then scooped a glop of spaghetti on my plate. Her hair stood out in a frizzy ball around her head, and dried-on food bits stained her blue uniform.

I moved on to Elsa. She could be Ilsa's ugly twin, only she had this crazy ability to roll her eyes in a circle whenever she looked at you. Elsa dumped a pile of steamed spinach next to the pasta, daring me with a roll of her eyes to complain.

I grabbed a tall carton of milk and, checking no one was watching, dumped out half of it into the crushed ice that held the cartons. Then I took a small blue bottle out of my pocket, emptied the white fluid into the opening, and popped in a straw.

"What are you doing?" Angie asked.

"You'll see."

The thing about Julia is she thinks everything belongs to her, including other people's lunches, and no one ever complains because, well, she's Julia Pillsbury.

As we walked past Julia's table, I said loudly, "You know, Angie, I love milk sooo much. I *cannot* eat lunch without it."

Predictably, Julia popped up and snagged the carton off my tray. "Gee, thanks, Phoebe. I feel the same way."

I made just enough of a fuss to be convincing, then scurried to join Angie at a table Damian had saved for us.

"What was that about, Katzy?"

"You'll see."

Julia drained the milk with her straw, slurping up the

last few drops, then flashed a satisfied grin at me over her shoulder. I smiled back and waited.

It took about ten minutes.

Julia squirmed, then her face scrunched up. Her arm went around her stomach. With a startled look, she pushed back from the table and ran out of the lunchroom.

I jumped to my feet. "Come on. This I want to see."

Damian stood warily. "Maybe I should wait here." But Angie collared him and dragged him out to the hallway.

"Which way did she go?" I asked.

"The girl's bathroom is that way," Angie said, pointing left.

We hurried to a set of green doors, one leading in, one out. I pressed my ear up against the metal. It sounded like a stray cat wallering inside.

"She's in there."

I pushed open the door. The sound of sobs echoed in the tiled room.

Damian held back. "I can't go in there. It's the girl's bathroom."

"Stop being such a sissy." Angie gave him a shove. "It doesn't have cooties."

I took a wary step in. Four stalls ran along each side. All the doors were open but one. A row of sinks under a steel mirror lined the back wall.

"Julia, are you in here?"

The girl sniffled loudly. "Here, take your stupid mirror and go away."

She slid the trinket under the stall door. I scooped it up, grinning triumphantly. We had just turned to go when there was an ominous gurgle from her stall.

"Julia, are you okay?"

A loud scream echoed in the small room. A second

later, a huge gush of water shot into the air, and with it, Julia. Her arms and legs flailed in the rushing spout, then she landed on the floor next to us.

The stall door burst open as a scaly green neck poked its way out of the shattered toilet, tearing the metal stall apart as if it were paper. A dragon-like head with serpentine amber eyes topped the long neck. Its spiny jaw was filled with big, sharp-looking serrated teeth.

As if one scary head wasn't bad enough, the toilet next to the first shattered, and the rest of the metal stalls were flung aside as a second, third, and then a fourth head appeared out of the pipes, tearing up the tile as the monster struggled to free itself.

"What is that?" I cried.

"It l-l-looks l-like a hydra," Damian stuttered. "This is bad."

Chapter 8

The monster clawed its way out, looming larger as it freed itself from the pipes. Once it was loose, there would be no stopping it. Julia screamed as the hydra heads let out a joint roar, and then thankfully, she fainted.

"Angie, help me with Julia."

We dragged the girl back toward the doors as I tried to think up a plan. Athena had said to be careful using my powers, but if I didn't do something, this four-headed toilet monster was going to destroy my school.

I opened and closed my fist. The lightning bolt came faster this time, a jagged bolt of glowing white fire. One of the heads swung toward me, and its maw opened. All I saw were drool-covered teeth and glowing eyes as it snapped at my head. I cocked my arms up and brought the bolt around for a home run. The bolt sliced through the neck, cleaving the head clean off and sending it bouncing against the wall.

"Yes!" I pumped my fist.

"No!" Damian grabbed my arm as I lined up for another swing. "Whatever you do, don't take a head off."

"Why not?"

"Two more will grow back."

At his words, the stumpy neck shuddered and split. A pair of matching heads pushed themselves out, making it a total of five snarling heads in the bathroom.

"Now you tell me!"

The hydra shook the destroyed toilet stalls off and walked forward on scaly three-toed feet. It looked like something that had crawled out of a swamp. Thick, muscular legs held up a fat, squatty body. Its tail whipped the air, smashing down on the sinks and destroying them.

It seemed to be afraid of my lightning bolt. I waved it in front of me, holding the hydra back. The heads snarled and snapped, trying to get at our little group.

"How do we kill it, Damian?" Angie clutched her flimsy switchblade.

"It's impossible. We'd have to cut off all its heads before it can regrow them."

"Not impossible. We just need a weapon," I said. "A really powerful one."

I clenched the lightning bolt and closed my eyes, ignoring the snarls of the hydra. The bolt grew hotter in my hand until it was almost unbearable. When I opened my eyes, the bolt was as tall as me and shaped like a staff. I was starting to like these powers of mine! I spun it in a circle, testing its strength.

"Damian, can you distract it?"

"Me? Why me?" But he reluctantly stepped forward, waggling his hands at the nearest head. "Hey, squid breath, come and get me."

The head whipped down, snapping at him. Its spiny teeth came within inches of Damian before I slashed down with one end of the lightning staff.

The crackling bolt cut through the flesh as if it were butter. Gooey green blood sprayed over us. I swiped it from my eyes and ducked as two more heads swooped down toward me.

Spinning, I brought my weapon around in a slicing arc. Head number two bounced on the ground. I jumped on it, using it to lever onto the stump of its neck, and leaped toward the third head. I managed to swing my arms down, but before I could land a blow, it knocked my feet out from under me with its tail, sending me flying against the wall.

While I picked up my bruised body, Angie got in on it, shouting, "Over here, you slimy bucket of fish guts."

Two heads veered toward her, snapping at her waving hands. She slipped in the green muck that smeared the floor and ended up flat on her back. The pair of slavering heads went after her. I took a running leap and swung the staff with two hands, slicing both heads off in midair.

She gave me a relieved nod of thanks.

"Hurry, Phoebe, we've only got a few seconds," Damian warned.

The stumpy necks were shaking and vibrating as the hydra regenerated.

The last head was bigger than the others. It hovered high, keeping out of reach. It swung its body around, taking out more stalls as its spiked tail came down with a *thwack*, aiming for my friends. Angie tackled Damian, sliding in the gunk out of reach.

I jumped on the hydra's back, coming face-to-face with the last head. I was about to swing the staff when our eyes locked. There was something familiar about them. I had seen those amber eyes before. I hesitated, and it bit down on my thigh. A burning fire tore through my veins. I didn't have the strength to swing the bolt, so I settled for shoving it in its glowering eye. The beast thrashed, tossing me off as it tried to shake the lightning bolt loose, and then it exploded, spattering the walls with gooey green flesh.

I blinked away the goo and looked around.

The bathroom was utterly wrecked. Water sprayed from the broken pipes. We were covered in hydra slime from head to toe. My skin was on fire, like I was burning up with a fever. Damian helped me up while Angie put an arm under Julia, and together we limped out into the hallway.

Spots danced in crazy circles behind my eyes. Principal Arnold came rushing toward us, shouting, "What is the meaning of this?"

The hall rapidly filled with students and teachers.

"The bathroom pipes exploded," Damian said. "A sewer accident. You do not want to go in there."

"It was a monster," Julia said, dazed eyes blinking. "I saw it. It was huge and it had, like, eight heads."

Angie laughed. "Poor Julia slipped and bumped her head. She's talking a little cray-cray right now." She waggled her finger in a circle at her temple.

Mr. Arnold put a consoling arm around Julia, leading her away. "There, there, Miss Pillsbury, let's call your father." He glared at us over his shoulder. "You three, clean that mess up."

I didn't bother to point out the bathroom was destroyed and far beyond our ability to clean up. We were alive. And in one piece.

And then I fainted.

CHAPTER 9

When I came to, I was lying on a sofa in a darkened room. My leg throbbed where the hydra had bitten me. I looked around, recognizing Miss Carole's office. My uniform was shredded and stained, but someone had left a stack of clean clothes, probably from the Lost and Found. I quickly changed into the jeans and clean T-shirt, then slipped on the denim jacket as the door opened and the spry guidance counselor entered, holding a small plastic cup. She turned on a small lamp.

"Oh, good, you're awake. Drink some juice. You've had a nasty shock." She handed me a small cup filled with amber liquid.

I swallowed it, surprised by the sweet taste.

Her silvery eyes watched me closely. "All better now?"

It took a moment, and then a rush of coolness washed over me, extinguishing the burning pain in my leg. Strength flowed back into me, and I sat up, nodding at her. "Much."

"The bathroom was quite a mess," she went on. "You're lucky you didn't get seriously injured when those . . . er . . . pipes exploded."

No kidding. That hydra could have bitten my head off.

"I pulled this piece of tile out of your leg. I thought you might want to keep it." She dropped a triangle-shaped chunk of porcelain onto my palm.

I stared at it, glad my hand didn't shake, because it wasn't a piece of tile.

It was a hydra's tooth.

I slipped it into my pocket, relieved when my fingers touched my mirror. "Thanks. Can I go to class now?"

Her eyebrows raised. "School's almost over, dear. You should probably go home and start packing."

"Packing?"

"Didn't you hear? Your transfer paperwork came in. You will be moving tomorrow to a new foster home. A lovely farm in Nebraska."

Shock nailed me to the floor. "So soon?"

She shrugged, holding her hands out. "Circumstances beyond my control. I'm sure Carl meant to tell you. He was supposed to be here. I can't imagine where he's gotten to."

As I limped to the door, my eyes slid over to Leonard's cage. The glass had a big crack, and the basilisk lizard was nowhere to be seen.

I stopped. An image of the hydra's last head came back to me. That's why its eyes had looked familiar—they were the same amber color as Leonard's.

"Where's Leonard?"

Miss Carole waved a hand. "Oh, he wasn't himself today. Quite lost his head, I'm afraid. Run along now."

I stumbled out into the hallway and was immediately tackled by Angie and Damian.

"You all right, Katzy?" Angie grabbed my shoulders, then crushed me in a hug.

"Miss Carole wouldn't let us see you," Damian said, adding his arms to hers. "We were so worried."

"It was just a scratch. I'm fine."

I wriggled free, needing air. My head was still a little woozy.

"Just a scratch?" Damian's voice cracked, the way it did when he was upset. "Hydra bites are quite poisonous. You could have died."

Odd. Ever since Miss Carole had given me that apple juice, I'd been better than ever. Except for the fact I was leaving tomorrow for some gawd-awful corn state in the middle of nowheresville. I shrugged. "Still here."

"Good, because we have bigger problems," Angie said. "Come on, there's something you have to see."

They dragged me down the hall to where a crowd of students had gathered, whispering and pointing at a message scribbled on the wall in red paint.

Daughter of Zeus, come out, come out!

The hydra was just the beginning

Meet in the cafeteria after school

"Someone knows who you are," Angie whispered. "You think it could be Ares?"

"Who else could have sent that hydra?" I said. "Which means there's no way I'm showing up. After tomorrow, he'll never find me."

"What's that supposed to mean?" Damian asked.

"I'm shipping out. Athena wasn't joking. I'm off to Nebraska."

"But they can't do that," Angie wailed. "You belong here. With us."

"No, I'm property of the state," I said bitterly. "Zeus might be my father on Olympus, but here, no one gives two rats about me."

"I give five rats, at least," Damian said quietly. "Big ones, you know, like the ones you see by the subway tracks."

We looked at Damian in surprise. He was always so serious—but his attempt at humor worked. I laughed, and Angie joined in.

"We could, you know, check it out," I said, turning toward the cafeteria. "One last adventure."

Angie hooked arms and we started walking. "I've always wanted to meet a Greek god. I hear they're *gorgeous*."

"You're both certifiable," Damian protested after us. "If Ares *is* there, we're walking into a trap."

"It sounds more fun than Nebraska," I said over my shoulder. I was pleased when he sighed, shook his head, and followed.

We peered in through the window notched in the door. One of the scuzzo lunch ladies was pushing a mop across the floor. The other was stacking chairs.

"Looks safe enough," I said. "The lunch ladies may smell bad, but they're harmless."

Angie nodded. "I say we go in, check it out, and then order the biggest pizza my dad has to celebrate your last night."

Sounded like a plan to me.

We stepped inside, letting the door close behind us, and stood there, not sure what to do. The lunch ladies came to a halt, staring at us with their usual hostility.

"Just looking around," I said cheerfully.

The two sisters looked at each other, and then Ilsa let her mop clatter to the ground. She cracked her neck to the side, then flexed her shoulders up and down in a weird stretching motion.

"Uh, Phoebe, we should go," Damian said.

No kidding. We started to back away.

Ilsa stopped flexing, and then something even stranger than a two-headed dog happened. A set of leathery wings sprouted from her back and fanned out. Her fingers curved into hooked talons. She hissed, revealing a pair of pointy fangs.

"What the—" I stepped back and bumped into someone.

I turned to find Elsa crouched behind us. She, too, had sprouted wings that flared outward. Her eyes rolled in a circle as she glared at us.

"What are they?" I whispered to Damian.

"I think they . . . um . . . I'm not positive . . . but I think the lunch ladies just turned into harpies."

"Stay back," Angie said, making her hands into fists.

"Or what?" Elsa clawed at the air with her yellowed talons as Ilsa snarled at us, baring wickedly sharp teeth.

"Or I'll fry your brains," I said, deciding to take matters in hand by calling up a fat lightning bolt. I stepped in front of my two friends and raised the bolt over my shoulder.

The sound of clapping echoed through the room.

"Bravo, Phoebe, bravo."

A tall fair-haired man stepped out of the kitchen dressed in a knee-length white tunic. A golden breastplate was strapped across his chest. Leather sandals laced up to his knees, and a gilded sword hung in a sheath at his side.

"Back off, whoever you are," I said, keeping the lightning bolt in a firm grip.

He gave a short bow. "Allow me to make introductions. I am Ares, god of war, at your service. And you are Phoebe of Argos, daughter of Zeus. You can put the fireworks away. I'm not here to harm you."

I gripped the bolt tighter. "Could have fooled me. That hydra nearly killed us all."

He laughed. "Sorry about that, but I had to be sure it was you. If I wanted you dead, you would be." His eyes glinted with a sudden power that quickly cooled. "Honestly, I'm your biggest fan. You see, you're going to help me topple Zeus from his reign over Olympus. The Oracle of Delphi told me herself."

He took a step closer, but I waved the bolt, warning him off.

He held his hands up. "I speak the truth. I went to the oracle and asked her what would happen if I attempted to knock Daddy off his throne."

"Daddy?"

"Zeus, dear, we're related."

Yuck. I'd rather be related to a cockroach.

"Do you know, she had the most awful look on her face?" Ares mused. "As if she had swallowed hydra guts. Shall I tell you what she said?" He went on without waiting for my answer. "It was so delightful, I can recite it by heart:

If you battle your father to take it all,
A mighty god will surely fall.
A child of Zeus will be the difference.
Daughter of Danae and sister to Perseus.
She alone will hold the key
To reach that final victory.

"Sister, now you understand? You are the game-winning piece. Come, give your brother a hug." Ares threw his arms out.

I stared at him with disgust. "If you think I'm going to help you, you're missing a brain."

His voice lost its charm. "Oh, you'll help me, Phoebe, or lose the one thing you love the most."

I almost laughed in his face. "No problem. I don't love anything."

"No?"

Ares snapped his fingers, and the harpy lunch ladies dragged a familiar figure out from the kitchen.

Carl. Bound and gagged and looking terrified.

Ares drew his sword and held it to Carl's throat.

"Then you don't mind if I kill him?"

CHAPTER 10

"**N**o!" The word was wrenched from me. *Not Carl. Anything but that.*

Ares lowered his sword. "Good. Then you'll do exactly as I say."

He stepped up into the double windows and flung them open. Outside, a golden chariot awaited, floating in thin air. It was pulled by a pair of gleaming black horses with wings, each with a single white mark on their forehead.

The two harpies lifted Carl out the window, dropping him into the chariot.

Ares paused in the opening. "Return home, Phoebe, and see the oracle. She will confirm what I say. It is your destiny. You cannot escape it."

"I'll never help you," I said, trying to think of a way to stop this while my brain went in circles around one thought: *He has Carl. My Carl.*

"Never is a very long time. We are not enemies, sister. The sooner you realize that, the sooner we can finish what is inevitable." He leaped into the chariot and disappeared in a blaze of light.

Panicked, I whirled on my friends. "I have to go after him. I have to get Carl back."

"We need to think this through," Damian said. "You were sent away for a reason. Going back could mean something worse happens."

"Worse than losing Carl? There isn't anything. I'm going and that's that."

"Okay, Katzy, chill. How do we do it?" Angie asked.

"We? You guys are coming?"

"Try to stop us." She folded her arms, and Damian folded his, matching her stance.

Relief made my knees wobble. "Okay, good, because I would probably mess everything up in the first five minutes. Damian, ideas?"

He cocked an eyebrow. "How to get to Ancient Greece? Sure, Phoebes, I have, like, ten a day."

"Come on, Damian, use that giant brain of yours."

He sighed and began pacing. "Ares flew on a chariot pulled by winged horses known as pegasuses."

"Which we don't have," Angie noted.

"Right, but we do have something." Damian stopped to look at me.

"What?"

"You. Or rather, your lightning."

I blinked. "Okaaay, what good is lightning?"

"The magic of Olympus turned an ordinary dog into a two-headed one, and our lunch ladies into harpies, right?"

A light went off as I caught his meaning. "So maybe with a little jolt, I can turn a plain horse into a winged one?"

He shrugged. "It's worth a try."

The bell rang, signaling the end of school, and the sound of shouts and lockers banging filled the hall.

"Where are we going to find a horse in Manhattan?" Angie asked.

I snapped my fingers. "Central Park. They sell carriage rides to tourists."

We bolted out of the cafeteria headed for the front door, when a stodgy figure stepped into view.

"Miss Katz, a word!"

Principal Arnold's beetle brows bristled as he marched toward us. "Someone destroyed that bathroom today. I don't believe it was an accident. I told you behavior like that wouldn't be tolerated."

I tried to think of an excuse, but my mind was blank, and besides, Ares already knew where I was. I didn't need to hide my powers anymore.

But before I could call up a lightning bolt, Angie shouted, "Fire!" and pulled the fire alarm on the wall. Water started spraying from the overhead sprinklers, and the alarm bells clanged in the hallway, sending everyone running in a panic. We dodged out in the chaos and didn't stop running until we were close to the park.

"Are you guys sure about this?" I asked as we caught our breath. Across the street, carriages lined up, ready to haul tourists around the park. "Aren't your parents going to freak out if you disappear?"

Damian shrugged. "My parents are in the middle of a three-month-long research trip studying migration patterns in whales somewhere in the Antarctic. They call once a week. *If* they have a signal."

"And Pops is out of town," Angie said, scrolling through her phone. "Business trip. I'll text his secretary I have a school thing and have her call Damian's housekeeper." Her fingers flew on the screen. "Ma's in Florida working on her tan. No one will worry about me for a few days."

"Seriously?" I shook my head. "If I don't text I'm going to be five minutes late, my foster parents think I've been kidnapped."

We crossed the street and walked along the row of carriages, eyeing the horses.

"What are we looking for?" I asked.

Damian shrugged. "A horse that looks like it can fly."

A gray mare caught my eye. I wandered over and ran a hand over her velvety nose. She whickered softly, pushing against my palm. Her owner was off having a smoke with some other drivers.

"She's a beaut," Damian said. "And the carriage looks sturdy. I'd say she's a winner."

"So what do I do?"

He nodded at the horse. "Give it a zap with a lightning bolt. You know, like a super charge."

"Seriously? What if I incinerate her like that dog?"

"Uh, you better do something," Angie said. "Because we got company."

A whistle blew shrilly. Mr. Arnold was at the corner with two police officers, pointing toward us.

"Okay, here goes nothing."

I clenched and unclenched my fingers, feeling the energy flow through me until I held a shiny silver bolt.

"Sorry about this," I whispered before touching the tip against the side of the horse. The mare jolted as a glowing shimmer encased it. But she didn't turn into a pile of ash. Encouraged, I pushed harder until the length of the bolt disappeared inside her, and then I stepped back.

A ripple ran along her flanks, as if the flesh was shifting and changing under her coat. She neighed sharply, tossing her head back, and then a glorious pair of feathery gray wings emerged, unfurling and spreading outward.

"No way," Angie whispered.

I looked at my hands and back at the winged horse. "Did I really just do that?"

"Come on, time to go." Damian pushed us into the carriage.

I took the reins and flicked them hard. The horse pitched forward, running along the street.

"Stop now, Miss Katz, or you will regret this," Arnold puffed, jogging up alongside.

He reached one meaty fist out and grabbed the side of the carriage. I flicked the reins again, shouting at the horse to hurry.

The carriage jerked upward, lifting a few feet off the ground until Arnold dangled, blustering away at us.

Angie pried his fingers off, waving as he tumbled back onto the lawn with a *thud*.

"Hold on!" I cried.

The wind whipped our faces as we climbed higher and higher until blinding light ripped the sky open in front of us. Then everything went quiet.

CHAPTER 11

Whatever wormhole had sucked us in knocked us out cold. When I finally pried my eyes open, bright sunlight made me wince. My bones ached as if I'd been dropped from a three-story building. Had we really traveled to Ancient Greece? Or more likely, crashed into the ground and destroyed an expensive carriage? Principal Arnold was probably sending the NYPD to arrest us. I cautiously sat up, ready to make a run for it, and gasped.

The New York City skyline was gone, replaced by stands of fig trees bursting with purple fruit. A faint breeze brought the smell of salt from the sea. Red poppies carpeted rolling hills under a vivid blue sky. A rutted road stretched out in both directions, one end pointing toward a distant mountain rimmed with clouds.

"Where are we?" Angie asked woozily, sitting up next to me.

"I'm not sure."

"Isn't it obvious? We did it! We're in Ancient Greece." Damian pointed excitedly overhead. "Look, that's a griffin. They pull Zeus's chariot."

The lumbering creature looked like an eagle that had been mashed onto a lion's body. It turned its head, gazing serenely at us, before winging on.

"That can't be real." I was beginning to wonder if I had been run over by a taxi and was dreaming all this. "Angie, punch me in the arm."

Angie knuckled me hard enough to make me yelp. "This ain't a dream," she said. "That griffin thing was real."

"Of course it's real. Which means—" Damian turned and pointed at the distant mountain—"over there is Mount Olympus. Home to the city of the gods."

A shiver ran through me. My dad lived there, according to Athena.

We climbed down from the carriage. I patted the mare's nose, reading the name etched into her bridle. "Hey, Pepper, nice work back there."

Pepper whinnied, turning her head to study her new wings with wide eyes.

"So now what?" Angie asked.

"Ares said Phoebe had to see the oracle," Damian said. "Maybe she can tell us how to stop him."

"You don't really believe that gasbag, do you?" I asked, kicking at the dirt. "That I'm going to help him?"

"Phoebe, he could have killed you back there," Damian said. "Why take Carl? Why drag you back here unless he believes it's true?"

"Damian's got a point," Angie said. "This oracle's bound to know something. It's their job, right? All we gotta do is find her."

"The oracle lives in Apollo's temple at Delphi," Damian informed us. "I'm sure if we ask for directions, someone will know how to get there."

I rolled my eyes. For someone so smart, he was absolutely clueless at times. I pointed at our clothing. "We don't exactly blend in, and I don't speak Ancient Greek, do you?"

He frowned. "Good point."

"Well, whatever we do, we better hurry," Angie said. "This looks like a busy road. Someone could come by anytime."

We crowded onto the driver's bench. I gripped the reins. "Left or right?"

Damian pointed at the distant mountain. "Let's head toward Olympus. I think Apollo's temple is south of it."

"Right it is."

I snapped the reins, and Pepper started pulling the carriage down the road.

Strange excitement bubbled in my veins as I looked around, taking in the sights and smells. I was home. Even though my father had banished me from the place, I felt like

I belonged here. Way more than I ever had back in New York. And somewhere out there was a brother I'd never met.

"Uh, guys? I think we might have a problem." Angie pointed at the road ahead.

A battalion of men on horseback rode our way, stirring up a cloud of dust.

I jerked my head at Angie and Damian. "There's a blanket in the back. Hide under it." They scrambled over the seat, ducking out of sight.

I pulled back on the reins as the lead rider approached. He wore a red tunic with a shiny breastplate and red-crested helmet.

But that wasn't what had me staring.

That would be the half man, half horse that pranced at his side.

The horse part appeared to be a black stallion and made up the back end and all four legs. The man part rose from the waist up. Silver armor covered his torso, leaving his muscly arms bare. Horse-man looked as though he could bench press a Mack truck. There were several others like him scattered among the troops.

The lead soldier held up a hand, halting the brigade. "I am General Egan, commander of the First Legion of the King of Argos. What business have you on the king's road?"

Either I had suddenly mastered Greek, or he was speaking English.

I squared my shoulders, trying to sound as snooty as Julia Pillsbury. "Out of my way, soldier. I have official business in Olympus. Zeus himself is waiting to greet me."

There was a moment of silence, and then Egan laughed. "If that's true, then I'm on my way to meet the goddess Aphrodite."

The men hooted and whistled.

Egan leaned in. "You know what I think? You stole this carriage, and you're hoping to sell it for a profit in town." He snapped his fingers and his men encircled us. They tore the blanket off the back, hauling Angie and Damian up by their collars.

The general frowned. "What strange garments you wear. And you possess a pegasus. Where did you say you were from?"

"I didn't."

Time to make ourselves scarce. A lightning bolt wouldn't cut it, not with this many soldiers. But maybe something else weather-related . . .

In my mind I saw dark clouds forming. The temperature dropped as a chill wind rolled in, sending goosebumps up my arms.

"Don't do it, Phoebe," Damian warned, but he was too late.

My blood hummed with a clamoring energy, and a pressure built up inside my head. Gripped by a sudden impulse, I thrust my fist into the sky and shouted, "*Chalazi!*"

The general's horse tossed its head, surprised by my outburst. The rest of his men looked around in confusion.

But when nothing happened, General Egan snapped his fingers. "Arrest these children and let the magistrate interrogate them."

He turned his horse away as the first ball of hail pinged off his helmet. A second and third followed. Ice missiles shot from the sky in every direction.

Apparently *chalazi* is another word for freaky hailstorm.

The horses reared up, unseating several riders.

"Hold on!" I snapped the reins, urging Pepper forward. She took three running steps before her wings lifted us off the ground. The carriage bobbed and weaved through the stinging storm as Pepper spirited us away from the mass of confused soldiers.

When we were a safe distance away, I guided the carriage down and parked on a grassy spot behind a stand of fig trees.

I jumped down, pumping my fist. "That was awesome!"

Damian and Angie climbed out. Damian wore a frown. "That was reckless."

"Why are you always so negative? I put those soldiers in their place." I raised my hand to Angie, expecting a high five, but she folded her arms and glared at me.

"Have you forgotten you've been banished from Olympus?"

My excitement fizzled out. "So?"

"So quit showing off."

"Angie's right," Damian said, a bit more gently. "We need to keep a low profile until we figure out what to do."

I nodded, blinking back tears. It wasn't fair. I'd just saved their hides from being tossed in some stinking jail, and they acted like I was out of line!

"Did you notice General Egan spoke English?" Angie asked.

Damian nodded. "It must be the magic of Olympus. I understood him perfectly. Did you see that centaur? It was massive."

"You mean horse-man?"

"It's like every myth I've ever read come to life. This place is remarkable."

Flying lions and horse-men? No thanks. The sooner we got Carl and found our way back, the sooner life could go back to normal.

"One question—how do we get home?" Damian's question hung in the air.

I bit my lip as it hit me—we hadn't given a thought to how we were going to get back. Based on the tense looks on my friends' faces, they had the same worry on their minds.

What if we're stuck here forever?

I mustered all the confidence I had. "We'll figure that out when the time comes. For now, the oracle awaits. Which way do we go?"

Before Damian could answer, a snicker of laughter came from some bushes behind the carriage.

"Who's there?" I asked.

The shrubbery rattled, and a voice growled, "Stay back. I am a manticore with sharp teeth and a poisonous tail."

"You don't sound like a manticore," I said. "Not that I know what one sounds like."

"A manticore is a lion with a Neanderthal head and a serpent tail," Damian explained.

The bush rattled louder, sending leaves flying. "Leave the carriage and be gone, or I will eat the flesh from your bones."

"If you're a big bad manticore, I'm a toaster oven." Angie reached into the brush and hauled a figure out by the nape of his neck.

It was a scrawny boy, maybe nine or ten. His fair hair was ragged, his features grimed in dirt. His eyes shone a deep blue that reminded me of the sea.

He twisted in her grip. "I am a son of Apollo. I command you to leave me be."

"Son of Apollo?" Damian said. "Perfect! You must know the way to his temple!"

The boy flushed, slipping free of Angie's grip, and straightened his tunic. "'Course I do. Been there loads of times."

"So you'll take us there?" I asked.

"That depends." He folded his arms. "Can you pay?"

"Pay?" I looked at the others. "We don't have any money."

He plucked a worn knapsack from the bush. "Then I'll be on my way." He whistled as he strode off.

"Wait!" I cried. "Please. We haven't a clue where we are."

He stopped, glancing over his shoulder. "No money, no help. That's the rule of Macario."

"Rule of Macario?"

He gave a short bow. "Macario, favored son of Apollo."

"I prefer the rule of Brooklyn," Angie growled, punching one hand into the other.

He arched one eyebrow. "If you so much as touch me, my father will send a bolt of sunlight so powerful you will sizzle to ash in the blink of an eye."

Something was off. For a son of an important god, Macario's clothes were as ragged as his haircut.

"Look, Macario, give us a break. We're not from around here."

He wavered a moment, then gave a slight shrug. "Maybe we can work something out."

"I'm listening," I said warily.

"Take me with you to see the oracle, and I'll guide you there."

I looked at my friends for approval. Seemed simple enough.

Damian hesitated. "Why do you need us to take you to your own father's temple?"

He eyed Damian coolly. "That's my business. Do we have a deal or not?"

I thrust my hand out. "Deal. I'm Phoebe, by the way, and that's Angie and Damian."

Macario flashed a grin. "Phoebe, did you say? How interesting."

CHAPTER 12

The son of Apollo took the reins, insisting he knew the way. We bounced along a hard-packed road through low hills and stands of olive trees. I sat up front while the other two lounged in the back.

Macario flicked me a curious glance. "So what parts do you hail from? They dress very funny there."

"Actually, I'm from around here somewhere. But I've been away."

"Where'd you go, Sparta?"

I laughed. "Nope. New York City."

"Where is New York City? Is that one of the new territories?"

"You could say that." *So new it hasn't been discovered yet.* "We met a guy earlier, General Egan. Seemed pretty intense."

"You're lucky he didn't conscript you into his army. King Acrisius is behind on his duty to provide more troops to fight in the Trojan War."

The name sounded familiar. *Isn't he my grandfather or something? The one who wanted my brother dead?*

"How long until we reach this oracle's temple?" Angie asked from the back. "I'm so hungry I could gnaw my arm off."

"There is a small village not far from here," Macario said idly. "We can stop there, if you like?"

There was a chorus of assents, but Macario had a secretive look on his face I didn't like. The sooner we were rid of this pest, the better.

Spirals of smoke soon rose through the trees, trickling up from whitewashed houses. The town itself was small, just a few buildings and a marketplace in the center plaza. Colorful stands displayed wares for sale. Earthen pots hung from wires, and the smell of roasted lamb turning on a spit made my mouth water.

"Come on," Angie said, jumping down and rubbing her hands together. "Let's have some of that."

"We don't have any money," Damian reminded her.

"Here." Macario flipped them a silver coin. "A drachma should be enough for all of us. Phoebe and I will see to the pegasus."

Damian and Angie rushed off with shouts of thanks.

While Macario led Pepper to a water trough, I wandered over to a stall stacked with beautiful fabrics. Three spinsters sat behind the counter, their gray hair piled up on top of their heads in knotted messes.

The first spinster had a loom in front of her. She racked and wove the thread so fast it was a blur. The second one held a needle, her fingers flying as she stitched her handiwork into the fabric as it came off the loom. The cloth was marked with beautiful symbols in all shapes and colors, like a strange language. The third one waited, a pair of scissors clasped in a swollen, clawlike hand.

"That's so beautiful," I said.

"She likes it, does she?" the one with the scissors said, snapping them open and closed.

"Yes, very much. How much is it?"

The three brayed with laughter. "She thinks she can buy her fate," the middle one said.

"Her fate is not worth much," the first one said, never slowing in her weaving.

"Not even half a drachma," the third one said. "See, it says here, dead she is by end of day." She pointed with the tip of her scissors at a silver arrow with a flaming tip next to a broken lightning bolt.

A trickle of fear made my hands clench. "Dead? That's not funny."

The second one paused in her sewing. "We only sew what we see, dear. It's perfectly clear your fate is to die today. Best to accept it."

Accept it? I wanted to plant a fat lightning bolt in her face for being so horrid to a stranger, but before I could open my mouth, a blast of white fire hit the ground next to me.

"Daughter of Zeus, you have broken the laws of Olympus," a voice boomed.

A woman with silvery wings descended from the sky. Her face was framed by long dark locks and a shiny headband. She wore a simple tunic and golden boots laced up to her knees. In her hands, she held a bow nocked with an arrow. A ball of white fire encased the tip—exactly like the arrow stitched in the fabric.

"I am Alekto of the Erinyes. You were banished for all eternity for the treasonous acts you will one day commit."

Without thought, I clenched my hands and called up a bolt of lightning. I launched it forward, aiming straight at her head. She spun away as she released her arrow, dodging my blast but sending the arrow wide. Another winged being came in from the other side.

"You are a traitor to Olympus!" the second one shouted. "You must die!"

She sent her own flaming arrow at me. I dove to the side, and it exploded in the dirt, sending clods flying.

A third one appeared, arrow nocked and ready.

Jeez, how many of them does it take to kill me!

I ducked under the table for shelter. The three spinsters continued to work on their weaving.

"Dead she will be, wait and you will see," they sang in unison, repeating the verse over and over again.

I scrambled along the length of the table past their stubby legs and fat feet. More arrows pinged in the dirt. If I could only get to the end, I might be able to dash to the next stall.

The table was flung backward, exposing me.

"We told you, daughter of Zeus, your fate was at an end," scissor-hands sneered in my face, catching me by the collar and lifting me up.

"The story ends here, princess," the middle one screeched, clutching the fabric. "It says so right here."

I wrenched free, a lightning bolt in my hand. I was really getting tired of being told what my fate was. In one swift move I brought the bolt down, splitting the loom into a pile of kindling.

The three hags screamed like banshees, wringing their hands over their ruined machine.

The marketplace erupted into chaos as villagers ran for shelter. A pair of squealing pigs ran by. An empty carriage thundered past, pulled by frightened horses. Another arrow struck the ground next to me, stinging my legs with sharp stones.

"Phoebe, over here," Damian called.

He waved from behind a low wall in front of the stables.

I sent three bolts in the direction the arrow had come from and darted in their direction, diving over the wall. Arrows pinged against the masonry, exploding with silvery light.

"Now who did you cheese off?" Angie said.

"I don't think my dad's all that happy I came back," I gritted out. "Who are these Erinyes anyway?"

"They deliver justice in Olympus," Damian said, sounding slightly awed. "If you break the law, they hand out the punishment."

"But I haven't done anything wrong," I protested.

Like most things in my life, it wasn't fair, but if they thought I was giving up without a fight, they didn't know me. I needed something bigger than my lightning bolt. Something better than hail.

The idea formed in my head like a dark storm cloud. I stood, hands clenched tightly, chin down. The trio of avengers hovered in the air across the market, bows drawn. As one they flew straight for me, unleashing their arrows at the same time I clapped my hands over my head.

"*Megalo Fortuna*!"

Forked lightning speared down from the sky, incinerating the arrows in a three-pronged strike. A black cloud blotted out the sun, and a blast of thunder shook the ground hard enough to rattle my teeth.

And then the rain came.

It rained so hard sheets of water quickly flooded the ground. Wind whipped across the empty marketplace, sending the rain sideways, tearing the flimsy stalls to shreds, and making it impossible to see. The Erinyes winged toward me, but they were tossed and tumbled backward.

"Over here!"

The faint shout came from the trees. Macario waved, holding on to Pepper's bridle with one hand.

I hooked arms with Angie and Damian, and crouching low, we fought our way against the buffeting wind to the carriage. We jumped in as Macario flicked the reins over Pepper's head, and we lifted off. The carriage swayed wildly as Pepper mightily winged us away from the storm.

My stomach was twisted into knots. I couldn't breathe. The same thought kept turning over and over in my head.

Zeus wanted me dead.

My own father.

"Put us down," I said.

"In a minute," he answered.

Bile rose up in my throat. "Put us down now."

The carriage dropped, hitting with a thump, and rolled forward.

I leaped out and rushed to some bushes, where I proceeded to empty my guts.

Angie jumped down and started shouting, "You little rat, you sold us out. Get down here so I can teach you a lesson."

Macario said nothing, but I could see guilt smeared all over his face like a rash.

Wiping my mouth, I stalked over to the carriage and hauled him down. "Tell us what you did, or so help me, I don't care if your dad is god of the universe, I will shove a lightning bolt down your throat."

He pushed my hand away and stepped back. "Fine. The Old Three said if I found a girl named Phoebe to bring her by. I was going to get five drachmas if it was the right girl."

"The Old Three?" I asked. "Who are they, and why do they care about me?"

"I think those were the Fates," Damian said, a deep frown etched in his brow. "They record the destinies of the gods on their loom—which you just destroyed. That can't be good."

I shrugged. "Who wants to know their fate? Not me."

Damian smiled grimly. "Remember, Zeus sent you away because a prophecy said you were going to destroy Olympus. We've only been here an hour, and you already nuked the loom of the Fates. I'm just saying, it's not a good sign."

Anger made my voice rise. "So you're saying I should have just let those winged avengers fill me with arrows? I should have just given up?"

He sighed. "No, it's just that we have to be careful, that's all. Not play into Ares's hands."

Frustration burned a hole in my gut. Why was everything always my fault? I wanted to punch a hole in the sky and let the universe explode in a cloud of dust.

Angie gripped my shoulder, steadying me. "Message received, Damian. So what now?"

"Same as before. We need to find this temple before anything else happens."

"My father's temple is only a few hours away," Macario said. He'd been quiet through our little argument.

I pointed down the road back the way we'd come. "You're not part of this discussion. You can walk back to wherever you came from."

He folded his arms. "Fine—then you'll never get in the temple."

"What do you mean?"

"The Erinyes will be staked out there. Your only chance is to sneak in a back way."

"And I suppose you know just the spot?"

He smiled. "Of course."

"Katzy, you're not seriously going to listen to him?" Angie protested.

I put my hand up, silencing her. "Do you really know another way in?"

He nodded, crossing his fingers in an X over his heart. "On Apollo's life, I swear it."

"Then take us there."

Damian looked worried. "Phoebe, I'm beginning to think we shouldn't have come here."

"I told you to stay home," I snapped, still reeling from everything that had happened. "You had your chance."

Damian looked hurt, and remorse kicked in.

"Look, I'm sorry. It just kind of sucks that the one place I thought I'd feel welcome sent out a hit squad to get rid of me."

He gave me a quick nod. "It's okay, Phoebes. We just need to . . . you know . . . be more careful."

He was right of course.

The problem was, I didn't know how to do that.

CHAPTER 13

Damian claimed the spot up front next to Macario—just as well, because I still felt like punching the worm. Thankfully the clatter of the carriage wheels muffled the sounds of Damian's voice as he interrogated the boy—I, for one, was already sick of this place.

"You all right, Katzy?" Angie asked quietly.

We had our feet up on the siderails, heads resting next to each other on the seat.

I took the piece of straw I'd been chewing on out of my mouth and waved it in the air. "Sure. Great. You know me. Nothing gets to me."

"Still—finding out your dad put a hit on you—that's pretty low. I'm sorry."

I faked a laugh. "What did I expect, a big warm hug?"

I refused to cry about it. What did I care about a dad I'd never met? Carl was the reason I was here. Carl was the one who had always been there for me.

I must have fallen asleep, because I jolted awake when the carriage stopped.

We were at the base of a knobby hill covered in pines and scattered boulders. The tip of a white column was just visible at the top.

The temple of Apollo.

"This is the back way," Macario said, jumping down and leading us to a gaping hole in the side of the hill. "From these tunnels we can make our way to the oracle's chamber."

"How do we know it's not another trap?" Angie asked. "This sewer rat's probably not even related to Apollo."

His face tightened. "I am so a son of Apollo!"

Angie made a mocking face. "Liar, liar, your tunic's on fire. I'll bet you're a fake."

A slash of color lit up his cheeks. "Take it back."

"Make me."

With a sudden flick of his wrist, a golden beam appeared in Macario's hand. It was a lot like my lightning bolts, only where mine were white, his was yellow and looked to be searing hot, judging from the heat waves radiating from it.

"Macario, put it down," I warned.

"Tell her to take it back before I plant this sunbeam in her big mouth."

"I said put it down." I called up my own lightning.

We faced off until Damian stepped between us.

"Macario, the question was fair. We're not welcome in Olympus. It can only bring you trouble being with us."

His arm wavered, and then he scowled, lowering his sunbeam. "Fine. I want to get my father's attention."

"What do you mean?" I let my lightning sputter out.

His shoulders hunched. "My mother was a tree nymph Apollo loved for about five minutes. I've never even met him."

"Right. So that makes us the same," I said a bit more gently. "I've never met my dad either. At least Apollo doesn't want you dead."

"Close enough." He kicked at a rock. "I grew up in the woods with my mother and her people. One day, a forest fire killed them all. I've been trying to reach my father, but—"

"He won't give you the time of day," I filled in.

Macario gave a tight nod. "It seems a powerful god like Apollo can't be bothered with a mere tree nymph's son. I am meant to do great things. I have the power of the sun."

He threw the sunbeam into the sky. It burst into a golden shower. Sparks fell to the ground and sputtered out.

"I just need to prove to him that I am worthy."

"I still don't trust him," Angie grumbled. "He led us right to those three uglies. This cave could be an even worse trap."

Macario's shoulders stiffened. "A son of Apollo doesn't apologize to mortals. Follow me or not." He strode off toward the entrance.

I turned to my friends. "I'm going in. Maybe you guys should wait here."

"Oh, can it, Katzy. I'm not leaving you alone with that rat." Angie brushed past me and stalked off inside.

I grabbed Damian's arm as he made to follow. "Are you sure about this, D? Angie could be right. It could be an even bigger trap."

He backed away, smiling like a goof, and pointed his fingers cockily at me. "You worry too much. Come on, this will be fun!"

I sighed as he disappeared into the tunnel.

Sometimes my friends were even crazier than me.

The inside of the cave smelled musky, like a zoo. Puddles of water dotted the ground. Macario held a small sunbeam that lit our way.

"As I recall, Apollo's temple used to be guarded by a giant python," Damian said.

"Used to be? Python is quite alive and still guardian of the temple," Macario said over his shoulder. "She uses this tunnel to travel outside when she must hunt."

I glanced over at Angie. Her frightened eyes told me she was thinking the same thing I was: *What if this Python gets hungry and decides we're handy snacks?*

A soft hissing noise blew through the tunnel, and something feathered across my skin, like a faint ripple of air being disturbed.

"Um, should we be worried about that noise?" Angie said.

"Don't be frightened," Macario assured. "Python sleeps this time of day. We'll be fine."

He let his sun bolt die out as light appeared ahead.

We emerged into a cavernous room lined with row after row of towering bookshelves. The warm air was humid, and green vines hung from the ceiling, twisting themselves around the shelves. Thick tomes were crammed on every shelf, stacked up in piles, and spilling onto the floor. Moisture dripped from the ceiling, and the entire floor was covered by several inches of water.

"Welcome to Apollo's temple," Macario said. "This is the archives, where they store all of the past prophecies."

I whistled. "That's a lot of prophecies."

"Gods and mortals have been asking questions about the future for centuries upon centuries. Every prophecy is recorded in a book. When the book is filled, a new one is begun," Macario explained.

"Why is it so hot in here?" Angie asked, fanning herself.

"Python likes it this way," Macario said.

"Doesn't the water ruin the books?" Damian asked.

The boy shook his head. "They're enchanted with powerful magic. Nothing can damage them, not even fire."

"So how do we find our way out of here?" I looked around. There was no sign of an exit—the towering shelves made it impossible to see around them.

Macario craned his neck. "Sorry, I'm a bit turned around." He pointed to the left. "You three have a look that way, and I'll go this way." He darted off before we could argue.

I sighed. "I really don't like him."

"He got us this far," Damian reminded.

"Yeah, so he can sacrifice us to some snake," Angie muttered.

"We should go after him," I said, but Angie gave me a shove.

"That's just what the little creep wants. Let's go around the other way, and then when we find him, I can strangle him."

Chapter 14

We waded into ankle-deep water. Shelves rose up on either side, blocking our view. Dangling vines brushed against us as we walked. I glanced over the spines. The books were different colors and thicknesses. I wondered what was inside—if the prophecies had all come true or not.

A distant splash made me pause.

"Did you hear that?" Angie asked.

I nodded. "Damian, how big did you say this snake was?"

"Big. Come on, let's find a way out of here."

We waded faster until we came to an intersection. Aisles of bookshelves extended in every direction like spokes on a wagon wheel.

"Which way?" Angie asked.

"Let's go right," I said, heading determinedly down the next aisle.

Another splash sounded, closer this time. We couldn't see anything but glimpses of other rows through gaps in the books. I thought I caught movement two aisles over but couldn't be certain.

We began making turns at random. The rhythmic splashes sounded closer and closer, as though something was slithering along.

"Anything?" Angie looked anxiously over her shoulder.

"Nope."

I was about to climb one of the stacks and shout out Macario's name when something tugged at me, like an invisible hand on my arm, pulling me toward the aisle to the left.

It wasn't worse than any other direction, so I turned. "This way."

We splashed down the aisle until we came to another intersection. I stopped, holding my breath, waiting.

There. Another slight tug.

I turned right, jogging now.

A faint hissing rippled across the air. Whatever was following us wasn't being quiet any longer. Books splashed into the water as it stepped up its pursuit.

"Phoebe, something's definitely following us," Damian said.

"We're almost there." The thread yanked me along, reeling me into a dead run. I had no idea where it was leading me, but my top choice was a quick exit.

The water grew deeper, reaching my knees and slowing us. Halfway down an aisle, I halted. Angie slammed into me, nearly knocking me over.

"Katzy, a little warning next time."

"Sorry. It's just . . . something made me stop."

"We don't have time to read some old prophecies," Damian said.

"I know, but something called me here. It must be important. Help me." I began pulling books off the shelf and tossing them.

Angie and Damian followed suit. "What are we looking for?" he asked.

"I don't know, but I'll know it when I find it."

Angie pulled out a scarlet tome with an eagle crest on the front. "Ooh, look at this one."

The crest glowed brightly to my eyes, lifting off the cover like a hologram. "That's it!"

Damian took it and opened the cover. The pages were filled with neat writing. We huddled around it, but before we could read a word, a massive snake the size of a subway train broke through the shelves, sending books flying as it snapped its gaping maw at us.

"Python!" Damian screamed.

The bookshelf came crashing down as we fled. Python shot after us, toppling shelves as it gave chase.

We made turn after turn, trying to evade it. A section of the snake's thick body crossed in front of our aisle, blocking our way. We turned to run the other way, but its diamond-shaped head swooped down over the top of the shelves, open jaws revealing glistening fangs longer than my arm.

Angie threw a pair of books at it, making it rear back long enough for us to escape down another aisle. But no matter which way we turned, the snake was there, heading us off until we were backed into a corner with nowhere to run.

Python towered over us, its massive head swaying. Its eyes glowed green as it hissed, "Intruder*sss*, *sssss*teal my mi*sss*stresses' book. You will be punished."

"I'm Phoebe, daughter of Zeus. This book belongs to me."

The snake's eyes widened. "You're the daughter of the prophecy."

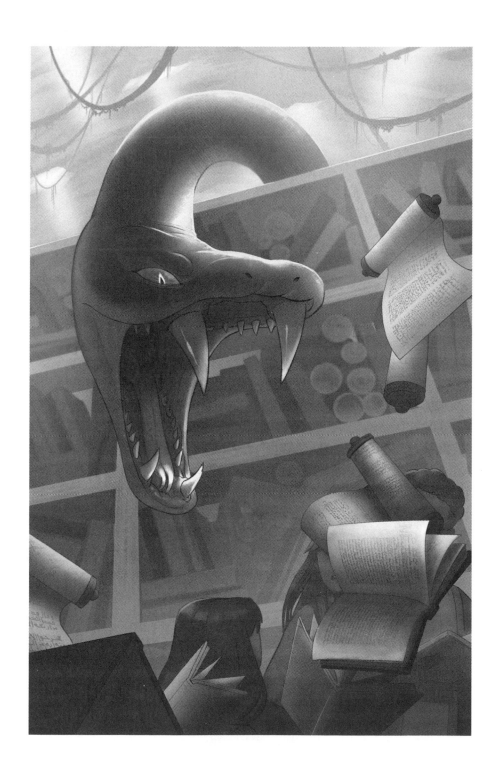

For half a second, I thought we were in the clear, until Python's eyes flared with rage. "De*sss*stroyer of Olympus! I shall eat you first."

It struck in a blur of motion, seeking to swallow me whole in its massive jaws. I didn't even have time to call up a lightning bolt. I threw my arms up in a lame attempt to protect myself, but something knocked me to the side.

Damian.

Python's outstretched jaws snapped shut, swallowing Damian along with the red book. The snake didn't see who it had swallowed, too busy tilting its head back to get its prize down its gullet as it slithered away.

Horror kept me rooted to the spot. Damian was gone. Really, truly gone.

"Come on, Phoebe, we have to help him!" Angie shook my arm. "We can't let it get away!"

What did she think we were going to do? Chase after the snake and ask him nicely to barf Damian up? My lips were numb as I said, "It's too late—he's gone, Angie."

Tears ran down her cheeks as she shook her head. "No, we do not give up on him. Do something. Use your powers."

I had never seen Angie cry. Ever. It snapped me out of my funk. She was right. I had to at least try. I clenched my hands as tight as I could and thought of the coldest, wintriest day, and the words burst from me.

"*Kryo Pagos!*"

I sucked in a deep breath and then blew it out. A frost cloud billowed over the knee-deep water, and it froze solid, trapping the snake in place. Python howled in rage as it struggled to break free.

Calling up a lightning bolt, I took three running steps and went into a slide, skating over the slick surface to the bulging part of the snake's belly.

Gripping the bolt, I sliced open the side of the snake as I slid past. Yellowish blood sprayed me, and Python screamed in pain. Its tail thrashed about, destroying more rows of shelves. I reached inside its belly. It was warm and gross. I pushed past layers of coiled muscle, searching, until a hand locked onto mine. I dropped the lightning and tugged with both hands. Damian's head came out first, then his shoulders, but the snake's coils tightened, locking him in place. Python's head swayed overhead, eyes blazing emerald fury.

"You will die for thi*ssss*, daughter of Olympu*sss*!"

Its fanged jaws hovered over me, ready to strike. I couldn't move—if I let go of Damian, the snake's muscles would drag him right back in.

Then Angie was there, swinging on a vine as she vaulted off the top of a bookshelf. In her hand she clutched her puny switchblade.

"LEAVE MY FRIENDS ALONE!" She plunged the little blade right between its eyes.

Python bellowed in pain, tossing Angie through the air. But it did the trick—the snake's coils unleashed enough for me to pull Damian free with a burping squelch. The snake broke free of the melting ice and slithered away, hissing to itself.

Damian sat up, clutching the red book and covered in snake goo. He wiped his eyes clear, looking abnormally pale. "It is hi-hi-highly unlikely to su-su-survive a p-p-python attack," he stuttered.

A whistle pierced the air. Macario stood atop a distant bookshelf, waving his arms. "I found an exit," he shouted.

I helped Damian to his feet. "Come on, let's get Angie and get out of here."

We found Angie groaning in pain two aisles away. The three of us limped over to where Macario stood waiting.

"You set that snake on us!" Angie snarled, lunging at him.

He backed up a step. "No, I found the exit. Look." He pointed to a stairwell tucked behind a thick layer of hanging vines. It was impossible to see until you were right on it.

"Sure, now you find it—that's convenient," Angie sniped.

"Let it go, Angie," I said. "It's time to meet the oracle."

CHAPTER 15

At the top of the stairs, a heavy wooden door opened to reveal a corridor lined with gleaming torches. The polished white marble floor reflected the flames. We gulped in fresh air, glad to be out of the steamy basement.

"This way." Macario walked confidently toward an archway at the end of the corridor.

We entered a high-domed room. Tall columns lined the open-air front, which offered a full view of Mount Olympus. The setting sun cast an orange glow over its snow-capped peak.

The back half of the temple was built into a rock-hewn wall. A set of marble steps led to a raised dais in the center of the room. Unlit torches had been placed in each corner of the dais.

We huddled at the base of the steps.

"So now what?" I asked.

We all looked to Macario.

"If you want your future read, you need an offering for the oracle," he said.

"But I don't have anything."

"Here." Angie slipped a silver chain from around her neck. "Pops spent a ton of dough on it."

"Angie, I can't—"

"You can. Go on." She closed my fingers around it and gave me a shove.

I stumbled up the steps on weak legs. Between freezing the python and calling up countless bolts of lighting, my energy stocks were low. For a moment, I wished I was back at Dexter Academy with nothing more to worry about than Julia Pillsbury and a ruined history project.

And then I remembered the terrified look on Carl's face as Ares hauled him off, and I pushed the fatigue aside.

When I stepped onto the dais, flames instantly lit up the torches. A marble basin of water rested on a stone pedestal. A shadowed archway opened into the rock wall.

"Hello?"

A whispery voice replied from the shadows, "Who seeks the Oracle of Delphi?"

"Uh, hi, my name is Phoebe."

Puffs of steam shot up from the floor, making me dance sideways.

"Your prophecy has been read before," the voice said carefully. "Not by me, but by one of my sisters."

"Someone else asked the question, not me. I'm here to ask my own."

I could just make out silvery eyes glittering at me. The rest of her was hidden. I thought she was going to tell me to get lost, but she asked, "Do you have an offering?"

I held the chain out, letting it dangle from my fingers.

"Put it in the basin."

I let it drop into the water. Immediately the surface bubbled and steam rose up. It smelled of eucalyptus and menthol. As I stared into the basin, the chain dissolved, and the water glowed with a faint aura.

A woman stepped gracefully out of the shadows. She was slender and tall. Dark hair was coiled atop her head. She wore a sleeveless gown of pearl silk, knotted over one shoulder.

"Phoebe of Argos. What a surprise."

Her tone was fluid and even. I couldn't tell if it was a good surprise or bad.

"I know there's some prophecy about me destroying this place," I said, "but that's not why I'm here. You see, Ares took my social worker. His name is Carl. He's the . . . I mean . . . I have to . . . I . . ."

"You care for him," she prompted.

"Yeah, you could say that. He's the one who found me when I was kicked out of Olympus. He's been looking out for me my whole life."

"I see." She walked to the basin, trailing her fingers in the water before looking at me. "And what question have you for the oracle? Be mindful, you may only ask one."

"How do I get Carl back home in one piece?"

Her silver eyes glittered with anger. "You wish to know how to rescue a mortal?" Steam shot up into the air around my feet, higher this time.

"Yes. Tell me how to save him, and I'll disappear again, and you can all forget about me. And I promise not to destroy Olympus while I'm here."

The oracle tilted her head stiffly. "Allow me to consult with the mists, and I will return with an answer." She backed away into the shadows.

"You all right up there, Katzy?" Angie called.

"Yeah, peachy." I rocked back and forth, my feet squelching in my wet tennies.

After a long moment, the oracle returned. She had a

funny look on her face, as if she'd just eaten some bad clams. Her hands were clasped behind her. "You were not supposed to return, child of Zeus."

I stepped back. "Right, but here I am, so how do I—you know—rescue my friend?"

"The prophecy was clear," she continued, swinging her arms forward, revealing a heavy sword. Its sharpened edges gleamed in the torchlight. "If the child of Zeus returned to Olympus, a mighty god would perish. You cannot be allowed to live." She raised the sword over her head with both hands, readying herself to cleave me in half.

Seriously? Does everyone in this place want me dead?

"Phoebe, run!" Angie yelled.

I grabbed the nearest torch and knocked it over, spilling flaming oil over the dais. The hem of her dress caught fire. Sparks and ash flew as the flames leaped higher, but it didn't slow her down.

Her face twisted with anger. "You cannot escape me, daughter of Zeus! Perish you must before the gates of Olympus crumple."

She flew forward, her feet skimming the ground as whatever magic she had propelled her along. I quickly threw a lightning bolt at her, pleased when it landed dead center in her chest.

The bad news was, it didn't have the intended effect. She grew even larger, glowing with a bright light as flames swirled and burned at her feet.

"You cannot kill me, puny mortal!" Her voice was a roar, booming off the ceiling as she grew to the size of a ten-foot-tall linebacker.

"I'm not a mortal," I shouted back, "I am the daughter of a god. I may not be able to kill you, but I can do this."

I squeezed my fists, calling up two lightning bolts, and

sent them both at the ceiling. They exploded in a flash of bright light. Stones tumbled down, striking the oracle and knocking her to the ground. An ominous crack sounded as the ceiling split open, revealing the twilight sky.

I hurried down the steps as more stones tumbled down. The first column cracked and split, falling in slow motion with an ear-splitting crash. One after the other, the columns began to splinter and fall.

"The temple is coming down," Damian said. "We have to go."

"But I don't have my prophecy," I wailed.

"Too bad!" Angie dragged me out, closely followed by Macario.

Behind us there was an explosion of dust and the roar of collapsing rock as the entire mountain seemed to cave in on itself. We ran headlong down the hillside to escape the tumbling boulders.

We didn't stop until we reached the bottom, and looked back up. I had to bite my knuckle to stop from crying out. As the dust settled, all that remained of the magnificent temple was a single broken column.

"It looks like the destruction of Olympus has begun," Damian joked.

I punched him on the arm. "Not funny."

Angie looked pale. "What if he's right, Katzy? What if none of this is supposed to happen?"

"It has happened. And Ares still has Carl, so if it means I have to destroy Olympus to get him back, I will."

Macario clucked softly. "This Carl must be some god."

"He's not a god," I said, blinking back tears. "He's like an old sweater that keeps you warm on a cold day. He's a pair of worn shoes that fit just right. He's hot chocolate when it's snowing outside. He's home. And I'm going to save him."

There was dead silence.

After a long moment, Angie put her fingers to her lips and whistled sharply. There was a thrumming of wings, and then Pepper sailed over the treetops, skidding to a stop in front of us.

We climbed in, and Pepper rumbled us away through the darkening trees.

A cloud hung over me. I wasn't any closer to knowing how to rescue Carl, and I had just wrecked the temple of Apollo.

If I was indeed the destroyer of Olympus, I was right on target.

Chapter 16

We made camp in the shelter of some trees near a bubbling stream. Macario built us a fire, using a spark of sunbeam to light the wood. We were hungry, with nothing much to eat but olives we picked from the trees. Still, no one complained. In fact, no one said much of anything. I lay back on a thick bed of leaves and stared at the twinkling stars, seeing the temple crumble to the ground over and over again in my head.

"Hey, Phoebes," Damian said. "You need to see this."

"What?" I rolled over, tossing a stick in the fire.

He was reading the red journal we'd found. I'd forgotten all about it.

"I think it's a prophecy about you."

I sat up, a mixture of fear and excitement making my pulse skitter.

"Well, what does it say?"

His eyes were stricken as he looked at me. "Sure you want to know?"

I nodded, swallowing back the lump of dread. "Whatever it is, can't be worse than what Ares said, right?"

Damian's eyes zagged away from mine. He cleared his throat and began to read.

"To Zeus, king of the gods, I have come to warn
The fate of Olympus rests on a daughter not born

From the same womb as Perseus will she arise
To a mighty god, she will be his demise

For she will bring the kingdom down
In ruins round and round his crown."

The air went out of me in a *whoosh*. "So Ares was right? I really am this . . . destroyer?"

Damian turned the page. "Hold on—it looks like there's more, although the writing is different." He held up the book. It looked like someone had scrawled more lines hurriedly. He continued reading:

"To stop this future from unfolding
Six talismans must she be holding

A single feather from the Sphinx's wing
The Crommyonian Sow's tusk shall she bring

Strength she'll need for the Nemean Lion's claw
For next she'll pry the Hydra's fang from its jaw

From mighty Cerberus, his tail be shorn
And finish it off with the Chimera's horn

When the Eye of Zeus is finally complete
Only then this prophecy will she defeat."

"Are you saying I have to battle all of these monsters?" I squeaked.

Damian frowned. "From what I can tell, you need only collect a talisman from each. But yes, that seems to be the only way to stop Ares."

I scrambled up. "Then we do it. We collect the talismans, put Ares in his place, and get Carl back. Who are these monsters and how do we find them?"

I looked at Macario.

He had a doubtful look on his face. "These creatures are all Echidna's children. She gave birth to six of the most fearsome beasts ever. Did you know the Lernean hydra has nine heads? And the Crommyonian sow can rip out a man's insides with its tusks." He shook his head. "The others are equally awful."

"We can't go after the talismans until we know what the Eye of Zeus is," Damian said. "I've never heard of it before."

Macario shrugged. "Neither have I."

My brain raced as I paced in front of the fire. "If no one's ever heard of it, maybe it's because it wasn't written about." I stopped. "Because no one knew about it." I pulled the old mirror out of my pocket and studied the shapes on the back.

There were six of them—the same number of monsters I had to get a talisman from. Taking the hydra's fang out of my pocket—the one Miss Carole had given me—I held it over the mirror. The fang vibrated in my hand, tugging itself toward the mirror. I let it go and it dropped into the triangle-shaped slot, changing size to fit. Then, with a sudden spark, it was spit out, turning to dust.

My eyes bulged. "Did you see that? It tried to fit itself in."

"But since it wasn't the real hydra—" Damian added.

"It was rejected," I finished, brandishing the mirror.

"This is the Eye of Zeus! All we have to do is collect a few trophies, and we're home free."

"Hold on—you're not thinking we're gonna trot out and face a bunch of monsters?" Angie had been quiet throughout our discussion, but her voice was angry. "That's just brilliant, because I really wanted to die here! Come on, Katzy, I like Carl too, but look at that list. You're talking a hydra, the real thing, not some bathroom monster. And a Nemean lion? I don't even know what that is, but it sounds deadly."

"Its hide is stronger than steel," Macario piped in. "Impossible to kill."

"See?" She pointed at the boy. "Even the rat knows we're doomed. I say we go home now before anything worse happens."

"Go," I said, ignoring the sting of pain at her words. "I don't care. I'm not leaving without Carl."

Angie glared at me. "Why do you always do that? Act like you don't care. You can't possibly think it's okay to destroy this place all because of one person—I mean, what about the rest of the people that live here?" She shook her head. "I've got a bad feeling about this. It's not going to end well."

She was probably right, but I was too stubborn to admit it.

"You know what the last thing Carl said to me was? He said I had potential, but if I didn't start using it, I was going to lose it. Guess what? This is me using my potential. Just because someone said I'm going to destroy Olympus doesn't mean I will. They didn't know I was going to meet you and Damian, because if they had, they would know I'm smarter and stronger with you guys. Maybe the oracle doesn't know everything, and maybe, just maybe, we can make our own fate."

Her face slowly relaxed. "Okay, Katzy. We'll do it your way."

"Thanks—I don't deserve a friend like you." She rolled her eyes, muttering how right I was, and my spirits lifted a notch. "Damian, what's first on the list again?"

"The sphinx. I think she lived near a place called Thebes."

"Macario, can you take us there?"

He shook his head, averting his eyes. "I have business elsewhere—"

"A son of Apollo could really make a name for himself, taking on all these monsters," I cut in.

His face brightened. "I guess my business can wait. Thebes is two days from here."

We set off at first light, an aura of excitement floating over us. There was a chance, a real chance, everything was going to be okay. I just had to face six terrible monsters.

At least I wasn't alone.

"Tell us about this sphinx," I asked Macario.

"Around these parts we call her the Flesh Eater."

"Uh, I think I prefer sphinx," I said.

He cocked a glance at me. "We also call her the Pagan People Eater."

"No."

"The Monster of Thebes?"

"Anything else?"

He sighed. "I once heard someone refer to her as Miss Kitty. She's half woman, half lion, and ugly as the rear end of a manticore."

"She doesn't sound so bad," I said, thinking of the ferocious hydra we had battled back in the bathroom.

"Macario's leaving out her tail, which is a deadly serpent," Damian said, clearly eager to show off his knowledge. "If you happened upon her lair, she would challenge you to answer her riddle."

"Ooh, I love riddles," Angie said, clapping her hands.

"Hers were deadly," Damian said. "According to legend, if you answered incorrectly, she would eat you alive."

"That's why she's called the Monster of Thebes," Macario said. "The people live in terror of taking the road that leads through the valley to their city, but it's the shortest route."

"How do we defeat her?" I asked.

"We have to answer her riddle," Damian said. "It's the only way."

"I don't suppose you know it?" I asked.

He tossed me an eye roll. "Of course. It went something like this: What creature is first four-footed, then two-footed, and finally three-footed?"

"It's impossible," Macario scoffed. "No one's ever solved it."

"I give up," I said, looking at Damian. "What's the answer?"

"Man. He's first on all fours, as a baby crawling. As he gets older, he walks on two feet. It's only when he is old and needs a cane that he has three feet."

Macario gaped. "By the gods, how did you know that?"

"I read," Damian said. "Everything that happens here has already been recorded in history."

"What do they write about me?" Macario asked eagerly.

Damian hesitated.

"Come on, they have to talk about the most powerful son of Apollo. They've probably written entire books about me," he boasted.

"Boring ones, I bet," Angie scoffed. "What's to eat?"

"That one only thinks about her stomach," Macario griped.

"That one is hungry—that's why," she snapped back.

They were like two cats in a fight. I sighed. "I'm kind of hungry too. Do you have any more drachmas, Macario? Maybe we can buy some food without three old ladies and a pack of Erinyes trying to kill me."

His eyes gleamed. "I know just the place." He flicked the reins, and Pepper let out an aggrieved sigh as she spread her wings and took flight.

We soared over the countryside. I liked seeing things from up high. Mount Olympus jutted up in the north, but the rest of the place was green-and-brown rolling hills bounded by a deep blue coastline. Small villages dotted the country. A dark haze muddied the horizon. A city squatted under the clouds of dust and smoke.

"What's that place called?" I asked Macario.

"That's Avalon, the black market of Olympus, filled with robbers, thieves, and outlaws. It's the one place where you won't be the most wanted person there."

CHAPTER 17

Macario was right about Avalon. The place was crawling with all sorts of lowlifes. Furtive eyes assessed us as we made our way into town, probably looking to see if we had anything to steal, but the carriage was streaked with dirt, and the wooden siding had been dinged by arrows. One of the wheels had several broken spokes. Plus, we probably smelled, and our clothes were stained and rumpled from sleeping in the dirt.

Macario tied Pepper off to a post with a row of other carriages. We had tossed the blanket over her back to hide her wings.

"You sure it's a good idea to leave the carriage untended?" Damian asked.

"No one wants this heap as long as they don't find out it's pulled by a pegasus," he said.

Pepper promptly buried her nose in the water trough and ignored us.

"So where do we eat?" Angie asked, rubbing her hands.

"We have to make some money first," Macario said, flipping a silver coin in the air. "Follow me."

He led us down a cobbled street toward an open square. The marketplace was more crowded than a mall on Black Friday, packed with stalls selling wares, spices, and dried fruits. People milled about, trading, eating, and shouting out wares for sale. Street performers juggled flaming torches. A squawking rooster ran between my legs, chased by a small kid.

Macario passed by the booths, his head bobbing left and right as if he was looking for something.

"There." He scurried toward a knot of people huddled around a table.

We pushed ourselves to the front. A shifty-eyed man wearing a red skullcap sat behind the table. On his right hand, he wore a thick ring made of dull metal. In front of him were three battered tin cups. He placed a shiny ball on the table and covered it with the first cup, then swiftly moved the cups in circles, switching them out. A pair of well-dressed teens watched avidly. I followed along, making sure I didn't lose sight of the cup with the ball.

When he stopped, he folded his arms. "Which one, lads?"

They looked at each other and nodded. "The middle one," they said in unison.

He lifted it up, but it was empty. He lifted the cup to the right, and the ball rolled out.

My eyes bulged. I had been certain the middle cup was correct.

"Impossible," one said.

"Do it again," said the other.

They put more coins on the table.

The man put the ball under the cup and began the ritual again. When he was finished, I was certain, absolutely positive, it was under the left cup.

They pointed to it, and he lifted it up.

Nothing.

"Sorry, lads, you have to keep your eye on it." He grinned, turning over the right cup to reveal the ball.

The teenagers grumbled, shoving off through the crowd. But I glimpsed something as the man passed his hand over the ball—it wavered. Like it was attracted to his ring.

"Macario, let's bet," I said.

"No, this one's a cheat."

"They're all cheats," I pointed out. "But I know his trick. Come on."

Reluctantly, Macario put a drachma down. I elbowed him, and he fished two more coins out of his pocket.

The man grinned at us. "Welcome to Avalon, travelers. Where have you traveled from? You wear such strange garments."

"Here and there," I said.

He tilted his head. "Let's play then. Rasputin plays a fair game." He put the ball under the first cup and began sliding the cups side to side. I didn't even bother to watch, whistling as he moved them around the table. He frowned, moving them faster as I whistled, rocking on my feet.

Finally he stopped. "I take it the lady is throwing her money away?"

"No. I know which one it is." I turned a cup over before this Rasputin could stop me. A metal ball rolled out.

The small knot of people watching gasped.

His eyes narrowed to slits of rage. "What a fortunate guess. How did you know which cup?"

I tapped my head. "Lucky guess. Now pay up." I held my hand out.

"Double or nothing?" Rasputin grinned, showing off silver-capped teeth.

"Sure, why not."

"Katzy, we should quit now," Angie whispered. "These guys are con artists."

"I got this," I whispered back.

He covered the ball and began moving the cups. His hands were a blur. Again, I didn't bother to watch.

"The odds of selecting the right cup are against you, Phoebe," Damian said in my ear.

"Have a little faith." I was a street kid. Con artists I could handle.

A crowd gathered as word of my win spread.

Rasputin kept up the show for a long minute, stopping with a flourish of his hands.

"Point out the cup, child, and I'll turn it over," he said with a greasy smile.

"Oh, any one will do," I said.

His eyes glittered. "You have to choose one."

"Fine. I'll take the one on the left."

He reached for it with his ringed hand, but I reached it first. "How about I turn the cup over?"

His eyes grew mean as I turned the cup. The ball rolled out.

The crowd cheered.

I bowed to my fans, grinning. His hand shot to my wrist, gripping it painfully and pulling me in close enough to smell his garlicky breath. "You'll pay for this," he hissed.

"Be glad I don't blow your scam," I hissed back. "Or do you want everyone in the crowd to know that ring of yours is a magnet?"

He released my wrist. I scooped up the pile of coins, and we headed for the nearest food stand. Behind me, a crowd pressed in, eager to try their luck.

As we ordered some kabobs of roasted lamb, I noticed a hooded figure watching us. Whoever it was wore a heavy woolen cloak pulled low. When I stared at the figure, it slipped away into the crowds.

"How did you know which cup?" Macario asked, gnawing on his kabob.

"It's an old scam. He has a ball under every cup. When he turns it over, his magnet ring attracts the ball, and you can't see it because it's stuck to the side of the cup."

We spent more coins on food and a bushel of carrots for Pepper. It had been a pretty perfect day. Our bellies were full, and not one person had tried to kill me.

A burly hand landed in front of me, then grabbed Macario by his nape and lifted him. The arm belonged to one of those half man, half horse dudes. *Centaurs* Damian had called them. He studied the boy. "Demigod or human?"

Macario squirmed in his grasp. "Demigod, you fool. Unhand me before my father, Apollo, incinerates you."

The centaur dropped him like he was contaminated. He trotted forward and scooped up Damian.

"Demigod or human?"

Damian hesitated.

That was a mistake.

"Welcome to the king's army." The centaur began dragging him away by his collar.

"Hey, let him go," I said.

Damian tried to wiggle free, but he was no match for the centaur.

I stepped into the center of the road, hands clenched at my side. "I said let him go."

Something about my voice must have penetrated his thick brain, because the centaur paused. He turned to look over his shoulder, his eyes tightening at the lightning bolt in my hand.

"Bad idea, Katzy," Angie said.

"She's right," Macario said. "The Erinyes can track you if you use your magic."

Seriously, what choice did I have? Damian was about to be conscripted into the king's army!

The centaur dropped Damian. The horse-man cracked his neck as he brandished his sword and turned to face me. "You are the demon who sent hail down on us. General Egan will be most pleased when I bring him your head."

I liked my head just fine where it was. I dug my front foot in the dirt and cocked my arm back, prepared to hurl lightning at his hairy chest, but before I could launch the crackling bolt, a cloaked figure holding a sword whirled into view. A bow was strapped across their back.

In a spinning move, the figure disarmed the centaur, sending his blade flying. One powerful kick of the stranger's booted foot sent the four-legged beast soaring through the air and crashing into a trough of water.

The figure whirled on me. "Put the lighting away, you fool."

That voice. I knew it.

Athena.

My half-sister in the flesh this time.

Crud. I was in so much trouble. The lightning sputtered out in my hand.

She shepherded us away as a crowd gathered. "We must leave Avalon immediately. There is no time to waste. The Erinyes are tracking you."

A silver-tipped missile hit the dirt next to me, sending us all diving for cover. Athena recovered first, drawing her bow and shooting an arrow back. She aimed wide by inches. A warning shot.

She hurried us into an archway and down a long corridor. Tapers lit our way, casting shadows at our feet. The rustle of wings made us scurry faster. Ahead, a set of stairs descended into inky darkness.

Athena paused, looking over her shoulder before giving us a shove. "Go, children. At the end of the crypt, you'll find a door. Seal it behind you. Do not return to Avalon."

"What about our pegasus?" I asked.

"Do you realize what you've done?" Her eyes flashed with anger. "You've put our entire world at risk. There are bigger things at play here than the whims of a child."

Her words stung, raising my temper. "Ares took Carl. I have to get him back."

"Your intentions are noble, but one human life is not worth all of Olympus."

"Carl's life is. While my real family was here, living it up, he was the one who looked after me. What did you ever do, *big sis*?"

Her eyes softened. "A conversation for another day. Go. We will talk again."

Damian took my arm, tugging me away.

I hated my family.

"If it's any consolation, my family fights every holiday," Angie said as we hurried past tombs. "They love each other, but the way they express it would peel paint off walls."

"Thanks, Angie," I said, biting back the tears. "I guess no one's family is perfect. Too bad mine hates me or wants me dead."

"At least Athena helped us," Damian said as we came to a door. He twisted the knob, and the door swung open on squeaky hinges. "She got us safely out of Avalon."

We stepped into bright sunlight—only to find an army of soldiers waiting. In the midst of them, the tin-cap-teethed swindler Rasputin stood pointing us out to a familiar figure.

General Egan.

Crud.

CHAPTER 18

Being a prisoner of General Egan had its benefits. We were given three meals a day, comfortable beds, and a room with a nice view.

Of course, I'm lying.

They tossed us in some dark dungeon with only rats for company. We slept on a stone floor without even a blanket to keep us warm. The food was terrible—maggoty rice with a side order of stale bread.

"I'm certifiably starving to death," Angie moaned.

"For once, I agree with this one." Macario sighed. "The rats are looking at us like we're their next meal." He threw a pebble at one that ventured too close.

"Damian, ideas?" I asked for the eleventh time.

He lay on his back staring up at the ceiling, fingers laced across his chest. "I told you, Phoebe, I don't have any ideas," he said calmly. "We are in an underground cell. We don't have a key or any willing gods hanging around that want to free us. So please stop asking."

"What's his problem?" I grumbled to no one in particular.

"Oh, he's just worried he's going to spend the rest of his life down here, or worse, be inducted into the army at age twelve," Angie carped.

I sighed. "I could call up a lightning bolt."

"No!" they shouted in unison.

"It will bring the Erinyes back," Damian said. "Somehow I think that will be worse than General Egan."

Boots clomped down the stone corridor. Was it already time for our afternoon gruel?

The door was flung open, and the general himself appeared. We sat up, instinctively drawing closer to one another.

He entered and came to a stop in front of me, staring down with a frown. "So you are the one?"

I raised an eyebrow. "The one who beat a cheat at his con game? Yeah, that's me. Might as well stone me to death."

He laughed. "They're still talking about the girl who outsmarted old Rasputin. But no—you are clearly more than that." He tilted forward and dropped his voice to a whisper. "The lightning bolt might have given you away." He straightened and began pacing the length of the cell. "Do you know the bounty on your head is quite substantial? Ten thousand drachmas. I could use those funds to help pay for more weapons for my men."

So that's how much my life was worth. It smarted, but I didn't let it show. "So turn me over to my father. I'm sure it will be a happy reunion."

"Zeus isn't the one paying it," he said. "It's the council of gods. They want to be rid of you. It makes me wonder, how much trouble can one small girl cause, even one who can send hail down onto my head?"

"Beats me. I haven't done anything wrong yet, but

those winged avengers want me dead because of something they think I'm going to do."

"We take our prophecies seriously," Egan said. "Rumor has it you will one day destroy Olympus. The city of the gods. I've never been, but I hear the streets are paved with gold."

I hesitated. Was he for that or against it?

"She's a daughter of Zeus," Macario said. "She can stop the prophecy from happening, but she has to complete her quest."

Egan's eyes grew curious. "Tell me about this quest."

I looked at Damian. "Show him."

Damian pulled the red book out of his bag and handed it to Egan. "If she completes the Eye of Zeus, we think she can break the prophecy."

Egan flipped through the pages, then sighed and thrust the book back at Damian. "It can't help me win my war against the Trojans. Ten years we've been fighting. There are hardly any men left to conscript into the army. I'm down to recruiting children."

"What if I could help you?" Damian said.

Egan raised one eyebrow. "Help me how?"

"I know how to end the war. To defeat Troy once and for all."

He scoffed. "How can a boy such as yourself know these things?"

"You believe she is the one who can destroy Olympus, yet you question whether or not her companion can show you how to defeat a mere army of mortals?" Macario said.

Egan laughed. "Okay, I'm listening."

"No, first we make a deal—I tell you how to win the war, and you let us go," Damian said boldly.

"And give us horses and supplies," Macario added.

"And some weapons," Angie said.

Egan looked us over and shook his head. "May the gods have mercy on me for unleashing you, but yes, you have a deal. Tell me how to end this war."

Damian leaned in and whispered in his ear. I couldn't hear much. Something about a horse, a gift, and a total fake out.

Egan's eyebrows rose. His eyes grew wide, then skeptical, and then understanding dawned.

"And you swear this will work?"

"On my honor," Damian said, crossing his heart.

Egan sighed, scrubbing his hand across his forehead before nodding. "We're desperate enough to try anything. I will pass it along to our leader, Odysseus, on my return. Maybe he won't take my head off for my lack of new recruits. Are you sure you don't want to come with us? You'd make a fine lieutenant."

Damian flushed proudly. "Thanks, but I have to keep Phoebe from destroying this place."

Egan laughed heartily. "Be off then before I change my mind."

He called for the guards to unlock the cell door. We were led up and out into the bright sunlight. I wanted to drop to my knees and kiss the dirt, but I kept it together as we were loaded onto fresh horses and shown out of the garrison. Damian waved goodbye to the general as we trotted down a road.

"I h-hate h-horses," Angie stuttered out, her pigtails bouncing up and down.

"Which way to the sphinx?" I asked Macario, holding on to the saddle horn with both hands.

"Thebes is a day's ride. You'll love it there. Even better than Avalon."

CHAPTER 19

Another night sleeping on the ground left my body aching as if I'd gone eight rounds with a cement mixer. On the bright side, Macario caught a pair of speckled trout in a nearby stream and roasted them wrapped in leaves over a fire for breakfast.

The horses were fresh and crisply trotted, jarring my teeth into the back of my head. Macario entertained us with stories about his exploits, including a tale of slaying a manticore and saving an entire village from a rampaging sea monster.

Little liar.

I didn't believe a word that passed his lips. But his nattering on helped pass the time until Thebes rose before us at the other end of a valley, a city of graceful spires and warm sandstone buildings.

"Where do we find this Miss Kitty?" I asked Macario.

"Her lair is down there." He pointed to the middle of the valley, where a mound of boulders rose up from the trees. "In order to reach the city, travelers must pass by it."

"Why would anyone be dumb enough to go in there if she's a flesh-eating monster?" Angie asked.

"She promises a fortune in gold to the one who can answer her riddle," he explained. "Many are tempted, thinking they are smarter than Miss Kitty or that they can defeat her in combat if they lose."

"And do they?" I asked.

"No one has ever lived to tell such a tale."

"Well, since we know the answer, it should be a piece of cake."

The horses picked their way down the rocky trail. It switched back and forth, leading us to a well-marked road at the bottom of the valley.

Tall pine trees towered overhead, letting in dappled sunlight. The faint humming of bees zooming here and there was relaxing. I was almost enjoying it when a snide voice called out, "Look, it's the misbegotten son of Apollo and a tree."

The voice came from a dark-haired youth. He sat on a branch, swinging his legs. He was sharply dressed in a black tunic with a gold sash across his chest.

"Deimos." Macario slid down from his horse. "What are you doing here?"

Macario's fists were tightly clenched, but it didn't stop them from trembling. He was afraid, I realized. And trying not to show it.

"Keeping an eye on my father's charge, of course." Deimos dropped from the branch, landing nimbly on his feet. "I can't allow his plans to unravel because a reject like you led her astray."

"I don't know who you are, but we don't need any help." I climbed down from my horse and stood by Macario. "So back off."

Angie and Damian joined on the other side. "You heard her," Angie said, folding her arms. "Move it along."

Deimos ignored her and slowly eyed me from head to toe. "So you're the famed daughter of Zeus. You don't look like much. I can't see why Father is so convinced you're the one."

I frowned. "Father? Wait—are you a son of Ares?"

He bowed. "I am Deimos, son of Ares, and this"—he waved a hand, and another figure stepped from behind a tree—"is my brother, Phobos."

They were like identical supermodels, handsome with sculpted high cheekbones and sleekly combed hair. The only difference was Deimos's eyes were green like chipped emeralds, and Phobos's were a glacier blue. A pair of black pegasuses stamped their feet behind them. Each had a white diamond on their forehead; they were exactly like the ones that had driven Carl away in Ares's carriage.

"Not nice to meet you," I said, hating them on sight.

Damian tugged on my arm. "Careful. Phobos is the god of fear, and Deimos is the god of panic."

Panic and fear—*they had gods for that?*

Ignoring the warning, I said, "We're on our way to Thebes, and you're kind of in our way. So if there's nothing else . . . ?"

"Just one thing," Phobos said. "Father is curious what the oracle said that made you destroy her temple?"

I flushed guiltily. "Nothing much. It went something like I should tell Ares to stuff it."

"We can make you tell us, you know," Deimos said, leaning in. His pupils expanded, blotting out the green. They began to glow with a pulsating yellow light.

A tidal wave of panic washed over me, followed by a rush of adrenaline that made my heart pound.

"She looks so scared," Phobos said, prowling forward, "like she saw a ghost." His eyes were like pools of ice.

Fear trickled up my spine, and my skin grew clammy.

"She's going to panic. Just look at her," Deimos said, tilting his head to the side.

Panic. Yes. I wanted to jump out of my own skin. Run screaming down the trail. And I would have if my feet weren't suddenly glued in place. Sweat ran down my face. I stared at the ground, willing myself to stop being so scared—and failing.

The clearing was deathly silent. The only sound was a loud buzzing from overhead. Angie whimpered faintly. Damian trembled where he stood.

"So scared, isn't she, brother?" Phobos crooned. "I see her screaming all the way to Mount Olympus."

"Father thought you were different," Deimos said in my ear, his eyes glowing like neon coals. "But you're nothing special at all."

"Just a girl who's going to cry herself to sleep tonight," Phobos said in my other ear, "an unwanted offspring like poor Macario."

That was the wrong thing to say.

Something snapped inside of me, lighting the fuse of my temper. Macario hadn't asked to be born the son of a god and a simple tree nymph, any more than I had asked to have this stupid prophecy hanging over my head. Blood flowed to my brain again. Whatever force was making me pee-my-pants scared faded as my anger took over.

The twins were too busy gloating to notice.

"I'm bored with this pathetic little band of nobodies," Phobos said. "Shall we leave them trapped in their own nightmares?"

"We shall," Deimos answered. "Father will just have to find a new champion."

Laughing, they headed back to their rides. By the time they reached them, I had enough crackling energy to blow a hole in the side of a mountain.

"Hey, duck butts!"

They paused.

"I'm not scared of you. And Macario's got more class in his big toe than the pair of you have between you."

They turned stiffly.

"What did you say?" Phobos's voice was deadly as a serpent.

A fat lightning bolt appeared in my hand. I looked up from beneath the curtain of hair that hung over my face. "I said I'm not afraid of you." I raised my arm, holding the glowing bolt.

"Throw that at your peril," Deimos sneered. "Touch us with your powers, and we will destroy your mind. You'll dribble into your porridge with terror the rest of your days."

"Oh, I'm not going to touch you."

I threw the bolt.

Straight up.

Over their heads.

At the hornet's nest that dangled from a branch.

The bolt hit the branch, splintering it. The twins looked up in shock as the giant hive fell in slow motion, bouncing off one branch to land on another, shattering into pieces and sending a bazillion angry yellow jackets swarming in search of the culprit.

The hornets descended on the pair, making them dance wildly as they swatted at them. We scrambled onto our horses and whipped them down the trail, leaving the pair screaming as the hornets had their way with them. I half hoped the Erinyes showed up so they could meet Ares's horrid offspring face-to-face along with the charming swarm of stinging insects. The thought kept a smile on my face until we had left them far behind.

We slowed the horses down. Their chests were heaving, and foam flecked their flanks. I patted mine on the side of the neck as Macario rode up beside me.

"Thanks," he said gruffly. "No one's ever stuck up for me before."

I glanced over at him. "How come you didn't just send a sunbeam at their yap traps?"

He scowled. "My father limited my powers when I was born. He gave me the gift of sunbeams, but I can never use them against another god."

"Hey, sun-brain, is that it?" Angie pointed at a black cave that loomed between a stand of trees.

Macario pulled up his horse, nodding solemnly. "Yes. The sphinx's lair."

We tied off the horses to some scrub. Macario marched into the entrance, followed by Angie and Damian. I lingered outside. This was step one of getting Carl back. I should have been excited, not choking back a softball-sized knot of dread that made it hard to breathe.

Angie paused in the opening. "Coming, Katzy?"

I nodded, moving forward on leaden feet.

CHAPTER 20

There was no need for light. Blazing torches were placed every few feet as if welcoming guests. Distant strands of violin music drifted down the tunnel. The melody was horribly out of tune, as if the players didn't know how to play. It grew to a deafening racket as we came through an archway and entered into a cavernous room.

It kind of reminded me of the inside of a harem. Canopies of red silk hid the rocky ceiling. A colorful brocade rug covered the ground. Sequined dressing gowns hung from a rack, each gaudier than the next. Candelabras held racks of gleaming candles. A trunk in the corner spilled over with gold, jewels, and the odd goblet. Seated on the oversized plush sofa in the center of it all sat Miss Kitty.

Her homely human face was square, with a jutting chin and thick bushy eyebrows. Wild ringlets circled her head. Her eyes were made-up with violet eyeshade, and her garish lips were painted crimson. She wore a purple dressing gown open in the front, embroidered with sequins and trimmed in white fur. The rest of her tawny lion-shape sprawled across the sofa, rear paws lazily drooped over one armrest. Her claws were painted the same bright red as her lipstick. A set of golden wings jutted up behind her.

Three misshapen, oversized rats played violins, thumping their tails in rhythm. Or maybe they were bats. They sported leathery black wings. The trio of bat-rats each wore a vest and a red cap. Miss Kitty's foot tapped along to their wild tune.

We'd taken two steps into the chamber when she sat up sharply, her nose scenting the air. "Quiet, you fools. I think Miss Kitty has visitors." She stood up, balancing on her hind legs. A long tail swished the air behind her and then curved over her back in an arch, revealing a hissing snake head.

She spied us and pointed her paw at us. "Fetch them here! Don't let them escape!"

One of her musical minions whistled shrilly and then joined the other two in taking flight, flapping furiously around our heads, driving us forward.

More bat-rats appeared, scurrying out of every crack and crevice, hissing and snapping at our ankles, herding us onto the rug in front of her sofa.

We warily huddled together. Angie drew the small sword General Egan had given her and waved it. "Back off, or I'll slice your tail off."

The sphinx laughed. "Aren't you a feisty little thing? Miss Kitty thinks you will make a delicious first course." She pranced forward on her back paws, licking her lips in anticipation.

"You can't touch her," Damian said firmly, stepping in front of Angie. "First you have to ask us a riddle. If we answer it correctly, we can leave unharmed with a sack of gold."

126   THE EYE OF ZEUS

She stopped and drew one curved claw down Damian's cheek. "Sadly, no one has ever answered Miss Kitty's riddle correctly. You children shall be no different."

"Ha, he knows the answer already," Macario boasted, jerking his thumb at Damian.

I could have knocked the kid sideways.

Miss Kitty's eyes narrowed. "But how can that be, when Miss Kitty hasn't asked it of him? None who have heard my riddle have left here alive." With a leap she knocked Damian down, planting a paw on his chest. "What lie is this? Tell me this instant before I devour you."

"I read it in a book," he said. "The answer is man."

Miss Kitty jerked back from him as a chorus of cries rang out from her minions. "But . . . how is this possible? What magic allows you to know my secret?"

"It's not magic. It's called history," Damian said, getting back on his feet.

"The details aren't important," I cut in. "We just need to borrow a feather from you, and we'll be on our way."

But Miss Kitty wasn't listening. She paced the length of her sofa, wringing her front paws. "No, no, no, this is all wrong. You've ruined Miss Kitty, ruined her." Her snake-tail hissed at us, waving in the air as she marched back and forth.

"Don't be so dramatic," Angie said. "Just make up a new riddle."

Damian and I both gaped at Angie as if she had lost her mind.

If the sphinx asked us a new riddle and we couldn't answer it, we were all dead.

Angie slapped a hand to her mouth as she realized her mistake.

Miss Kitty stopped pacing, a gleam entering her eye. "Yes. A new riddle. One I've never shared out loud, so it won't be in any history book." She seated herself back on her sofa, patting the head of the snake with one paw. It nestled into her, enjoying the scratch of her claws.

She turned her eyes on us and began to recite the riddle.

"I have a head but cannot think or care.
Four legs to hold me but only one foot to share.
Spend time with me, and you can go anywhere.
What am I?"

She clapped her paws together, and one of her rat-bats dragged a tall hourglass over. It shook the piece until all the sand was in the bottom and then thumped it over on its head.

"Come, children," Miss Kitty said. "The sands of time have begun to run. When the hourglass empties, you will belong to me."

The sand looked like it was running out pretty fast. I turned to Damian. "Come on, genius, put that super brain of yours to work and come up with an answer."

"I'm thinking." His face was screwed up in a tight knot. I could almost hear the wheels turning in his head.

Angie squeaked. "Uh, Katzy—I think we have another problem."

The army of rat-bats were prowling closer, encircling us. And they had a distinct predator's gleam in their eyes.

"That's not fair," I said, giving one a swift kick. "You have to give us time to solve the riddle."

"I didn't say I had to make it easy," Miss Kitty purred, eyes glowing. "My pets are hungry. If they eat you before you solve the puzzle, I didn't break the rules. They did." Her serpent tail flicked out its forked tongue. I could swear the thing was smiling at us. Like it couldn't wait to get its share of my flesh.

I called up a small lightning bolt. "Angie, Macario, flank Damian while he concentrates."

We formed a triangle around him. Damian was mumbling the riddle to himself as his brain churned it over. If anyone could solve it, I put my money on Damian.

One of the rat-bats nipped at my ankle. I swung at its head with the lightning bolt, knocking it aside.

"Damian, we really need an answer now," I said as Macario threw a small beam of sun fire into a cluster of them, sending them squealing as their tails caught fire.

"Stop interrupting me," he snapped.

Angie hacked at three of the flying pests that got too close.

"No pressure, Big D, but"—she swung at one—"we're really"—she swung at another—"out of time."

"You're not helping!" he shouted. "Just, everyone, be quiet."

We backed into a small knot. Sweat rolled down my back. The sands of the hourglass trickled down until there were only a few grains left.

As the last one fell, Miss Kitty stood up from her sofa. "Children, it appears that you have run out of time."

I was trying to think of a Plan B, something that involved a lot of lightning and maybe some luck, when Damian started shouting.

"I've got it! I know the answer. It's a bed. It has a head, a foot, four legs, and it can take you anywhere when you dream."

Mottled splotches colored Miss Kitty's cheeks. Her wings flared behind her as she prowled forward and kicked the hourglass aside with one paw. "You ran out of time, boy, and now you belong to me."

"No." I lunged forward with my lightning bolt. "We answered your question. That means you can't touch us."

The sphinx snarled, slashing the air with a paw. "Fool, I make the rules here. Just because you answered my question doesn't mean I have to let you go. I can kill you anytime I want to." She launched herself into the air and began flying in a circle over our heads. "Which one of you shall I eat first?"

She swooped down with her claws outstretched. "I think this one looks juicy!" She headed for Angie. Her jaws opened unnaturally wide, and her teeth grew into curved fangs.

Macario and I both launched our bolts, but Miss Kitty rotated sideways, dodging them, reaching greedy claws out for Angie. I leaped up on the sofa and jumped off the armrest, tackling the sphinx in midair.

Her wings flapped, lifting us higher as I grappled with her. She snapped her nasty jaws at me, but we crashed into the back wall before she could tear a bite of flesh out of me. I hit the ground hard, rolling back onto my feet as she thumped down next to me

She rose on her back legs to tower over me. "Now your flesh will be mine," she sneered, raising her paw to swipe my head off. She was so intent on killing me, she didn't see Damian come up beside her.

"You're nothing but a cheat," he said. She lifted her gaze from me to him. That's when he punched her.

Yup, my brainiac friend had a mean right hook.

He buried his fist in her pudgy chin. In slow motion, she backpedaled across the rug, tripping over the edge of her gown. She fell into a candelabra. The candles toppled over, spilling wax and lighting her wings on fire.

"No, not my pretty wings!" She screamed in pain, hopping from paw to paw around the room as she furiously patted the flames. She flailed around, knocking into the rack of gowns and entangling herself. The flimsy fabrics went up like rocket fuel.

We watched in horror as the flames began to consume her, turning her into a raging spire. The silk canopy caught fire, filling the cavern with choking smoke. Her minions scattered in every direction.

"Damian what about the feather?" I pulled my jacket up to protect my mouth from the smoke.

"We need to put out the fire," he said, coughing and holding one hand up to ward off the heat.

I clenched my fists and thought of the rainiest, wettest day ever. I shouted the word that popped into my head.

"*Vrocheros!*"

A thick cloud swirled over our heads. Thunder rumbled in the cavern. And then the rain came. Buckets and buckets of water, dousing us and the sphinx.

When the rain fizzled out, Miss Kitty was nothing more than a pile of charred flesh. I gingerly poked the remains and triumphantly came up with a singed feather.

"Here goes nothing."

I laid the mirror on my palm and dangled the feather over it. It vibrated under my fingertips. When I let it go, it hovered over the mirror a moment before it settled into the oval opening, reshaping itself to fit. A layer of silver oozed over the top and turned solid, leaving a raised shape.

"That's powerful magic," Macario breathed in awe.

"But you fried the sphinx," Damian said with his usual frown.

"It wasn't my fault! We answered her riddle fair and square." A sliver of hope made my hand tighten on the mirror. I looked at Angie. "One down, five to go."

She nodded. "Time to find a giant pig monster."

"And hope we don't run into its gut-ripping tusks," Damian muttered.

CHAPTER 21

I chewed over Damian's words as we made our way out of the valley. *You fried the sphinx.* Wasn't that a good thing? One less flesh-eating monster in the world? So why did I feel like a giant wrecking ball? Like for every good thing I tried to do, ten bad things happened.

Given that half of Olympus seemed to have it in for me, we stayed well away from the city of Thebes. At least using my lightning in the cave hadn't called the Erinyes. Damian theorized it was because we were underground.

After another night sleeping on the ground, the horses trotted briskly under a searing blue sky. According to Macario, the vicious she-pig roamed the hills above a seaside village named Crommyon.

"Are we there yet?" Angie moaned, not for the first time.

"Angie, quit whining," Damian said. "Do you see a giant pig anywhere?"

"No, all I see is your annoying sunburned face. I'm hungry. I need to eat a meal. A real meal," she added before he could point out we had feasted on stale bread rolls that morning, the last of our meager supplies from General Egan.

Angie suddenly pulled up her horse, sniffing the air. "Is that—do I smell bacon?"

We halted, all of us eagerly testing the air. A sudden breeze ruffled my hair. Saliva flooded my mouth as the delicious aroma of fried bacon reached my nostrils.

"I think it's coming from over there," I said, pointing at a cluster of trees nestled between two low-lying hills. A thin tendril of smoke twined upward from the top of a chimney just visible through the pines.

"You think whoever lives there might be willing to feed us?" Damian asked hopefully.

Macario pursed his lips. "I don't know—it could be a trap."

"I hardly think anyone who cooks bacon that delicious smelling is setting a trap for us," I said, imagining the crispy pieces in my mouth.

Macario shrugged. "My mother always said, never trust anything that seems too good to be true."

"I don't care if it's a wicked witch that wants to throw us in her oven like Hansel and Gretel," Angie said, giving her horse a kick. "I'm going to knock on their door and beg whoever answers for some breakfast."

Angie trotted off toward the stand of trees with Damian close behind. I hesitated, until I caught the unmistakable smell of freshly baked cinnamon rolls.

"Come on," I said to Macario. "If it's a trap, we'll eat first and then figure a way out."

He grumbled but followed along. As we entered the woods, the temperature dropped and the air cooled. Soft grass grew underfoot. The horses began grazing, refusing to carry us any farther. I couldn't blame them, as they'd been living off scrub brush for days. We left them behind and walked down a narrow trail that wended through the trees.

A tiny cottage came into view. It was surrounded by swathes of purple and pink bougainvillea that provided cover for the chorus of crickets that chirruped a loud welcome. The white adobe walls had thick brown beams framing an open window. A neatly pebbled path led to a round front door with a brass knocker.

Angie was already rapping loudly. Pans banged in the kitchen. A cheery voice called out through the window, "Door's open, children, come right in."

She must have seen us come down the path, I reasoned, as Angie eagerly opened the door. More delicious scents assaulted my nostrils. I caught the smell of cinnamon and nutmeg. Surely that wasn't maple syrup . . . and *ooh* . . . the distinct odor of chocolate chip cookies made my head dizzy.

"If I'm dreaming, nobody wake me," Angie said as we stepped inside the cottage.

The white walls were offset by a colorful throw rug. The sofa held plump cushions, and next to it was a wooden chair in front of a spinning wheel. A small fire burned merrily in the stone hearth.

"In here, dearies," the voice called.

We followed the sound into a cozy little kitchen. Every surface of every counter was covered in platters of food. Cinnamon rolls dripped with icing. Stacks of waffles oozed maple syrup. A plate piled high with bacon still sizzled. The woman had her back to us, busy serving up food.

My eyes bugged out.

Either I was seeing things, or the woman had six arms. Three on each side. Her movements were a blur as she deftly served up our plates. She turned, giving us a bright smile. She was younger than I expected, with long black hair coiled in a knot on top of her head. In four of her hands, she held a heaping plate of food. The other held a jug of milk and the last, a platter of cookies. "Welcome, welcome, children, please find a place at the table."

We didn't say a word. Even Macario didn't argue, his eyes bigger than any saucer as she set the plates in front of us. "I saw you coming, and I thought to myself, Ara, they look hungry enough to gnaw on a tree trunk, so I fixed this lovely meal for you."

"Thank you," I managed between stuffing my mouth with fluffy waffles. I took a bite of bacon and swooned . . . sooo crispy and perfectly cooked. "We really were starving."

"Mmfhmmf," Angie muttered. "I could've eaten my arm off."

Ara laughed, clapping her hands. "Younglings can be so ravenous. They need a fresh meal when they come out into the world."

She sounded oddly excited. I swallowed a bite of my cinnamon roll, exulting in the sugary taste, and pushed back an uneasy feeling that prickled my neck. "This is a lovely cottage, but it's so far from anywhere. Don't you ever get lonely?"

Her hands went to her hair, patting stray strands into place. "Sometimes, but soon, I'll have all the company a mother could ask for."

"Are you expecting?" This freaky-armed lady didn't look pregnant to me.

"My babies will be here before the day is gone. They're practically bursting to be born." She clapped her hands. "Come, enough talk. Finish your milk, and then perhaps you'd like a little rest before you continue on."

We drained our glasses. Before I could cry out in protest, she swept our plates up and began rinsing them in the sink. "There's a nice soft couch in the main room. Make your-selves at home, and I'll pack some food to take with you."

That sounded heavenly and made up for the fact that I didn't get to wipe my plate clean with my biscuit.

Macario grabbed my arm as we rolled ourselves into the other room. "Something's off about this one," he whispered.

"You mean because she has six arms?" I joked.

"That. And why is she being so nice? And where are these babies she speaks of?"

"I don't know, and I don't care." I plopped down on the sofa, so tired I could barely keep my eyes open. "Maybe she's a nice lady who—" a yawn split my face "—who likes to do . . . nice . . . things." My eyes were slits as I fought to keep them open.

"Katzy, I can't stay awake," Angie mumbled, and then she keeled over across the top of me, landing facedown at my feet.

Damian sat down in the center of the room. "A little . . . nap . . ." He sprawled backward.

Something is wrong, my brain screamed at me. The last thing I saw was Macario looking at me with sleepy eyes that still managed to look angry, and then I began to snore.

CHAPTER 22

I opened my eyes to a fuzzy white world. My mouth felt stuffed with cotton. I worked my jaw, trying to spit it out. Gauze wrapped around me as if I'd been rolled up in a burrito. I couldn't move. Was I dead? Had the six-armed lady poisoned us? No, if I was dead, I wouldn't feel this sick. My head pounded and my stomach was doing somersaults. A putrid smell made me gag.

My arms were trapped behind my back. If I could get a lightning bolt, I could maybe get out of this. I clenched and unclenched my hands until the tingle started and managed a small bolt. It cut easily through the gauzy covering, and with a *whoosh*, I fell backward out of my cocoon and landed on my butt.

A dark paste covered my arms. I sniffed it. *Gross.* It was the source of the icky smell. I was in a storage room with no windows. Shelves lined the walls, stacked with jars filled with brown goop. Three matching white cocoons hung from the ceiling. A pile of bulging gray sacs the size of basketballs were piled up in the corner. They were pulsing, as if something inside wanted out.

Using my small bolt of lightning, I slashed at the first hanging bundle. Angie spilled out onto the ground, choking and coughing. I quickly freed Damian and then Macario, who came out yelling, "I told you this was a trap, but no, you didn't listen."

"Quiet!" I snapped. "You want her to come back?"

Angie wrinkled her nose. "Why do we all smell like we rolled in horse manure?"

They had the same dark paste smeared on their faces and arms. Damian rubbed some of it between his fingers.

"We've been basted with cricket guts if I'm not mistaken. The smell is a sort of spider aphrodisiac." He smacked his forehead. "Of course! Six arms, two legs, eight limbs. Our hostess must be Arachne. Athena cursed her to be a spider for boasting she was a better weaver."

"So Arachne dowsed us in cricket guts so she can eat us?" Angie asked, rubbing at the caked gunk off her arms.

"No, not Arachne," I said, pointing. "Them."

They turned and saw the pile of pulsating egg sacs. As we watched, one hairy black leg poked itself free of a sac, followed by a head.

A gnarly, beady-eyed spider's head with a pair of nasty pincers.

"Damian, we could really use one of your ideas right now before those babies of hers start to eat us," I said.

Because they were definitely hatching. The first spiderling stepped out of its sac, and it was anything but little. Its cantaloupe-sized body had eight spindly legs and unblinking red eyes that were focused on us. We backed away as the pile of discarded pods grew, and the teeming mass crawled forward on tentative legs.

"Spiders don't actually eat their prey," Damian said. "They spit acid on them to dissolve them, then slurp them up."

We stopped to glare at him. "Not helping," I said as one began skittering closer. I kicked at it, making it draw back.

The only exit was a wooden door that I had a pretty good idea was barred from the other side. Angie rattled the handle, but it didn't budge.

"Damian, anytime." I gave another spiderling a boot. It snapped at my foot, spitting something nasty at me.

"Um, I'm thinking," he said, blinking rapidly.

Macario drew a glowing sunbeam. "I say we fry them."

I grabbed his arm. "And us at the same time. We're locked in, so if they burn, we burn."

"No, Macario has a good idea," Damian said.

We turned to goggle at him. "Explain," I said.

"We need Arachne to open the door. If we stack our discarded cocoons, we can light them and create a barrier between us and the spiderlings. The door's not sealed tight. Arachne is bound to see the smoke."

"So she opens the door, and I crack her a good one," Angie said, smashing her fist into her other palm.

"No, we slime her like she slimed us." Damian took a jar off the shelf and twisted the lid, reeling back at the strong odor.

It was just crazy enough to work.

Macario touched his sunbeam to the mound of cocoons. Flames licked up, and smoke quickly filled the room. We ducked down behind the door and waited, each with a handful of cricket guts. The smell and the smoke made my eyes water.

The newly hatched spiders retreated from the fire, clacking their jaws in fear.

The door flew open.

"My babies! What have you done?" Arachne stomped and stamped on the burning cocoons, which were largely ash by now.

She spun around, her face twisted into a mask of rage. "You will pay for this!" She flung her hand forward, and a stream of webbing spit out. I dodged to the side as Damian shouted, "Now!"

We flung our handfuls of cricket goo, nailing her in the face and chest. Arachne screeched, swiping at the sticky paste. The spiderlings stopped their march toward us and, as one, turned toward her, hungrily encircling her. Their pincers clicked and clacked as they scented the air.

Arachne took a step back, shaking her head. "No! My babies, not me. Them, eat them!" She pointed a finger at us, but the odor of fresh cricket goo was too tempting. One of them spat out a green hunk of spit at her, melting a hole in her dress. She screamed as another spiderling joined in. They climbed up her skirts, swarming over her and burying her under their hairy legs and clacking jaws.

We slammed the door shut and bolted it, running from the house as her screams followed us.

Chapter 23

The only good thing about running into my sister's web-spinning nemesis was our bellies were full for the first time in days. The horses were eager to trot, having feasted on lush green grass. There was a charge in the air, a sense of anticipation. We had defeated the sphinx and escaped from a nasty spider lady. We were on a roll. That crummy she-pig didn't stand a chance.

"Where exactly are we headed?" I asked Macario after we'd stopped to bathe in a stream. It felt good to scrape off days of dust and cricket guts.

"Crommyon. You'll like it. They have the best clams in all of Greece."

"Too bad we don't have much money," I said, rubbing the few coins I had left from my gambling win in Avalon.

Macario grinned, shaking his pocket. A jangling sound rang out. "I helped myself to Miss Kitty's treasure chest while you were getting that feather. I can buy all the clams you can eat."

"Forget clams. I need a warm bed," Angie muttered. "One that doesn't have rocks in it."

After a few hours of riding, we crested a hill and pulled the horses up. Below us was a small fishing village. Boats bobbed in the water. White buildings with tiled roofs sprinkled the hills around the town.

"Is that it?" I asked.

Macario nodded. "Welcome to Crommyon."

We rode into town, hoping to find a shop selling roasted kabobs, but the place was deserted. Every shop was shuttered closed. We got down from the horses and left them drinking from a trough.

"Where is everyone?" Angie asked, turning around. "It feels like eyes are creeping on us."

"Do you think it's that crazy she pig?" As I said the words, a chill trickled up my spine. A sudden panic washed over me.

Angie's eyes grew frantic. "Something horrible's going to happen. We have to run."

Damian was hyperventilating. "I feel it too. We're in terrible danger. We have to go now."

Macario's terrified eyes searched every corner for the threat.

There was the sound of laughter, and then Ares's pair of brats, Phobos and Deimos, stepped out into the street.

"Look who we ran into," Phobos said, his glacial eyes glittering with hatred. His face was covered in blotchy red welts.

"Father's chosen one and her band of misfits," Deimos added, sporting his own angry bites. His eyes took on that ominous yellow glow.

"I can't wait to make you feel the most intense pain of your life," Phobos blazed, taking two steps closer. "A thousand times worse than any hornet's sting."

"Stop," I said, fighting the fear back so I could work my jaw. "If you hurt me, your dad won't get his wish."

"What would that be?" Phobos asked.

"To see me destroy Olympus. I'm doing what he told me to. I destroyed the temple of the oracle and the lair of the sphinx. We left Arachne to get eaten by her baby spiders, and we're on our way to destroy a crummy sow. If you interfere, Olympus will stand, and Ares's plan will be for nothing."

Phobos hesitated, and then a nasty smile crossed his face. "Agreed. But that doesn't include your little friends, does it?" He flicked one hand out. Instantly, Damian dropped to his knees, clutching at his throat. "They are expendable, are they not, brother?"

"Yes. Indeed." Deimos stepped forward, and Angie joined Damian on her knees, both hands grasping at her chest.

"My heart," she gasped.

Deimos clenched his hand tight.

Angie's face turned red. "*Eaagh*, he's squeezing it. Do something, Katzy."

Macario stood helpless. He couldn't use his powers against these two goons.

But I could.

I dug my front toe in the dirt, clenching and unclenching my fists. If it brought the Erinyes, so be it. I was going to call the biggest, fattest, lightning bolt I could and run them through.

Only I never got the chance.

A loud squealing noise made the brothers turn. A tusked pig the size of a Volkswagen ran down the middle of the street, head down. Its cloven hooves pounded the earth. An elderly woman clung to its back, gripping a harness, her gray hair streaming wildly behind her.

"Grab Damian," I shouted to Macario as I tackled Angie out of harm's way. The sow headbutted the odious pair, sending them flying through the air to land behind our horses, scattering the animals.

The woman reined in the sow, bringing it skidding to a halt, nearly unseating her.

"Get on if you want to live," she said.

Phobos and Deimos were already getting to their feet. Horse dung clung to their once pristine tunics. We hurriedly climbed on behind the woman, and she dug her heels in, sending the sow into a run.

"Get back here!" Phobos screamed.

I turned and got one last look, enjoying the look of outrage on their snooty faces.

The sow turned off the road and raced up into the hills above the town. We came upon a well-worn trail that wound through the trees and led us to a small clearing. Chickens pecked in the dirt. Smoke trickled out of a stone chimney built into a grassy knoll. Carefully placed bushes obscured the entrance to a cave.

The woman sawed back on the reins and slid down. She rubbed the sow fondly on the snout and fed it a large mushroom she pulled from her pocket. She didn't seem bothered by its enormous pointed tusks at all.

We jumped down. Angie had her color back. Damian's knees wobbled, but he was able to stand. Macario stepped warily back.

"Thanks," I said to the woman. "You saved our lives."

"Don't thank me." Her voice was low, harsh. "I know what you came to do, and I won't let you harm my Agatha. Come inside and we'll talk."

She led the sow into the cave by its harness. For a huge man-eating terror, Agatha seemed docile enough, butting her snout against the woman for another treat. Inside, a bright fire burned in a hearth made of stacked stones. Scattered pillows provided seating. A wrought-iron bed took up one corner. The sow headed for a thick pile of rugs.

Something was moving on the rugs. Were those baby piglets? Three pink squirmy shapes began squealing. Agatha settled down with a contented sigh, and the piglets latched on to her, nursing with loud sucking noises.

The sow was a mother. How was I supposed to rip its tusk out?

We sat down on the pillows and took the offered mugs of soup she ladled from a cauldron over the fire.

"My name is Phaea." She settled herself across from us. "I used to be an oracle of some renown. I was forced out of

Apollo's temple several years ago when I gave a prophecy to a great king that didn't turn out as he expected. He accused me of being wrong."

"Were you?" I took a sip from my mug. It was a delicious chicken stew with chunks of meat and vegetables.

"Of course not. There has never been a prophecy that didn't come true."

I felt the air rush out of me. Angie gripped my shoulder, squeezing it hard.

"So why did he think you were wrong?" I croaked.

"The king wanted to know if he went to war with his archrival, would he win. I told him if he went to war, a powerful army would fall."

"And?"

"And a powerful army fell," she answered with a small smile. "It was unfortunately his army, not the other side's. Prophecies are tricky things. Often, the receiver hears what they want to. He blamed me for his loss."

"That doesn't seem fair," Damian said. A piglet waddled over and crawled onto his lap, nudging under his arms. He scratched its belly and it sighed contentedly. Another climbed onto Angie's lap and the third onto mine. Its bristly little pink body was warm. One of its tiny tusks was missing.

"It wasn't fair," Phaea agreed. "But I had tired of life at the temple. So much pressure to tell people what they wanted to hear. I was wandering the countryside when I found my Agatha, crying her head off. She had been abandoned by her mother and left to die."

"Her mother was Echidna," Damian said.

"Yes, she was better off without that monster." She looked over fondly at the now sleeping sow.

"This makes no sense," Macario blustered. "Everyone

knows the Crommyonian sow is a man-eating menace who terrorizes this part of the country."

Phaea laughed. "Does she look menacing? They are stories I spread. A few scattered cattle bones and rumors of missing people no one actually knew, and the lies became myth. Now no one bothers us."

"Why did you help us today?" I asked.

"Being gone from the temple hasn't stopped me having the visions. I had one about this day. That you four would arrive." Her eyes darkened. "That you would attempt to take Agatha's tusk and cause her great harm."

"I don't want to hurt her. I couldn't." I looked down at the sleeping piglet in my lap.

"I'm glad to hear that, because I won't allow it." Her words had steel.

"Phoebe, the prophecy," Macario urged. "It's just one tusk. Do you want this Carl of yours to perish or, worse, for Olympus to be destroyed?"

I didn't need reminding what was at stake. Searching for a distraction, I asked, "What happened to this little one's tusk?"

"Those are its baby tusks. The permanent ones will grow in soon."

An idea came to me. "I don't suppose you have one of Agatha's baby tusks?"

Her eyes brightened. "I think it might be here." She threw open a trunk and rummaged around. She lifted a small jeweled box and opened it. Inside, nestled in pink satin, were two tiny yellowed tusks. She held one up. "Do you think it will work?"

"Only one way to find out." I dug out the Eye of Zeus.

Phaea held the small tusk over the mirror. Nothing happened at first. It seemed as if it wouldn't accept the talisman. She closed her eyes, muttering words to herself, and released the tusk. It dropped and then hung in the air, suspended by some magic. It spun slowly, first left and then right, as if the Eye were inspecting it. With a loud *pop*, it shot into the boomerang slot, shrinking into place as the silver sealed it inside.

"We did it," I whispered. "And we didn't destroy anything."

CHAPTER 24

I woke to the smell of breakfast cooking. Phaea had fixed us scrambled eggs with some toasted flatbread, which we devoured in seconds. When the dishes were wiped clean, Phaea led us outside, where the giant sow waited.

"Agatha will take you to the crossroads. You will find a ride easily to wherever you are headed." She raised a hand when Damian opened his mouth. "No, I don't want to know where. I have a feeling if I did, I would have to stop you."

We waved goodbye as Agatha trundled us along a rocky ridge. The sea sparkled in the distance, making me wish for a time-out, a day we could play in the waves and not worry about the fate of Olympus, Carl, and how I was going to get my friends home in one piece.

Agatha came to a stop at the edge of the tree line at the top of a hill. Before us, a well-marked road stretched in both directions. Clouds of dust marked the passing of wagons. We climbed down and waved goodbye to Agatha as she snuffled out her farewell and began her slow climb back into the hills.

"What's next on our list?" I asked Damian, rubbing my hands.

"The Nemean lion." He looked the most cheerful I had seen him in days. A good night's rest and belly full of food had that effect on us.

"Great. A lion. Can't be worse than Miss Kitty," Angie said, flexing her arms.

"Oh, he's worse," Macario said. "In fact, this is where we part company."

Shocked silence filled the air.

"Excuse me?" Most days Macario annoyed the snot out of me, but I had kind of grown used to him. "What happened to impressing your father?"

"I'm not going to impress him if I'm dead," he said darkly. "The Neman lion is called Leather Back because its hide is so tough, none can kill it. None."

"Hercules was able to kill it," Damian pointed out. "He strangled it with his bare hands."

"Not yet, he didn't," Macario glowered. "Another reason I'm leaving. You and your strange stories and odd clothing. You three don't belong here, and it's time I made my own way."

"So you're leaving?" Angie gaped at him. "You scum-licking toad—we should have left you to be petrified by those scare-creeps."

"Drop it, Angie," I cut in. "Macario's done more than enough to help us. If you can point us in the right direction to find this Leather Back, we'd appreciate it."

Macario pointed south. "If you keep to this road, you'll catch a ride in no time and be there by noon tomorrow." He backed away as a wagon carrying a load of chickens trundled past in the other direction. "This is my ride," he said, hopping onto the back. "Travel safe, daughter of Zeus."

It was happening so fast, I didn't know what to say. "You too, son of Apollo. I hope things work out with you and your dad."

"He's really leaving?" Angie said, staring after him in shock.

"It is rather unexpected," Damian said with a slight frown.

"We'll survive." People came and went all the time in my life. One more wasn't going to break me. "Come on."

We started walking. Several carts passed, but none were heading in the direction of Nemea. The sun beat down on our heads, and we were all grouchy by the time we called it a day under a small stand of olive trees.

"I sure wish we could find a nice inn," Angie said, stretching her arms. "And a hot shower with breakfast in bed."

We listed all the things we missed. Without Macario, our attempts at a fire were pointless, so we made do with some hunks of bread Phaea had packed.

The next morning, my feet ached and had two blisters, and there was still no sign of a wagon heading for Nemea.

As the third cart passed heading the other way, Damian shook his head. "This doesn't make sense. Nemea is a big city. Everyone went there to trade. Hold on."

He raced after the peddler, shouting at him to stop. The man pulled up his cart and leaned down. They spoke a minute. Damian held his hand up, as if he was asking him to wait, and ran back to us.

"Macario lied. We're going the wrong way."

"What do you mean?"

"I mean Macario sent us the wrong way. Nemea is back the other way."

Sudden suspicion made me pat my pockets. "Hey, Damian, where's the Eye of Zeus?"

He shrugged. "I don't have it. Where did you last see it?"

"After we put the tusk in. Macario asked to look at it. He said he gave it back to you."

Our eyes locked as realization hit at the same moment. "Macario!"

Angie exploded. "Aargh—that little thief! I told you he was a rat! Wait till I get my hands on him."

I was too stunned to react. I couldn't believe he had stolen my one chance at fixing things.

"Why would he do that?" Damian asked.

"Because he wants to kill the Nemean lion himself," I said numbly. "So he can impress his father."

"And I told him how to do it," Damian said, eyes stricken.

"Come on. We have to get to Nemea."

"Why?"

"Because there's no way he can kill that lion on his own. He's going to need our help."

"Help? I'll tell you the kind of help I'm going to give him. It involves my foot connecting to his backside," Angie said.

"Save it for when we get the Eye of Zeus back, Angie."

We ran after the peddler, who had started to drive off, and piled in the back of his cart.

Nemea turned out to be a bustling city of adobe buildings and the familiar red-tiled roofs. A pillared temple sat on a hilltop. White columns held up a domed ceiling. Tall letters inscribed across the front read TEMPLE OF ZEUS.

"What's the scoop on this place?" I asked.

With Macario gone, Damian readily resumed his role as our walking encyclopedia. "Nemea was ruled by a king named Lycurgus. He started the Nemean Games, kind of like a prequel to the Olympics."

"That explains the stadium." I pointed out the circular edifice that held rows and rows of seats carved into stone. Giant red flags with a golden lion pawing the air hung from every post. Crowds teemed at the gates, clamoring to buy tickets.

"I smell food," Angie said, wrinkling her nose. "I say we take a break, check out the sights, and eat. Then we'll find the little rat and whomp on him until he gives us the mirror back."

We paid for admission and bought some fresh skewers of roasted meat with the rest of my coins, then made our way down to seats toward the front.

Across the stadium, a broad platform jutted out, covered in a canopy of red silk. People milled about the terrace dressed in fancy gold-braided tunics, laughing and drinking from goblets. A trumpet blew and the crowd grew quiet. A couple came out wearing crowns, their raised hands clasped together. The woman was beautiful, with blond hair braided in two buns on either side of her head. The broad-shouldered man had a touch of gray at his temples. They waved at the crowd and took their seats on ornate thrones.

"That's the king and queen," Damian said with a touch of awe.

"Yeah, I got that from their crowns," I said, but I couldn't help smiling. It was strangely exciting.

The competition began with an archery display. Five men lined up, taking aim at straw bales across the arena, each pinned with a bullseye. One competitor stood out, hitting the target time and again. He wore a simple crown and his chest armor bore the Nemean crest of the lion pawing the air.

"That must be the prince." Angie rested her chin on her fist. "Isn't he dreamy?"

I rolled my eyes at her. "What's next?" I asked Damian.

"The sign outside said lion wrestling. Did you know the rules say they can't use any weapons? They have to use their bare hands."

"You think they wrestle Leather Back?" I asked.

"Who would be crazy enough to do that? Probably an old toothless she-lion."

The gates rattled up and the competitors turned to face the tunnel. The prince dropped into a crouch. The crowd grew quiet. Some half rose, trying to see into the opening. Nothing happened for a long moment. A scream rang out of the darkness.

A familiar scream.

What the—

A golden-haired boy ran out of the tunnel, pumping his legs as fast as he could. Behind him a lion bounded out, clawing at his heels.

The lion was super-sized with a glorious tawny mane. It stopped in the center of the arena, planting catcher's mitt–sized paws in the dirt, and threw its head back, letting out a roar that rattled my bones.

"That doesn't look like an old she-lion," Angie squeaked.

"Macario led the Nemean lion here." I jumped up. "Come on, we have to help him."

We pushed our way forward as the rest of the competitors fled over the side of the wall, leaving only the prince in the arena with Macario. Macario had a bleeding gash on his leg. The prince warily circled the lion. He had retrieved his lance, holding it out in front of him.

"Stay here," I warned the other two and slipped over the railing, dropping into the dirt.

"Child, get out of here," the prince shouted at me.

"I'm not a child. I'm a demigod. Macario, what did you do?"

Tears streaked the dust on his cheeks. "Nothing! I was tracking the beast when it headed for the arena. It was after one of the females in the cages. I tried to stop it from entering, but it attacked the guards. It nearly took my leg off!"

"Did you try a sunbeam?"

"Yes, it made it very angry."

Angie and Damian dropped down in the dirt next to me.

"So what's the plan, Katzy?" Angie held the short sword General Egan had given her.

"Don't you guys ever listen? I don't have a plan."

The lion paced, licking its chops, as if it knew we were lunch meat. The crowd had gone deathly still.

The prince decided to be a hero and stepped in front of us. "Stay behind me, children. This beast has been a plague on my kingdom for too long."

Without warning, the lion launched itself at the prince's head. The prince braced himself and then stabbed upward with his lance, driving it into its chest with a powerful thrust, but the metal tip snapped off, unable to penetrate its hide. He pivoted, tossing the lion to the side, but as it passed over him, it swiped at the prince with one paw, tearing a gash in the prince's chest armor. The blow knocked the prince sideways, sending him tumbling over the hard ground.

The lion spun, ready to pounce on him, but Angie stood over him.

"Eat my blade!" She raised her stubby sword with both hands and brought it down, stabbing Leather Back in its eye.

My heart soared as the blade went in deep. "Way to go, Angie!"

The lion screamed, tossing its giant maned head back and knocking Angie flying with a slash of its paw.

The crowd cheered as Damian and I rushed to help Angie to her feet.

"Is it dead?" she asked, swaying.

"Not yet."

The blade stuck out of the lion's eye at a crooked angle. Rearing up on its hind legs, it used both front paws to grasp at the hilt, and with a sickening squelch, the blade came spinning out and landed at Angie's feet.

The crowd went silent again. Blood poured down the lion's cheek as it dropped its head to glare at us with its remaining eye. I could have sworn steam came out of its nostrils.

"Damian, tell me you got something," I asked as we took a collective step back.

"Um, another version of the story suggests Hercules shot an arrow in his mouth. It's not as tough as his hide."

Macario and I looked at each other. He nodded. I called up a lightning bolt, and he matched it with a sunbeam.

"Angie, guard the prince."

She lifted her bloody sword. The tip was broken off, but she held it bravely as she stepped in front of his limp form.

I looked at Damian. "You know what to do."

"How come I'm always the bait?" he grumbled, but he stepped forward. "Here, lion, lion." He waved his hands as Macario and I took a position on either side of him. "I'm nice and juicy. Tasty as can be."

The lion roared again, so loud the stadium shook and the audience screamed. It crouched, its muscles coiled into a tight spring.

"Ready?" I asked.

"Ready," Macario answered.

Damian ducked into a tight ball as the lion sprang at him, claws out, jaws wide open.

"Now!"

Macario and I launched our bolts at the same time. They joined in the open mouth of the lion and exploded in a bright burst of yellow and white light.

The beast's razor claws dug trenches in the ground as it skidded to a stop directly on top of Damian. It swayed once, then twice, as tendrils of smoke rose from its mouth. Then it teetered over and thudded to the ground. Its glassy eyes stared up at the sky. A roar of cheers sounded in the arena as the crowd leaped to their feet.

The good news was it was dead.

The bad news was Damian was buried somewhere underneath a mountain of tawny flesh.

"Damian!"

We raced to the lion's side. "Grab that pole," I said to Angie. She took the broken end of the prince's lance and stuck it under the lion's belly. Macario and Angie put their weight on it, lifting the lion's body enough for me to spy a familiar leg. I grabbed Damian's shin and began tugging.

When he was free, I dropped to my knees, rolling him over. His cheek had a scrape. I couldn't tell if he was breathing.

"Damian, wake up. It was only a little lion attack," I joked, hoping it would irritate him enough to rouse him. I took his chin and shook his head a bit. "Come on, you've survived worse. Look, I'll give you mouth-to-mouth if I have to."

That did it. Something fluttered across his face. His eyes blinked and then shot open. He lifted his head and saw the smoking jaws of the lion, then slumped back to stare up at the sky.

"Y-y-you kn-kn-know, it is stati-ti-tistically improbable I will s-s-survive another a-t-t-tempt on my life."

"Sorry, Damian, I promise I'll never ask again." I stuck my hand out and helped him to his feet as the crowd erupted in cheers. Guards rushed into the arena and carried the prince away on a stretcher.

I grabbed Macario by the shoulder as he started to slip away. "Hand it over."

He looked shamefaced as he pulled the mirror out of his pocket. "I was going to give it back, I swear. I wanted a great feat of my own for my father to hear about."

"Save it." I knelt by the lion. Angie lifted one giant paw. Its claws curved into razor-sharp points. Stretching out one toe, I used her broken sword to saw it loose. Holding it over the mirror, I waited for it to disappear. It vibrated under my fingers until, with a *pop*, it tucked itself into the crescent moon and sealed over. A pulse of power washed over me as the Eye absorbed this new talisman.

I tucked it safely away in my pocket. "That's three. We're halfway there."

A loud voice rang out. "King Lycurgus demands an audience." A soldier flanked by three more holding pointed lances stood waiting. "You will follow me."

"We really don't have time," I began, then seeing the set look on their faces, I smiled. "But we'll make time for the king, right, guys?"

They marched us down a street crowded with cheering spectators that threw flowers at our feet. Hands reached out to pat us on the back, thanking us for saving their prince and killing the beast.

It was kind of nice to be the hero for once.

Tall columns marked the entrance to the palace. The king waited outside in the shadowed columns of the steps, pacing restlessly. His eyes lit up as he spied us.

"There you are. Nemea's saviors." He hurried over and gave a short bow. "I am King Lycurgus. To whom do I owe a lifetime of gratitude?"

"No thanks necessary," I said. "We're no one special."

"I think not. You two are demigods," he pointed at me and Macario. "Who are your parents?"

"I am a son of Apollo," Macario said proudly.

"And you?" He looked at me.

"Daughter of Zeus."

He looked pleased. "We built a temple in honor of Zeus. I knew he would not abandon Nemea in our time of need." The doors to the palace swung open, and a woman hurried forward. He turned with a smile. "Meet my wife, Queen Thea."

She wrapped us in a hug. "You saved the life of my only son. I can never repay you. Please, you must stay and attend a banquet in your honor."

"Uh, we really can't stay—" I began.

Angie elbowed me aside. "Banquet? As in one of them all-you-can-eat shindigs? Sure, we'd be delighted."

"Wonderful." The queen clapped her hands and servants appeared. "Take these children to their rooms to freshen up. Tonight will be a celebration to end all celebrations."

Chapter 25

The palace was the biggest crib I'd ever been in. Think one of those artsy-fartsy museums you go to on field trips, only the artifacts on display were just part of the decor. Acres of marbled floors opened up to rooms filled with expensive-looking gilded furniture. We climbed a broad set of stairs. The boys were led off to their room while Angie and I followed a blushing serving girl named Mira. She threw open a set of double doors.

A steaming pool of water with lotus flowers floating on top greeted us. A bay window overlooked the valley. Two comfy beds piled high with pillows awaited our aching bodies.

"Last one in is a rotten hydra's egg," Angie said, eyeing the steamy water.

Mira left us to bathe in private. We stripped down to our underclothes, glad to be rid of the tattered clothes we'd been wearing, and stepped into the water. It smelled like roses and felt heavenly.

"Now, this is the life, Katzy." Angie stared up at the ceiling as she floated, dipping her hand into a plate of frosted dates.

"Do you think the boys have it as good?"

"Knowing Damian, he's thinking of all the reasons not to enjoy it, while Macario is stealing everything that's not bolted down." She sat upright, wet hair plastered to her head. "Why do you put up with that kid? He's nothing but—"

"A rat, I know." I sighed. "I guess he reminds me of me, or me if I hadn't had Carl."

His mustached face swam before my eyes, and I blinked back tears.

"Hey, Katzy, I didn't mean to make you sad. Carl's from Brooklyn. They make them tough."

"Yeah. I'm sure you're right."

I climbed out of the tub and dried off. Mira reappeared with two young women in tow, a stack of clean clothes in her arms. "For you, courtesy of the queen," she said, bowing low.

She held out a tunic made of a heavy, soft fabric. On the chest, a yellow lightning bolt was outlined in thick gold thread.

"Thanks!" I slipped it on, enjoying the cool, soft feel of it.

"And for the prince's savior." She held up a tunic for Angie. The front had the Nemean lion crest woven in red. There were new shoes as well, soft boots that came to our knees, inlaid with fine swirls of bronze.

Angie looked longingly over at her prized Doc Martens. They had a gash in them from the lion's claws, and the left heel was falling off. She sighed and accepted the new boots.

"Another gift, from the king," Mira said, beckoning the first girl forward. She held a tray in her hands. Mira lifted a towel off, revealing two small golden headbands.

One had a triangle pointing up in the center; the other had a lightning bolt carved into the band.

She slipped them over our heads. The metal fit my forehead as if it were molded to me. Angie couldn't wipe that silly grin off her face.

"And from the prince." She waved the second girl forward. Across her arms lay a sword on top of a shield. "To replace the one you lost," she explained, lifting the sword and handing it to Angie.

Angie's eyes practically bugged out of her head. "Tell the prince thank you very much." She drew the sword out of its sheath and slashed the air with it. The shield was small and round, carved with the Nemean lion in the center.

The servant girls helped us with our hair, giggling as they braided it and wove in flowers. Finally, they left us alone, promising to return when it was time to go to the banquet.

"I could really get used to this." Angie sighed, stretching out on the feather bed.

I wandered over to the window, hopping up on the ledge. I had a clear view of the temple of Zeus perched on the hill, the golden sun setting behind it. I had a sudden urge to see it up close.

"Hey, Angie, wanna go check out the temple?"

A rattling snore was my only answer.

Taking a hooded cloak off a hook, I slipped it over my head and opened the door. No one paid me any attention. The servants were too busy carrying flowers and platters of food into a great hall.

I raced down the steps of the palace and hurried through the city. With my hood up, none of the crowds recognized me as the day's hero. It was easy enough to find the way to the temple. It was always in sight, overlooking Nemea, as if the god kept an eye on the city.

I hiked up the hill, thrusting through tall grass that itched at my legs. At the top, I flung the hood back and paused to catch my breath. The temple had a domed marbled roof held up by a circle of columns, open on all sides. Purple silk banners hung down from the ceiling, stirred by the breeze.

A white marble basin sat in the middle on a raised dais. Piles of flowers—some wilted, some still fresh—littered the floor. A woman brushed past, glancing briefly at me before hurrying to the altar. She dropped her flowers, curtsied, then left.

A flicker of disappointment ran through me. I had expected an over-the-top statue of my father, like the one at the Lincoln Memorial. I waded through the piles of flowers and made my way to the basin. I had to step up on the dais to look down into it. Green algae slicked the inside. An insect skimmed across the surface.

I hadn't brought any flowers, but I had some in my hair. I untwisted a few petals and dropped them in, watching them drift lazily. I didn't know what I'd expected, but I guess part of me was hoping my father would just appear like magic.

Which was pretty dumb, even for me. When had my father ever shown up when I needed him? I was just about to turn away, eager to get back to the palace and the banquet in my honor, when a sudden ripple wrinkled the surface.

I hesitated, staring down into the bowl.

The water swirled as if something were moving. I leaned in closer, then yelped as a familiar face swam into view.

"Athena!"

"Phoebe, what are you doing here?" Her angry image glared up at me.

"Nothing." My cheeks flamed with embarrassment. I

wasn't about to admit I had been hoping to catch a glimpse of my father.

"You used your powers to slay the Nemean lion. The Erinyes have tracked you there. You must leave at once."

"The Erinyes are here?"

"Yes, even now they circle the palace. You can't go back there."

"But I have to. My friends are there."

Her eyes glowered at me from the reflection. "You dare defy Athena? Do you remember what is at stake?"

"Yes, I do. All of Olympus. Boohoo. I'm starting to think destroying that place isn't the worst idea. The gods live up there behind golden gates while down here the people suffer from all kinds of monsters, and you do nothing."

"You don't mean that. Phoebe, I beg you—do the right thing."

"I am doing the right thing. I'm going after my friends. I only wish you were the kind of sister that understood." I dashed my hand in the water, erasing her image.

I ran all the way back to the palace, rushing up the steps and into the hall. It was easy to find the banquet with all the noise of the people dining and laughing. I burst in, half expecting to find my friends in chains with the Erinyes standing over them, but they were happily stuffing their faces.

The boys hovered around a table holding plates stacked with food, looking uncomfortable in their new tunics. They each wore a red sash across their chest. Angie stood next to them, gnawing on a chicken leg. Her shield was strapped to her back, her new sword dangling from her side.

I clapped Angie and Damian on the shoulders. "Party's over. It's a trap."

Damian paled. "The Erinyes?"

Angie dropped the chicken on her plate. "Here?"

I nodded. "Yup. Just had a chat with Athena in a fountain. She was pleasant as ever."

"Then we'd better go," Damian said. "Now."

"What about our feast?" Macario longingly eyed his heaping plate of food.

"No time." I scanned the room, suspecting every person. The guests were all eating and drinking. The king and queen sat at the head table. They raised their glass to me. The prince sat next to them; his arm wrapped in a sling. He tilted his head at me with a smile.

Everything appeared fine. Still, Athena might be annoying, but she hadn't steered me wrong.

"If you want to stay, go ahead," I said to Macario, "but we're leaving."

He sighed, adding another hunk of meat to his towering plate. "I'm coming, but I'm taking this with me."

We were hurrying for the door when a figure stepped out from behind some long curtains, threw back her cloak, and drew a bow holding a flaming silver arrow.

"Daughter of Zeus, you have betrayed the laws of Olympus." Alekto shot the arrow straight at me.

I didn't have time to react. The arrow would have gone straight through my heart, only Macario stuck his plate up, and the arrow plonked into his pile of meat and mashed potatoes. The plate dropped with a clatter as we bolted for the door.

Another of the Erinyes stepped out, blocking our way. *Crud.*

The king and queen stood, calling for their guards.

I drew a lightning bolt and threw it at the closest winged-nuisance. She leaped into the air, dodging it, and the bolt embedded in the long curtains behind her, which promptly caught fire. Guests began screaming as the silk

Nemean banners hanging in the rafters also caught fire. Flames shot up, licking across the ceiling. Chaos ensued as everyone scrambled for the exits, overturning tables as they fled.

Guards hurried the royal family out. I ducked behind an overturned table, yanking Macario down as silver-tipped arrows flew past.

"Phoebe of Argos, come out or your friends will perish."

I peeked over the top of the table. Angie and Damian were being held by two of the winged avengers. Alekto waited, a silver arrow notched in her bow.

I stood, raising my hands.

"Don't do it, Katzy—run!" Angie shouted.

"They'll be dead before you take two steps out of the room," Alekto said. "Come willingly and you may serve out your days in the underworld prison of Tartarus. Resist and you leave us no choice but to terminate your life and that of your companions. Choose now."

Smoke billowed in thick clouds. The curtains burned brighter, sending chunks of burning ash into the air. Alekto wanted me to choose? What kind of choice was death today or a lifetime in an underworld prison?

"I choose neither."

I didn't have a plan, at least not much of one. My thoughts swirled in my head, spinning and spinning as my frustration grew. I hated being helpless. I hated not being able to change my fate.

"Then you will die now," Alekto said, drawing back on her bow and gazing steadily at me over the clasp of her fist. "Last chance. Surrender now or die."

I did the only thing I could think of.

I created a tornado.

Clenching and unclenching my hands, I felt the power build in me. I sifted through my mind, searching for the right word. When I had it, I thrust my hands upward and shouted, "*Sifounas*!"

Alekto released her arrow. The shiny silver flaming tip headed squarely for my chest, but a sudden gust of wind took hold of the arrow, spinning it wildly before sending it into the flaming curtains, scattering embers.

A whipping wind lifted chairs and tables into the air, spinning them in a circle as the vortex grew bigger and stronger. Alekto took flight, only to be caught in the maelstrom and spun in a circle as she fought against it.

Angie elbowed her captor, breaking her grip, while Damian wriggled free and dropped to his knees as my swirling tornado swept toward them. The three Erinyes struggled valiantly to reach me, but the wind tossed and turned their winged figures away.

We crawled out on our hands and knees as smoke, fire, and flames danced together in a giant fiery cone. The ceiling cracked, and the flames leaped onto the roof as the freed tornado rose into the sky.

"I need to stop it," I said, hardly believing I had caused yet another disaster.

Angie tugged on me. "If you do, they'll be on you before you can say *death sentence*. We have to go."

She dragged me off as I stared behind at the destruction I'd caused. Flames jumped from building to building as my tornado continued unabated, painting the evening sky orange.

We didn't stop until we were free of the city gates and a ways down the road.

Damian looked back at the burning skyline, letting out a whistle. "You do realize you just burned down the entire city of Nemea?"

"Yeah, so?"

"So?" Damian raised his eyebrows. "That's the third place you've wrecked. You look a lot like someone who is destroying Olympus."

"Hey, I didn't do anything to Crommyon or Agatha!" I shouted. "So maybe give me a break. I'm doing the best I can."

I spun away and stomped off down the road. Did Damian not appreciate how hard this was for me? How hard I was trying?

"Phoebe, I'm sorry," he called as my three friends trotted after me.

"Drop it." I wanted to get as far from Nemea as I could and forget this day ever happened.

The last light was fading from the sky when a young man swaggered into view, whistling softly as he made his way toward the burning city. He had long hair tied in a ponytail. His chest was bare and muscled, as if he spent his life at the gym pumping iron.

"Greetings, travelers. Have you come from Nemea?" he asked in a deep baritone voice.

"Yeah, what's left of it," I said.

"I am Hercules. I am on my way to slay the Nemean lion. It's one of my twelve labors to prove my valor and strength." He rolled his shoulders back, flexing his biceps into impressive camel humps.

Angie sputtered with laughter. She tried to stop it, but it caught on, and Damian let out a snort. Macario followed, and the three of them bent over laughing. Hercules stared at my friends as if they had lost their minds.

"Good luck with that," I said. "I hear he's hard to kill."

Hercules raised his hand in goodbye and sauntered off.

"Do you think he's going to be bummed when he finds out we handled it?" Angie asked, wiping tears from her eyes.

"Naw, he'll probably send a thank-you card," I said.

Macario grinned. "Wait till he hears we killed the hydra of Lerna."

"We haven't done it yet," I reminded him.

"But we will," Damian said. "Knowing you, we will, and I'll be the bait."

Macario added, "You do know the hydra has nine heads and—"

"Regrows two when you cut one off? Yeah, been there, done that, got the souvenir scar." I lifted the hem of my tunic and showed him the jagged scar on my leg. "Tell me something I don't know."

"Its bite is poisonous."

"And yet I survived."

"How?"

I shrugged. "Dunno. Miss Carole gave me something to drink. Like extra sweet apple juice."

Macario shook his head. "Then that is a miracle, because without ambrosia to cure you, its poison can kill the strongest of mortals, even demigods."

"I wish we could have stayed in Nemea longer," Angie sighed. "I really wanted a night in that feather bed."

"I don't miss the Erinyes trying to kill us," I said.

"There is that." She grinned, and we burst into another bout of laughter as we walked away from the flaming skyline.

CHAPTER 26

After torching Nemea, we made good time on foot heading south toward the swamps of Lerna. None of us were particularly excited about facing a hydra again. The first one had nearly bitten off our heads and poisoned me half to death. And it had been a cheap imitation.

Macario proved useful, finding a place to camp near a stream and keeping spirits up with his tall tales. In the light of the campfire, he rambled on about a bottomless lake that fed the swamps and hid monstrous creatures we couldn't imagine.

When the hour grew late, we burrowed into nests of leaves, staring at the stars as Damian pointed out the names. I tried to stay awake, but my lids grew too heavy to keep open.

For as long as I could remember, I'd never been the kind of person who had dreams. Some demigod genetic defect, I supposed. I'd slept like a zombie at night without a single memory the next morning.

Which is why I didn't know I was dreaming at first. One minute, I was listening to Damian drone on about alpha centauri, and the next, I was floating. It was kind of cool. My body was next to the fire, but I was above it, weightless and free. It was like being in a zero-gravity chamber. I drifted along, seeing the countryside below lit by moonlight, until weight returned. I floated downward, flinching when my bare feet touched the cold ground.

It was stony and hard. Real. But it couldn't be, I told myself, because this was obviously a dream.

In front of me, a red door with a brass knob awaited. It hung in the air like an invitation.

I looked around, but there were only silent trees and twinkling stars. A powerful curiosity seized me, and taking a tentative step forward, I lifted a hand to the knob, then let it drop, suddenly wary. I walked around the back.

Nothing. Just the other side of the same door, hanging in place.

I went back to the front and grasped the knob. It was warm under my hands. I twisted it, and the door swung open. I could see clean through it. So it went nowhere. *Duh. What did I expect?* On a whim, I stepped through, ready to have a laugh and maybe pinch myself to wake up.

My foot touched down—and I found myself in a bright new world.

I blinked several times in case I was seeing it all wrong, but no—on this side of the door, the sun was shining. Green grass spread out like a lush carpet, replacing the rocky soil. I wiggled my toes, testing out the feeling. Birds sang sweet music. A light breeze brought the smell of honeysuckle.

I turned, gasping at the sight of a small lake. Weeping willows encircled it, touching their branches down to the water. A single swan paddled serenely across its mirrored surface. It was jet black, with gleaming feathers and massive wings folded at its side.

I walked to the shore, curious to see if it would come closer. It swam in a slow circle, never looking at me.

"Hey," I called. "Here, birdy, birdy." I wished I had some bread to feed it.

The swan floated to a stop. Its elegant neck twisted around, as if seeing me for the first time. It began paddling smoothly toward me.

"There's a good birdy," I crooned, holding my fingers out as if I had a treat.

The bird's feathered brows lifted, and then it spoke. "Do I look like a simpleton to you, child?"

I backed up a step. "Sorry. I didn't know you could talk. Who are you?"

"You may call me Cygnus." The bird tilted its head in a greeting.

"I'm Phoebe."

"Ah, the destroyer of Olympus. Have you come to destroy my home?" Its round eyes gleamed at me curiously.

I picked up a rock and skipped it across the water. "No. And I'm not going to destroy Olympus. That's just a stupid prophecy."

"Aren't you?" The swan paddled in a slow circle. "Word is the oracle's temple at Delphi was ruined. The sphinx's lair is rubble. And the city of Nemea burned to the ground. I won't even mention the loom you destroyed."

"Hey, those weren't my fault! And besides, they're not part of the fancy-schmancy city of the gods."

Cygnus stopped and craned its head toward me. "Did you not cause them to happen?"

"Yes, but—"

"Then by definition, you are at fault." It continued its paddling. "Everything here is connected to the city of the gods. Think of Olympus as a giant tree. The cities around it are its branches. Destroy one and it's like cutting at the heart of it."

"But it was for a good reason," I protested.

The swan drifted a moment before answering. "So the ends justify the means?"

"Sometimes."

It nodded its head. "So when your parents sent you away—justified or not?"

"Not!" A flush of anger raised my voice. "They should have kept me, given me a chance."

Cygnus paddled closer, extending its head toward me. "Even if it meant you would have died?"

"Well, no—but they should have found a way to stop that from happening. My father is a god, after all. What good is it to have all that power if you can't stop something bad from happening?"

The swan swung its head to the side, looking disappointed. "They did find a way. They sent you someplace safe. You weren't supposed to return."

"So I suppose that makes everything my fault," I said with heavy sarcasm. "Because they did *alllll* they could to help me."

"Correct."

"WRONG!" I shouted. "WRONG, WRONG, WRONG."

The swan flared its wings, backpedaling as I stomped toward the water.

"They didn't make sure I was okay. And they didn't tell me who I was. I've spent my whole life thinking there was something fundamentally wrong with me, and guess what? There is, because I'm a DEMIGOD, so yeah, I think they should have told me that part."

The swan lowered its head as if in shame. "Perhaps you have a point, young Phoebe. These things are never easy. Doing what you think is best—it always carries a cost. On both sides."

I sighed, tiredness creeping into my bones. "This is a pretty sucky dream. If it's all the same to you, I'll wake up now and count stars till morning."

I walked away from the edge of the lake back toward the floating red door.

"Be well, daughter of Zeus," the swan called. "Be well."

CHAPTER 27

"Wake up."

Damian was shaking my arm. I groaned, rolling away onto my side. He shook me again.

"Wake up, Phoebe. It's time to go."

I opened my eyes, squinting at the bright sunlight.

"You've been snoring like a chainsaw," Angie said, squatting in front of me. With her shield strapped to her back and her headband on, she looked an awful lot like Athena.

I sat up, rubbing my eyes. "I had a dream."

"I thought you didn't dream," Damian said.

"I don't, which is why it was so weird." I told them about the red door and the swan.

Damian's eyes widened. "That swan sounds like Zeus. He has the power of transfiguration."

"Trans-fig-what?"

"Transfiguration. The ability to take the shape of an animal. Maybe he was sending a message. Communicating with you in your dream."

"He's right," Macario said. "Zeus often appears in the form of a swan."

My head spun. "You think that dream swan was Zeus? Then why didn't he tell me?"

Damian shrugged. "Maybe he just wanted to talk."

I felt gobsmacked. If Damian was right, I had met my dad. He was a swan, but still—monumental.

"Come on, time to find us a hydra before ol' Hercules beats us to it," Angie said, rising to her feet.

As we walked, I played back every word the swan and I had exchanged. I'd shouted at him. Of course, I would do that. My first time meeting my dad and I had basically ripped his head off.

A plus, Phoebe, A plus.

The smell of sulphur and rotting vegetation was the first clue we were getting close to the swamps. That and the dark cluster of gnarled trees whose twisted limbs formed a solid wall before us.

I couldn't help the shiver of fear that ran up my spine as we stopped in front of the thorny barrier. We'd faced a hydra once, and it had been a close call. How many of these monsters were we going to face before something bad happened to one of us?

"Welcome to the swamps of Lerna," Macario said. "There is no road through it, because no one is foolish enough to enter."

"Except us," Angie said.

Damian hesitated. "Maybe we should wait for Hercules. You know, let him do the dangerous parts, and we get what we need."

"No. We do this on our own," I argued. "He may not even head this way next. I can't make Carl wait a second longer than necessary."

Angie drew her sword. "I got your back, Katzy. Let's do this. I'm not afraid of a hydra."

"Well, you should be," I snapped, feeling the scar on my leg throb at the memory of the first attack. "Because this isn't a game."

A look of hurt flashed across her face, but then she nodded. "You're right. I'm sorry."

I studied the impenetrable wall of branches. "How do we get in?"

"Like this."

Angie began hacking at the twisted brambles. It took a few minutes, but she managed to carve out a hole big enough for us to climb through.

When we came out the other side, we were inside the swamp. Mist clung to the ground. Behind us, the branches knitted themselves back together, magically sealing the hole up as if it had never been there.

The sun had disappeared behind a bank of gray fog, making it hard to see through the dense trees. Insects buzzed around our heads, and birds flew past above us, sending out shrill cries that pierced the air. Glowing eyes peered out from tangles of brush.

"Does anyone else have the creeps right now?" Angie asked.

"Let's move," I said.

The hard earth gave way to marshy reeds. Soon we were wading in shallow water. We tugged our boots off and tucked them under the belts of our tunics. The water got deeper, reaching our knees. Something brushed against my leg, and I screamed, making everyone jump. A small water snake poked its diamond-shaped head up once before it swam rapidly away, leaving an *S* trail.

Hours passed, and we continued slogging through muck and water. There was nothing to guide us but the never-ending grim landscape. Occasional clumps of rock poked out of the water. An algae-covered spire twisted up into the fog. Another stinging insect landed on my neck. I slapped at it, grimacing at the green-splattered goo on my palm. At the rate I was getting bitten, I would run out of blood before the hydra had a chance to kill me.

"Katzy?" Angie stopped in front of me.

"What's wrong?"

"Do you hear that?"

"Hear what?" All I heard was the sound of my breathing.

"Exactly."

One second the place had been abuzz with swamp noises; the next, silence, as if someone had pulled the plug.

Angie drew her blade. Damian touched my arm. "Careful, if you use lightning, the Erinyes might come."

"Or we might get eaten by a hydra. I'll risk it. Maybe they're still stuck in my tornado."

I called up a lightning bolt, and Macario drew a sunbeam.

We walked on, listening intently for any sound.

"Do you hear anything?" Damian whispered.

"No," I said. "Maybe it's nothing."

The attack came from behind.

One second Angie was beside me; the next she was gone. A scaly green tentacle had wrapped around her legs, dragging her backward. The spire of rock began to untwist, revealing nine separate long necks.

The hydra.

Angie's scream was cut off by a mouthful of water. She recovered quickly, hacking at the limb as I sent a lightning bolt at it. It released her, and she staggered to her feet, dripping with muddy water. The hydra's swamp-green body was as big as a school bus, with nine different serpentine heads. A pair of jutting fangs curved upward from each of its lower jaws. The eyes were glowing emeralds. Wide nostrils exhaled steam. A row of jagged fins ran from its skulls down its back to a tail that arched up high, the end spiked and lethal looking. The tail was what had wrapped around Angie.

We ducked as all nine heads darted toward us, hungrily trying to eat us in one single attack.

Macario and I launched our missiles, momentarily shocking it in an explosion of sun sparks and electrical energy.

"Take cover!" I shouted.

We fled in different directions. Damian took refuge behind a scraggly tree. Angie ducked into some brush. I dropped behind a pair of fallen logs with Macario.

The nine heads spun every which way, searching for its meal. The tail slashed out, knocking the top off the tree shielding Damian. It clawed forward, moving its massive body toward him.

I knew better than to hack off a head until I had a way to get rid of them all. I took mental stock of our meager weapons.

"Damian?"

"Don't ask me to be the decoy," he shouted.

"I need you to be the decoy."

"So not fair."

"I know. But Angie has a sword, and Macario and I can use our powers. Please."

"No."

"If we each take three heads, we can defeat this thing in one go. Angie, are you up for this?"

She grinned at me from her hiding spot, not looking the least bit afraid. "Does a duck walk backward?"

"No? I'm not sure."

She rolled her eyes. "I'm saying yes, I got this."

"The son of Apollo is ready," Macario called, gripping his sunbeam.

"Okay. Damian, I promise you'll be fine."

"That's what you said about the python, and then it ate me!"

"But I freed you."

"After it swallowed me. And you let that lion nearly take my head off."

"But I didn't let it. I know I promised I wouldn't ask again, but are you in or not?"

There was a heavy moment of silence, then he grunted, "I'm in."

I pointed Macario off to my left. Angie took up a position to my right, her shield in front of her. Damian stepped out from behind the tree. His toga was stained gray with mud. He looked really small, not nearly strong enough to take on a hydra. He wasn't a demigod. He was just a kid.

"No, wait!" I shouted as Damian jumped in front of the hydra.

He waggled his hands and started shouting, "Here hydra, hydra, come eat me, you revolting nine-headed beast."

The heads swiveled toward him, nine pairs of eyes flickering, as if they were all thinking, *What is this puny human up to?* There was no way he could take them on. It was a suicide mission.

"Damian, no!"

The first head swooped down. I moved forward, throwing the lightning bolt in a spinning arc at the beast's head, hoping to slice it clean off. Instead, the beast snapped up the lightning in its jaws and swallowed it. Macario tried with his sunbeam, flinging it at the nearest hydra. It stuck into the side of its neck, glowing with yellow fire. The hydra howled, smashing down at the water to put it out.

Angie let out a rebel yell and launched herself at the closest head. She smashed at its snout with her shield, then brought the blade down on the fleshy part of its neck. She managed to cut deeply, getting sprayed with green blood in the process, but her arm didn't have the power to sever the head.

The hydra's body started to shake and shudder. I blinked away green slime. Was it—was it getting larger?

The beast rose out of the water, glowing with an inner white light. Not only did it swell three sizes, but more heads appeared, thrusting upward out of its body until the thing had—I counted nineteen heads.

"What did we do?" I shouted. A wall of water sprayed us as its tail slapped at the surface.

"I think your lightning supercharged it," Angie said.

Damian was still all alone out in front of it. The heads towered over him. He was paralyzed with fear, unable to move.

Everything went quiet. It was as if the world slowed down. Molecules of water floated in the air. I could see everything in slow motion. The position of the nineteen heads. Angie's sword over her head. Macario with his arm cocked back, holding another sunbeam.

This wasn't going to work.

No matter what we did, we were going to lose.

Not cool. Phoebe Katz doesn't give up.

And then it came to me.

The heart. The hydra might have nineteen heads, but it had only one heart. At least I hoped so.

"Forget the heads!" I yelled. "Go for the heart."

184   THE EYE OF ZEUS

The beast crawled forward, parting the water, roaring so loud the wind peeled my hair back. The heads swarmed over Damian. He swayed on his feet, too terrified to move, his hands limp at his sides as the heads snapped closer.

The lightning bolt I drew was cold fire in my hand. "Macario, the biggest sunbeam you have."

"Got it." He drew a flaming yellow beam of pure sunshine.

The hydra's green-scaled chest was built like a tank. The heart was in there—but could we penetrate the skin?

"Angie, got your sword?"

"Yeah, it's ready." She held it over her head, feet planted like a warrior.

"On my count, Macario and I send our bolts at its chest and crack it open, then Angie finishes it off. One, two, now!"

Macario threw his beam. It exploded in a burst of yellow fire on the hydra's chest. The beast reared up as flames danced on its skin. In the next instant, I launched my lightning bolt. Electricity crackled on the green surface of the creature, and it bellowed in pain. I threw another and then another until a small opening appeared, a crack in the skin.

Angie ran in with both hands on the hilt of her sword. "Taste my steel!" She jumped up, thrusting her sword into the crack.

The blade sunk in with a sickening sound. The hydra heads all screamed in unison, splitting our ears with the noise. It reeled backward, jerking Angie off her feet as she clung to the hilt. The hydra thrashed back and forth, trying to shake her off, and then took off across the water. I dove after Angie, grasping her ankles. Macario latched onto mine as green blood spattered us, staining the water.

We had failed.

The hydra would probably grow another ten heads, and we would never survive another attack. The beast dragged us backward through the swamp until, suddenly, it stopped. I let go of Angie and got to my feet, prepared to do what I could. I didn't even have the strength to call up a single lightning bolt, but I would use my fists if I had to.

The hydra staggered once, and then one after another, the heads tumbled into the water, slapping down until the beast lay still.

Angie pulled her blade free and turned to grin at us. She was covered head to toe in green hydra blood.

"That. Was. Epic!" And then Angie began dancing the Floss in front of the limp beast.

I blinked to clear my vision. Using that much lightning had left me light-headed, but there was no time to rest. "We need a fang. Quick, before it decides to come back to life and grow ten more heads."

We splashed over to the nearest head. Angie peeled back its upper lip, revealing double rows of deadly teeth.

"Hold it steady," I said. "I don't want it to snap closed on me."

I tested the fangs and found one that was loose. I wriggled it back and forth until I could tug it free. Taking the mirror, I pressed the fang into the triangle-shaped slot. This time it accepted it. A tremor of power ran up my arm as the slot sealed over.

Four down, two to go.

We sloshed back to find Damian standing stock still in the same place. I snapped my fingers in his face, and he startled, dragging in a deep breath.

"Am I really alive?"

I nodded. "We did it. We got the fang."

"Good. That was fun, wasn't it?" He was making light of it, but I knew he was shaken. Badly. And it was all my fault.

I put my hand on his shoulder. "No more being the bait."

He smiled weakly. "You said that before. It's okay. I don't mind."

"I mean it this time. I don't want to lose you. I won't do that again."

He nodded. But I wasn't sure he believed me.

CHAPTER 28

We made our way to the edge of the swamp. Our legs and arms were scratched and bleeding. Smelly mud and sticky hydra slime coated our once pristine tunics. It was a relief to slip our boots back on and be rid of the stinging insects. Only two talismans remained. The boys began arguing about which one to go after first.

"Cerberus is next on our list," Damian said.

"But the chimera is easier to get to," Macario argued.

"Tell me what it is again?" I asked.

"Mostly lion with a goat sticking out of its back."

My eyebrow went up. "A goat? Really?"

Macario nodded. "And a snake for a tail like Miss Kitty."

I shook my head. "Now I've heard it all. Cerberus is the three-headed dog, right?" I said, turning to Damian.

"He guards the underworld. If I remember my maps correctly, there's an entrance north of here where the Acheron river meets the sea."

"Where does the chimera live?" I asked Macario.

"Outside Lycia. It's across the Aegean Sea."

"Across the sea? How are we supposed to get there?"

"We can hire a boat. There are herds of wild pegasuses there. Once we slay the chimera, we can fly the pegasuses across the seas to Acheron. Their wings are so fast we'll arrive before we've even left."

"But the underworld is closer now," Damian said. "We should deal with Cerberus and then head to Lycia. Our last stop is Olympus."

"Exactly, which is a straight shot from Acheron."

"So is Lycia," Damian argued.

These two were giving me a headache. "So basically, it's a toss-up. Angie, what do you think?"

"I say we deal with the freaky lion-goat first and leave the underworld for last."

I had to agree. I had no desire to go deep underground where the dead lived. None at all.

"Chimera it is," I announced.

Damian protested but I held up my hand. "Your leader has spoken. No more arguing. Macario, how do we arrange this boat?"

"I know just the place," Macario winked.

Macario led us to a charming fishing village on the edge of the sparkling blue sea. The sand was white as sugar. Simple adobe huts with bundled sticks for roofs lined the shore. Old men played some kind of dice game in the shade. Olive-skinned street urchins dressed in nothing but white loincloths offered us strings of pretty shells.

Macario talked to one of the older boys.

Correction, he wasn't a boy, at least not completely. He looked about fourteen, but he had horns. Yup, small horns that peeked out of the mop of curly hair on his head. He even had a slight scruff under his lip. And did I mention his feet were hooves? His bare chest was human as could be, but he walked on a pair of what looked like goat legs. My jaw hung open. Angie's did the same.

"What is it?" I asked.

"I think it's a satyr," Damian said. "Epically cool."

Macario's hand flashed, and a coin passed to the other boy before our friend rejoined us.

Over Macario's shoulder, the satyr caught my eye and held it, gazing at me with an intensity that left me wondering if I had dirt on my face.

Macario filled us in. "Karisto says there is a small fishing boat we can use. Its owner has been sick for two weeks. He says he can borrow it to take us to Lycia."

"How do you know we can trust this Karisto?" I asked.

"Because I paid him well," Macario said. "You have to trust me. I've been here before."

We made our way out to the docks, stopping to buy a few supplies, draping casks of water and fresh fruits over our shoulders. Karisto stopped in front of a weathered boat that looked like it was about to sink. It listed heavily to one side, and its ragged sails hung limp.

"It's great," Macario said. "A fine boat."

"Um, it's got holes in it," Damian said, pointing at the missing strips of wood in the siding.

"It's a death ship," Angie blurted out.

"No, we are not taking this," I said firmly.

"You have a problem with my boat?" Karisto snapped, his eyes flashing disdain.

"I have a problem with dying out on the open water," I snapped back.

"Then the deal's off." He turned his back and clomped away.

Macario glared at me and scurried after him. "Karisto, my friend, she didn't mean it."

The satyr paused. "The price just went up."

Macario frowned. "What do you mean?"

"Because of her rudeness, I will need something more or the deal is off."

"We don't have any more money to spare," Macario said.

"That's okay. I need light." Karisto's voice turned a bit gruff. "For the kids. They work all day and do their schoolwork at night, but they don't have oil for the lamps."

"How are we supposed to give them light?" I asked.

He pointed at Macario. "This one can do it."

He wanted a sunbeam.

"Can you do that?" I asked Macario.

He shrugged. "If it's stored well."

Karisto called to one of the boys. The urchin ran into a bait shop and returned with a glass urn with a stopper on top.

Macario rubbed his hands and clapped them together. A glowing sunbeam appeared. It gave off a radiant heat that made my face warm. He carefully placed it in the glass urn and put the stopper in.

"Set this on a shelf. If you don't open it, the light should be good for several weeks."

The young boy carried it carefully down the dock, followed by a cheering group of urchins.

We boarded our sad-looking ship. I opened my mouth to tell Karisto the lamp was a nice thing to do, but he barked at me.

"How about you give us some wind, demigod, instead of standing there?"

Macario must have told him who I was—but what exactly had I done to get on his bad side?

"Are you sure it won't draw the Erinyes?" I asked Damian. They had left us alone in the swamp. I didn't want to push my luck.

Damian shrugged. "Should be okay. It's not major power."

I sucked in air, imagining the wind building and pushing. Exhaling, I whispered, "*Anemos.*" Instantly the sails filled, and the boat jumped forward, skimming sleekly across the water.

Karisto clip-clopped across the deck, leaving scuff marks as he adjusted the sails. He had a strong chest with tiny whorls of hair. His tattered canvas shorts were lashed around his waist with a length of rope. He went about his business, checking the lines and calling orders to Angie, who held the tiller.

The ship rode the gentle waves easily. The sun was shining, making the water dance with light. After the first hour, I relaxed. My job was simple: keep enough wind in the sails to keep the ship moving. It wasn't that tough, a little puff now and then. I lay in the back of the ship, tossing figs into my mouth as I let my fingers trail in the cool water.

"Are you always so lazy?" Karisto grunted at me as he swabbed the deck with a makeshift mop made of rags.

"I can't use my powers, or the Erinyes will come at me with silver arrows that are pretty much deadly."

"There are other things you can do," he said angrily. "You could help with the sails."

"I don't know anything about sailing." I tossed another fig in the air.

He swung his mop, hitting the fig and sending it sailing over the water. A silvery fish jumped out of the froth and swallowed it.

I sat up, annoyed. "Why'd you do that?"

"Because that fish needed it more than you did."

"You're impossible."

"You're lazy."

We glared at each other.

This was going to be a long trip.

Sailing is boring. Really boring. There's nothing much to do but watch the waves. Damian spent the time fishing with Macario, laughing as they reeled in wriggling silver fish. The two of them bonded over the best hook to use and what bait was better, moldy cheese or fish guts.

Yuck.

And Angie. Don't get me started. She and Karisto passed the time battling each other with makeshift swords. The satyr, apparently, was a world-class swords-goat and had fashioned a pair of wooden practice blades to teach Angie everything he knew.

I was left to sulk on my own.

On the second day, we passed by a small island off to our left.

"We should stop there," Karisto said. "We can buy some more supplies."

"We don't have a lot of money," Macario said.

"That's okay," goat-boy said. "We can sell some of the fish." He held up the string of fish the boys had caught.

We nosed into an empty slip. The wharfman accepted a small coin from Karisto to leave the boat there a few hours. A rocky path led from the harbor to a small village. The limestone houses were clean and well tended. Grape vines and vegetable gardens filled the yards. Women were out pinning laundry to the lines. White tunics flapped in the ocean breezes. The women stopped to stare at us as we made our way up the hill.

Damian stopped halfway up and tugged on my arm. "Phoebe, whatever you do, don't use your powers. We can't have the Erinyes tracking us."

"I won't."

"No, I mean it. You have to swear on Carl's life."

I sighed. "Fine, I swear, cross my heart."

"On Carl's life," he pressed.

I could feel Karisto's eyes watching me, and I flushed. "On Carl's life, jeez, I said I promise." I pushed past him, irritated by his lack of faith in me.

Macario and Karisto moved along the stalls of the marketplace with Angie and Damian. Karisto was haggling for a good price for our haul of fish.

 I lagged behind, feeling a tug toward a white building with a bell in the tower. It looked like a school. A crowd of boys had gathered out front.

I pushed my way in. A boy my age stood in the center of the circle. Three boys were taunting him, all of them bigger. The boy's tunic was soiled and ragged, and his untrimmed hair fell to his shoulders. He wore old leather sandals that had been tied together with string.

"You don't belong here, fisherman, so take your smelly feet elsewhere."

"Yeah, get lost."

They shoved the boy to the ground. His lunch spilled out of his bag, a green apple and some bread and cheese.

"Hey, knock it off," I said, thrusting myself into the circle. I helped the boy to his feet. "What did he ever do to you?"

They eyed me, studying my clothes to see if I was anyone of importance. The sight of my golden headband made them hesitate, in spite of the fact that my tunic was spattered with dried hydra blood.

"I don't need your help," the boy said to me.

"No? Because it looks to me like you're outnumbered."

"What are you, another fisherman's castoff?" the tallest boy sneered. He had blond hair and buck teeth as big as a horse's.

"No. I am a daughter of Zeus, so beware."

They looked at each other, then laughed. Bucktooth laughed the hardest, spraying spittle at me as he snickered out, "If you're a daughter of Zeus, I'm a centaur's uncle."

"I'm thinking more a son of a donkey," I said.

His face turned tomato red. "My father is the king. Boys, let's teach them a lesson about knowing their place."

I itched to call up a lightning bolt. Electricity tingled at my fingertips, and then I remembered my stupid promise. I hated Damian right then. I let my fingers uncurl.

"Got any ideas?" I asked the boy softly.

"Yeah, do what I always do. Run." He ducked into the crowd and took off. I followed two steps behind.

"Get them!" Bucktooth shouted.

We ran through the marketplace, weaving in and out of stalls. I tried to keep the boy in my sight, but after a few turns, I lost him.

Unfortunately, I found the three bullies from the schoolyard.

"Lookie here," Bucktooth sneered, "it's time to teach this peasant a lesson in manners."

They circled in closer, backing me into an alley. I looked left and right, trying to see where I could run, but I was trapped.

Unless I used my powers.

CHAPTER 29

When I opened my eyes, everything hurt. My cheek was bruised, and my lip was swollen. My body felt like someone had taken a baseball bat to it. I was lying on a thin pad in a shadowy room, a light blanket over me. Gauzy fabric separated the rooms, moving gently in the breeze. I could smell a fire and something cooking. A woman's voice murmured, and a boy answered.

I sat up, feeling a bit dizzy, and knocked over a bowl of water. There was a rustle of fabric, and then a woman stood in the doorway with the boy I had tried to protect. The sun was behind her, so it was hard to see her face. Long caramel-colored hair fell in waves over her shoulder. She looked kind, if a little sad around the eyes.

"You're awake." She gave the boy a push. "Go fetch her a bowl of soup."

He ran off and returned with a steaming bowl in his hands. The woman left us as he set it carefully next to me, squatting down to my level. I got a good look at his face then. His eyes were the same color as mine, a bright blueish green. "You look terrible," he said with a grin.

"Whose fault is that?" I said, lifting the bowl. "You left me alone with those bullies."

"I didn't ask for your help," he reminded me, "but thanks all the same. I'm sorry they got hold of you. I looked for you."

"Where am I?"

"Mother and I helped you home, once we found you in that alley."

"Thanks."

I spooned some soup up. It was a delicious lamb stew, with chunks of meat floating in thick gravy and potatoes. I finished it quickly, then set the bowl down.

"I really need to get going. My friends will be looking for me." I stood up, testing out my legs and arms. There didn't appear to be anything broken. Just my pride.

Outside the hut, the sun was high in the sky. I must've been out for a couple hours. The harbor sparkled down below. We were in a neighborhood of simple huts—stone enclosures with heavy canvas stretched over them to keep out the sun. Kids ran about, playing a game that involved tossing pebbles into a circle. Women were busy at work, washing clothes and pounding out flatbread, while men mended fishing nets. Dried fish hung on racks.

The boy's mother put her arm around his shoulders. "My son told me what you did for him. It was very brave."

"Stupid, but brave," he said with a wink.

The sound of hooves pounding made the woman turn. Clouds of dust swirled as men on horseback entered the small village. The men wore leather-girded vests, carried swords and pointed lances, and had shields slung over their backs. Their horses bore armor as well, shiny metal helmets over their heads and ornate chest plates. This was someone's army.

The woman turned to me, grasping my shoulders. "Hide inside! Whatever happens, do not come out." She pushed me back into the little hut. I moved to the small window, kneeling down so that I could see.

A man dismounted, handing his reins to one of the soldiers. "You have insulted the king's son," he said, grabbing the boy I had helped by the collar. "You will be thrashed within an inch of your life."

"Don't hurt him!" The woman flung herself at the soldier. He raised his hand to strike her.

A trumpet blared, and everyone froze as another man rode up, parting the throng of soldiers with his horse. A golden crown glinted in the sunlight. His shoulders were draped with a heavy red cape embroidered with gold stitching. He looked cruel, his mouth a slash in his face.

Four men ran up and helped him down. Gold inlaid boots came up to his knees. It didn't take a genius to figure out that this was a king, especially since every person he passed by dropped down to one knee, including the woman and the boy.

"King Polydectes," she said, keeping her head down. "To what do we owe this pleasure?"

"Rise. I want to see your face."

She stood, keeping her eyes downcast. The boy stood next to her, his hand clasped in hers.

The king raised her chin with a finger. "My dear, why do you hide such a pretty face?"

"Leave my mother alone!" The boy tried to step in front of her, but the king backhanded him, sending him flying to the ground.

The woman gasped, dropping down to help him back to his feet.

Ooh, how I wanted to teach this king a lesson, but it would only make things worse for this family.

"I could have the boy executed for speaking in that manner to his king," the royal bully said. "But I'm in a mood to be fair. You hide yourself in this fishing village, but I know the blood that runs through your veins. I will have you as my queen. Come of your own accord, or I will find a way to make you."

He spun on his heel, strode back to his horse, and waited to be lifted up onto the finely tooled saddle. He started to ride off, then pulled up to look back at her. "My son said there was also a girl about the same age."

"She was a stranger he met on the street. No one of importance," the boy's mother said.

Thankfully, he accepted her answer and galloped away.

The soldiers ransacked the little village, tossing tables over, emptying pots of food onto the ground, stomping out cooking fires, and throwing the dried fish into the dirt before leaving.

The woman stood with her arm around her son as the rest of the villagers set about righting the tables and picking up the pieces.

I came out of the hut. I think they had forgotten I was there. The woman saw me and wiped her damp cheeks with her apron. Rummaging in the debris, she pulled out a small bag. "Here, child, I packed this for you. Take it with our blessings."

I hesitated. I didn't want to leave. Something about the two of them tugged at me. I wanted to help them. Tell them it would all be okay. But they stood silent, a pair united in their own world, waiting for me to leave.

With a nod goodbye, I made my way down the hillside to the docks. My friends came running toward me.

"Where have you been?" Angie demanded, practically throwing herself at me to wrap me in a hug. "We were so worried."

"And what happened to your face?" Damian asked with a worried frown. "You look like you fell down a flight of stairs."

"It's nothing," I said. "Let's go. I don't want to stay another minute in this place."

Karisto eyed me but remained silent. As I stepped on board, he stopped me. "You kept your promise, didn't you?"

I tugged free. "What's it to you?"

He shrugged. "I'm just surprised. In my experience, demigods tend to throw their powers around."

"Guess that makes me unique. Now, if you don't mind, I'd like to leave this dump."

Karisto hoisted the sails, and I provided a hearty gust of wind to speed us away. As the island receded from sight, I thought of the boy and his mother. I hadn't even learned their names.

"I've always liked Seriphos," Macario said from his spot on the deck, where he lay in the sun. "They have the best candied figs in all of Greece." He tossed one in the air and caught it in his open mouth.

Damian was helping Karisto with the sails, but he paused, turning to look at Macario. "What did you say the name of that island was?"

"Seriphos. Why? Is it in one of your stories?"

Damian's stricken eyes went to mine. I sat up, knowing I was about to get some horrid news. "What is it?"

"It's just . . . I mean . . . I think . . ."

"Oh, just spit it out." Angie dropped down on the deck next to me. "Katzy here can take anything."

"Well, a long time ago—or maybe not, I'm not sure where exactly we are in Greek history—there was a king named Polydectes."

"Yeah, I met him. He's a real jerk."

Damian laughed nervously. "Okay, then, about that king—he fell in love with a woman. She and her son had come here from another land. She lived in a simple fishing village but was descended from a royal family."

"Sounds like a fairytale," Angie said, making gagging noises.

"It's not a fairytale. It's the story of Phoebe's family."

I froze. "What are you talking about?"

"I'm talking about your mother, Danae, princess of Argos, and her son Perseus, your brother."

I shook my head. "No, back up. I mean what does it have to do with that place?"

"Seriphos is the island Danae and Perseus washed up on after her father, the king of Argos, put her and her baby in a crate on the seas."

My head buzzed with anger. "And you didn't think to mention that to me?"

"I didn't know. I swear, Phoebe, I didn't know that's where we were."

Then it hit me, like a ton of hydra dung. "I met them." The woman had looked familiar. Now I knew why. She was my mother. I quickly told them what had happened, including how the king had threatened her. "It has to be them. We have to go back."

"We can't," Karisto said. "The tides are against us now."

"I don't care! That was my freaking mother back there. I didn't even get to tell her my name or who I was. I left them to that bully. He's going to do something terrible. I have to warn them."

I rushed for the tiller, but Karisto gripped my wrist. "It is too late to turn back."

I wrenched my arm free. "Why are you so heartless? Don't you have any family?"

Pain flashed in his eyes. "Yes. A brother named Mikos I would do anything for. But it doesn't change the facts. Macario has told me of your journey to save your friend. Every second you delay means another day he is a slave." His eyes burned with a fire I didn't understand, but I did get the Carl part, and he wasn't wrong about that.

Damian put a hand on my shoulder. "It's okay, Phoebe. Perseus turns out fine. You know the stories. He's smart and brave, and, well, he's just like you."

I sank down onto the deck. My mother had been right there. I could've hugged her. Asked her a hundred and one questions. I opened the satchel she had given me. Inside was a pair of small green apples, some dried lamb meat wrapped in flatbread, and three freshly baked cookies. Tucked beneath was a scrap of linen for a napkin. I held it to my face, inhaling, imagining I could smell her.

Angie sat next to me. "You okay, Katzy?"

I nodded through blurry eyes. "I should have recognized her."

"I bet she misses you."

I leaned against Angie, closing my eyes. I wasn't so sure. She seemed so close to Perseus, as if the two of them made a closed circle. Even though they lived in a small fishing village, they had each other. That was a lot more than I'd ever had. I had a sudden longing to be home, back in New York, with its smell of hot dogs and sewers, the bustle of traffic, and Carl taking me out for Sunday pancakes.

CHAPTER 30

After another day of sailing and brooding over missed family reunions, we came across another island jutting out of the sea in front of us. It was like nothing else I'd ever seen. An entire city had been carved into the steep sides of the sandstone cliffs. Ornate columns held up vaulted ceilings, hinting at dark openings. Oddly, there wasn't a soul in sight.

"Is that Lycia?" I asked Karisto. He had thawed considerably toward me since I had kept my promise not to use my powers.

"No. Those are the tombs of Kragos."

"Kragos?"

"The Lycians believe that if they bury their dead in these tombs, winged creatures sent by Hades will carry their souls into the underworld. They are tended to by priests called necros."

I looked at Damian. His eyes flared as he had the same idea. If it was true—and around here the craziest things were—we might be able to follow them to our next stop, the underworld.

If we survived the monstrous lion-goat, that was.

We beached the boat on a rocky shore, tugging it high so the tide wouldn't carry it out.

"So where do we find the chimera?" I asked, looking hopefully to Karisto.

He shrugged, perched on the prow of the boat. "Don't ask me. I've never been here before. But I've heard rumors it roams the hills in these parts. If you follow the vultures circling the sky, you'll find its latest victim. Just wondering, how do you expect to kill it?"

All eyes switched to Damian.

He cleared his throat. "According to legend, a guy named Bellerophon rode on Pegasus, the one Perseus rode, and attacked the chimera from the sky to avoid its deadly fire breath."

"Fire breath? Wait, you didn't mention it had fire," I said.

"Didn't I?" He laughed nervously. "I did mention it has the head of a lion."

"A fire-breathing lion?"

"No, as I recall, it's the goat that breathes fire, and its tail . . ."

"What about its tail?" I said, hands on my hips. "You said it was just a snake."

"Snake. Yeah, maybe more like a drakon."

"Drakon? That sounds bad," Angie said.

"It's like a small hydra head."

"Great, so how did this Beller-phone guy kill it?"

"He shot a lead arrow into its throat, and the fire melted the lead in its lungs."

I stared at him in stunned disbelief. "So all I have to do is learn how to shoot a bow and arrow from the back of a flying horse. How hard could that be?" My voice dripped with sarcasm.

"Don't be mad at me, Phoebe. It's not like I make the rules here," Damian said.

"I know." I sighed, picking up a rock and throwing it into the sea. "I just wish one thing was easy in this place. Macario, you said there were wild herds of pegasuses, right?"

"Yes, they roam the woods outside of Lycia."

"So first we capture a pegasus, and then we'll figure out the rest."

"About that." Now it was Macario's turn to look nervous.

"What now?" I asked.

"Uh, the thing is, the pegasuses are—"

"They're not fire-breathing things with serpent tails, are they?" Angie asked.

"No, no, they're harmless," Macario said. "They're not the ones I'm worried about."

"What he's trying to say is they're guarded by a couple of centarians," Karisto said, jumping down to the sand.

"What's a centarian?" I asked.

"A hundred-handed giant."

I blinked. "A hundred-handed what?"

"Giant. You know, very large creature, pretty dumb, but they don't like it when you mess with their herd." A haunted light entered his eyes.

"What do they do?" Damian asked.

"Boil you in a pot of oil, peel your flesh from your bones for their stew, and make a necklace out of the bones."

I stared at the satyr. "Seriously?"

He burst out laughing. "No, but you should have seen your faces." His face tightened as he went on. "They lock you in chains and put you to work as a slave in their fields."

There was something he wasn't telling us, but I didn't

have the patience to pry. "Damian's right, we can't defeat the chimera until we have wings, so job one is to find this herd and figure out how to steal a couple without tipping off the giants."

"Then what are we waiting for?" Angie said. "Let's go wrangle some winged horsies."

A steep ravine led up from the beach. Loose rocks caused us to lose our footing more than once. The hot sun burned our skin, and what little water we had was brackish and hardly touched my thirst. As we passed the tombs, a cold draft skated over my skin, chilling me in the heat of the day.

I lagged behind, curious about the place. A man appeared in one of the openings, standing silent in a black robe. His eyes were on me, as if he could see me, but that was impossible because someone had sewn them shut. Black stitches crossed his lids with knotted thread. The same thing had been done to his mouth.

Weird. And really creepy.

I hurried after the others. Karisto clopped along on those goat legs of his as if this was a simple stroll down Fifth Avenue. His back glistened with sweat. He used a walking stick to keep his balance as he steadily led us up the ravine. Finally, red-faced and completely spent, we reached the top and collapsed in a heap on a patch of dry grass.

After my lungs stopped aching and my legs had feeling in them again, I sat up. In the distance, a city of white adobe buildings rose from the valley.

Lycia.

I planned to give it a wide berth. My track record in big cities wasn't great. If I didn't burn something down, I destroyed a temple or got myself thrown in prison.

Karisto led us into a forest of what he claimed were

cypress trees. The air was cooler out of the direct sunlight. The ground underfoot grew soft with the covering of pine needles.

"Hurry up," he called as he rushed us along. "The giants will be sleeping this time of day."

"How do you know that?" I asked.

"Yeah, I thought you said you'd never been here," Angie added.

He stumbled to a halt, shoulders heaving as he stared at the ground. "That's right, I've never been here, but I've sailed around these islands. People talk. Now, are you coming or not?" And then the jerk turned and walked off, without even waiting for an answer.

I exchanged glances with Angie.

"What's his problem?" she asked.

"I don't know, but something's wrong."

The satyr stopped abruptly, cocking his head. "There." He pointed. "In that clearing." He waited for us to go ahead.

"And I thought sun-brain was annoying," Angie said.

"Hey, I heard that," Macario said.

We stepped out of the brush into a clearing covered in a thick layer of leaves. A pegasus stood on the other side.

My breath caught in my chest. It was so beautiful. I had seen Pepper turn into a winged horse, so I knew what a pegasus looked like, but Pepper was a carriage horse. She didn't have nobility woven into the fabric of her being.

The pegasus gleamed in the sunlight beaming through the trees. It was silver, glowing with an inner fire. Its regal head raised up, sapphire eyes watching us warily. Its wings were tipped with white feathers, and it flared them slightly, as if it were wondering if we were friend or foe.

Karisto held back as the rest of us took a step toward the pegasus.

Two things happened: the pegasus crashed away into the brush, disappearing in a thunder of hooves, and Karisto drew a curved blade from his waistband and slashed at a rope tied to the tree. Before I could ask what he was doing, my feet went out from under me as the net hidden under a layer of leaves snapped tight and hoisted us up into the air.

CHAPTER 31

We swung in the air, squished together, a good fifteen feet off the ground.

"Karisto, cut us down!"

We took turns yelling at him, but he didn't look up, remaining crouched behind the tree, as if he was waiting for something.

It didn't take long.

An ominous stomping sound grew steadily closer. The treetops parted, and my heart stopped as I caught sight of my first giant.

It was big. Not linebacker big; more like two-story-building big. He had a bushel of red hair on top of his head, a cauliflower-shaped nose, and tiny eyes that squinted down at us.

And then there were the hands.

I couldn't swear there were a hundred of them, but his beefy arms extended one after the other from the shoulder all the way down to the waist, three deep. He wore a singlet made out of animal hides. His bare feet sported four gnarly toes with dirt-crusted nails.

"Agor smells thief," the giant rumbled, wading closer through the trees. "Who dares steal Agor's pretty ones?"

Two stomps later he towered over us. Yellowed teeth sprouted from his gums like broken surfboards.

"Hey, Agor, down here," Karisto called. "I have something to trade."

"Trade?" Agor sniffed the air. "I know that smell. You try steal my pretties once."

"I escaped, but you took my brother Mikos prisoner. Look." He pointed at us. "I've brought you four new slaves. Take them and give me my brother back."

My jaw dropped. So that was what Karisto had been hiding—the traitorous snake!

Agor bent down to look in the net. His beady eyes passed over each of us, inspecting us like cattle. "This puny lot?"

"Two of them are demigods," Karisto said. "The other two will be hard workers. More than enough to replace one satyr."

The giant scratched his chin with one hand while he dug out earwax with another. "Deal."

He reached out a meaty fist, snatched the net out of the tree, and turned to go.

"Hey, what about my brother?" Karisto challenged.

The giant chortled. "Brother is nothing but bones at the bottom of the sea."

"You killed him?" Karisto flinched, as if he'd been punched in the gut. I almost felt sorry for him.

Almost.

"We not kill good slaves," Agor said. "The beast of the woods ate him. Now be gone before Agor change mind and keep you too." He strode off through the trees, carting us off and leaving that traitor Karisto behind.

"This calls for lightning." I rubbed my hands, ready to call a fat bolt.

"Don't, Phoebes," Damian said. "You know it will only make it worse."

Aargh. I was so tired of hearing that. "You really think those Erinyes are going to find us here?"

"I think they can track you to the ends of the earth."

"Guys, we've got company," Angie said.

Another giant approached—just as big, just as homely.

"What find you, brother?" It scented the air with its bulbous nose.

Agor thrust the net out. "Fresh slaves to help Boza work the fields."

The giant named Boza leaned in to get a closer look. "Boza like new slaves." He poked the net with one of his fingers.

"The son of Apollo is not a slave."

Macario drew a sunbeam and launched it into the face of the giant. The giant howled, swatting multiple hands at the burning sun embers on his face.

Angie slashed through the netting with her sword. We tumbled to the ground in a heap. She stabbed the first giant in his foot.

He screamed, hopping up and down. "That not nice," he roared as dozens of hands smashed down, trying to capture us.

We dodged between fumbling fingers and fat palms. "Split up!" I shouted as I jumped over a large thumb.

Angie followed me as Damian hotfooted it after Macario. We ran through the trees, dodging brush, jumping over rocks and across small rivulets. We raced down an ivy-covered hill, nearly tripping in the twisting vines. One of the giants chased after us, tossing trees aside like sticks.

"We have to shake this guy," I said to Angie.

"How?" she huffed.

"I don't know. I was thinking a lightning bolt in his forehead."

"Damian wouldn't approve."

We ducked behind some boulders, pressing up against the rock as the giant sniffed the air.

"We need to find the pegasus herd," I whispered. "I'll distract him while you go search."

"And miss out on battling a giant? I think not. Besides, you can't use your powers, and I have a sword. I'll be the bait, you go."

"I can't—"

"You can. I got this. Go rustle us some winged horsies." Angie stepped out from behind the rock, drawing her sword. "Hey, cheese-brain, over here."

Immediately a hundred sets of hands swiped at the trees and brush and rock to reach for her. Angie was swept up in a meaty fist. I hesitated at the edge of the clearing, torn between helping her and finding the herd.

"Get lost, Katzy," she shouted, raising her sword to jab at the giant's fist. "I got this."

The giant roared in pain. I ducked into the trees and ran until the sounds of the giants faded and the world grew quiet. I stopped, resting my hands on my knees to catch my breath.

Guilt pounded on me. I should have stayed and helped my friends. Erinyes or not, I had enough power to defeat a couple of knuckle-headed giants. *Not that my friends aren't capable.* The thought calmed me. Angie had probably already defeated the first giant, and Damian was bound to know how to beat his. Plus, he had a miniature sun god to help him.

I looked around, hoping to find a clue. Most of the shrubs were stripped of their greenery. I fingered one branch, studying the bite marks. Following the broken and gnawed branches, I prowled on until I came to an open field. That's when I lost the ability to breathe. Truly. My lungs stopped working at the sight of a herd of winged horses grazing peacefully and playfully rearing up with each other.

How in Zeus's name was I supposed to catch one of them, let alone enough for all of us to ride?

A sturdy black pegasus raised its head and gave a whinnying snort. The herd froze and, as one, turned to stare at me. I stood frozen as the black pegasus reared up and began running flat out straight at me.

It stopped and reared up a few feet in front of me, towering over me. Its eyes were sapphire, like the silver horse I'd admired, but its coat was a shiny ebony down to the tips of its feathers.

Its nostrils flared, and it reared up again, flashing its hooves. I held my ground, afraid if I moved it would stomp me to pieces. I winced as the hooves got dangerously close.

A high-pitched whinny pierced the air as another pegasus advanced. I recognized her silver color from the corner of my eye. The black one snorted a warning, baring its teeth, but the silver beauty held her ground, tossing her head and answering with a sharp neigh.

The pegasus from the clearing.

My feet moved me forward even as the black pegasus pawed the ground angrily. The silver one nudged it with her head, chiding it, and the leader finally settled, though it warily watched me. I reached for the silver pegasus and put a hand out to touch her velvety nose. She pushed back against my hand and tossed her head.

"Hey. My name's Phoebe. I'm kind of the destroyer of Olympus. I could use your help making that not happen. I'm supposed to fight a nasty fire-breathing creature called a chimera. It's going to be dangerous, I can't lie, but somehow, I feel like you and I belong together."

Her sapphire eyes looked intelligently into mine, and I could swear she understood every word. With a soft nod, she stepped closer to me, rubbing her nose along my arm.

"You think you could get a couple of your friends to join?"

She whinnied at the black pegasus. It stomped its hoof, shaking its head.

She whinnied again, and this time three more of the winged beauties stepped forward, joining her to face off against the black leader. One was a golden tan with black trim, the other charcoal gray, and the third, a reddish brown with streaks of yellow in its mane.

The black one neighed angrily, pawing the air, but they didn't flinch, and it gave in. It chased the rest of the herd away in a roar of thundering hooves, leaving me alone with the four pegasuses.

"What shall I call you?"

She whinnied at me, and the name sounded like a bell in my head. "Argenta. I like it."

Argenta lowered her head and knelt on one knee. I grabbed a fistful of her mane and levered one leg over, settling on a spot in front of the wings.

"Are you ready?"

My pegasus took off in a dead run, almost tossing me off her back. With a mighty spring of her legs, Argenta lifted up to the sky, making me dizzy as she veered left to circle over the treetops. Her wings moved up and down smoothly, carrying me easily. The other three followed behind. Across the valley, I could make out the top of one lumbering giant.

I leaned forward to whisper in her ear. "See that nasty giant over there? That's where my friends are."

She lowered her head, beating her wings faster. Tears streamed from my eyes as the wind blew my hair back. I wanted to shout for joy, but I settled for a fist pump.

Now to get my friends out of the clutches of those giants.

First up was Damian and Macario. I could tell it was them by the tiny blasts of sunshine. The giant, I think it was Agor, kept swatting at his russet hair with dozens of hands to put out the flames from the burst of sunbeams. Damian kept biting its thumbs. The giant would drop him from one hand only to snatch him up with another.

My pegasus circled over a field half cleared of rocks. The piles of small boulders gave me an idea how to rescue my friends without using my powers.

I urged Argenta down, whispering in her ear. The pegasus curled her front legs around a large rock, pressing it to her underside before launching into the air with it. The others quickly followed suit. We flew in a circle around the giant. The small red one attacked first. It swooped in, avoiding the swatting hands, and dropped the boulder on Agor's head. The boulder bounced off his forehead, leaving a dent.

Agor roared in anger, snatching at the red pegasus. "Get back here, pretty one!"

The gray one was next, flying in from behind to drop the boulder just above the giant's ear. Agor bellowed in pain, spinning around to try and snatch her. Damian and Macario were clutched in two of his fists. The golden pegasus flew past next, flinging its boulder at the giant's nose. It smashed in, spraying blood.

"Owie!"

The giant's hands went to his nose, and he forgot about the boys, dropping them. They flailed in the air, but the pegasuses were there to catch them.

My turn.

Argenta's wings flapped strongly as we circled around.

Agor tilted his head back, eyes gleaming with hurt and anger. "Give me back my pretties."

"Now," I yelled, urging Argenta closer. She arrowed down between a wall of hands the giant smashed together, and she released the boulder, dropping it right between Agor's eyes. The giant blinked once, twice, then tilted backward, landing with a crash.

The boys had no time to admire their rides; Angie was hollering for help.

We winged over the treetops, heading for the sound of Angie's shouts. They were coming from a small cave. Boza's hands were too large to reach inside, but he was tearing the hillside apart, digging out giant clods of dirt and tossing them over his head like a steam shovel.

"Phoebe, back there was a patch of ivy," Damian shouted. "Maybe we can use it to trip the giant."

I wheeled Argenta around, guiding her down and motioning what I wanted. The pegasuses ripped up mouthfuls of ivy, tearing out long lengths of it. Argenta held one end in her teeth while the gray pegasus took another; the other two did the same. The giant was so busy going after Angie he didn't see us. We flew in circles, going in opposite directions, winding the thick ivy loosely around its ankles. I jumped off Argenta, tumbling in the dirt, and rolled to my feet.

"Hey, you big ape, come and get me."

The giant stopped digging and took a step toward me, reaching out to grab me. I danced out of reach, forcing

Boza to lunge for me. The ivy tangled around his ankles. He got two steps before he lost his balance and tripped, falling forward to hit the ground with a resounding *thud*.

I wasn't fast enough to get out of the way, and a pudgy hand pancaked down on me, smothering me underneath. I pushed up on it, kicking and grunting, but it was too heavy. I couldn't breathe. Panic made it impossible to think.

And then hands wrapped around my ankles and yanked me to freedom.

Damian stood over me, grinning. "Being the bait's not so easy, is it?"

He stuck his hand out and pulled me up. We trotted back to our pegasuses, where Angie and Macario waited. The giant was groaning, trying to untangle his legs.

We took off as Boza gave chase, snatching at us with a flurry of grabs. He ran as fast as his legs could go, but not fast enough to catch up. Panting and out of breath, he shook all one hundred fists at us as we left him behind.

CHAPTER 32

W e landed our pegasuses in a clearing of tall grass. Angie whooped, jumping off her charcoal-gray pegasus. "Thanks for the ride." She rubbed its nose. "I feel like it wants me to name it."

"Yeah, I had the same feeling. Meet Argenta." I patted the neck of my ride.

Angie stepped back, studying the creature. "Hmm, I think I'll call you Nero." The pegasus whinnied and tossed his head in approval. "Hah, he likes it. Nero it is."

We looked at Damian. His golden pegasus had wings of black feathers and a black mane. "Hey," he said, gingerly patting its head as if he wasn't sure if it was going to bite or not. "I need a good name for something as fine and noble as you. How about Albert after my grandfather? I think he would have liked you."

The pegasus lowered its head and pawed at the ground, nodding his head up and down.

"Albert it is." Damian grinned at me. "Are they really ours?"

"I don't think we can take them home like souvenirs, but for now, yeah."

We turned to Macario, who stood staring at his russet pegasus. She was smaller than the others, and her wings were tipped in the same yellow that streaked her mane, like flames. It was the perfect fit for a son of Apollo.

"Stop staring and give her a name already," I said. "We still have a lion-goat to find."

"I'm thinking. Names are important. They have to mean something."

"Like Macario means sun-brain?" Angie teased.

He tossed her a glare, then snapped his fingers. "I have it. Zesto. It means fire."

"Zesto sounds like a pizza sauce," Angie said. But the name stuck.

"So where's this beastie?" I was suddenly eager to get on with it.

Angie was staring upward. "Remember what Karisto said?"

"Yeah, he said to look for the vultures."

"Look." She pointed at the sky.

A pair of ungainly birds made a lazy circle over a stand of trees.

Fear tightened my gut. "Let's see if the traitor was telling the truth."

I climbed onto Argenta's back.

"How are we going to kill it?" Damian asked. "We don't have a bow and arrow."

I shrugged. "We'll think of something. We always do."

Argenta took off first, and the other winged horses followed. We headed straight for the circling buzzards, chasing them off with a display of flared wings that had them squawking in annoyance before they hightailed it away.

Below, in a stand of brush, the chimera was finishing off its latest meal, a poor deer by the looks of it. The misshapen beast raised its head to study us.

I had to hold back a laugh. Sure, it had a fearsome lion's head, complete with a short mane and tawny eyes. But with a goat head sticking out of its back, it looked ridiculous, especially with those tiny billy-goat horns. Add to that the green snake wavering in the air in place of a tail.

Pretty silly.

"I thought this thing was supposed to be scary," I said, hovering overhead.

The goat bleated and the lion snarled at it. The snakehead tail snapped at a passing mouse that it just missed.

"This is like something from a freak show," Angie said.

"Damian, what say you?" I asked.

Sitting on the back of Albert, he looked uncertain. "I told you, Bellerophon shot it in the throat with a lead arrow, and the flames melted the lead and killed it."

"I don't want to kill the poor thing," I said. "I want to get that goat horn from it. I'm going to land and try to talk to it. You guys stay back."

"Are you crazy?" Damian cried, but I had already guided Argenta down to the clearing.

"Phoebe, how do you expect to get the horn off?" Angie asked, circling overhead on Nero.

"I'll use a small lightning bolt, guaranteed not to call the Erinyes." I wriggled my fingers, using just the tiniest power to call a thin sliver of lightning.

I approached the creature slowly, talking softly as I walked. "Hey there. You remind me of a movie I saw. It was called *Frankenstein*. The main character was made up of all these different parts like you. Maybe I'll call you Frankie? We can be friends."

The lion head lifted from the animal carcass. Blood smeared its jaws. It must have decided I wasn't worth eating, because it went back to its meal.

"So, Frankie, I just need a little piece of that horn," I said, taking another step. I plucked a handful of grass and held it out to the goat. "Here, don't you want some yummy grass?"

The goat sniffed the air as the lion end kept eating. I kept an eye on the snake head, but it was busy searching for mice in the grass. I got close enough to smell rotting meat. I could feel the warmth of the beast like a radiator. I held out the grass, and the goat gently nibbled on it.

"Nice billy goat," I whispered.

I raised my other hand, bringing the lightning bolt up toward one of its nubby horns. The goat spied the lightning and alarm entered its eyes. It bleated a warning like a fire bell. I stumbled back, tripping over my feet, and fell on my rear end.

And that's when Frankie began to morph. By morph, I mean the goat head sunk into the body, bulging out the sides as it moved forward. The lion's head stretched wider as the goat head pushed upward, merging their features. A pair of thick pointed horns as long as my arm pushed their way out. The lion's face thinned, and its fangs grew even larger. The eyes narrowed into almond-shaped slits.

The snake sank back into the hindquarters like a cord retracting. The beast's rear legs thickened, turning scaly and green with wicked claws at each toe. A lizard-like tail extended with a barbed tip to thump the ground.

This was not some freak show reject.

This was a monster.

It clawed at the ground, dropping its head to show us its wicked horns. The hind legs coiled as it crouched down. A forked tongue flickered out of its mouth. It drew in a deep breath and bellowed out a rolling ball of fire at me.

I was too shocked to move, still piecing together how Frankie had changed from silly to terrifying, so I would have been incinerated if Argenta hadn't swooped down to pluck me up in her teeth and toss me like a sack of potatoes onto her back.

The chimera howled in rage, belching another fireball upward.

Argenta nimbly dodged it, circling out of range to join the other pegasuses hovering overhead.

"Damian, ideas?" I asked desperately.

"We don't have a lead-tipped arrow," he said, bobbing on Albert's back.

"Right, so what's the next best thing?"

"Next best thing." His eyes flickered as his brain went to work. "We have to get something metal into its mouth that will melt in extreme heat. What do we have?"

Macario and I shouted it at the same time. "Angie's shield!"

"Not my shield!" Angie's face fell as her hand went to the strap at her chest.

"Toss it to me," I said.

She hesitated, then unstrapped it and flung it over to me. "I really liked that shield."

"I'll get you another one," I promised, gripping it tight. "We need it to open its mouth. I could use a volunteer." I didn't look at Damian. I couldn't ask him. But he volunteered.

"I'll do it, just don't let him fry me." He looked determined as he landed Albert in the clearing and stepped in front of his pegasus to face the chimera.

I circled over his head. "As soon as it opens its mouth, I'll throw the shield."

"You're only going to get one shot," Angie called out. "Don't miss or Damian's burned toast."

Great. No pressure.

Damian waggled his hands at the chimera. "Come and get me, fur-face. You're nothing but a goat with a bad temper!"

The chimera hunkered down, inhaling and exhaling, stoking the fire in its chest. It tossed its head up, letting out a roar.

I swooped down, cocking my arm back with the shield held in my hand like a frisbee. As the beast opened its mouth, I flicked my arm forward. The metal disc spun through the air, headed in a perfect line for that open maw, but at the last second, the chimera whipped its tail around, batting the shield away.

Fire-sucking balls of tar!

"Phoebe! Help!"

The chimera had Damian pinned. He stood in front of Albert, arms spread, as if he could stop the flames from consuming them both.

I landed Argenta and leaped from her back as the chimera drew in its breath, gathering itself to send another fiery blast. My hand twitched, ready to call up a lightning bolt, but someone knocked me to the side. Karisto moved past me on furred legs. He scooped up the shield in one hand and flipped it into the chimera's open mouth with a deft move.

The beast choked, trying to spit it out, but Karisto wrapped his arms around its snout, holding it closed. The chimera threw its head side to side, but the satyr held tight. Its body shimmied and shook as its internal furnace overheated. The barbed tail whipped around and jabbed at Karisto, but still he didn't let go. Smoke streamed from its nostrils, and a high-pitched whistling sound grew louder.

"Get back!" Damian cried.

I tackled Karisto, knocking him loose and rolling him away as the beast began to glow a bright shade of red. Waves of heat washed over us as flames began to lick along its mane, growing larger and spreading until the chimera burned like a funeral pyre.

When the smoke cleared, all that was left were the hooves, the horns, the barbed tail, and some teeth.

"We killed it," I said, getting to my feet.

"Good riddance." Macario kicked at the ashes. "It was a menace."

I squatted down, using a stick to sift through the ash until I found a horn. It had returned to being billy-goat sized. Pulling the Eye of Zeus from my pocket, I held the horn over it. The horn vibrated, shimmying in my hand, and with a *whoosh* disappeared into the matching shape. My arm shivered as the mirror throbbed with power.

"That's five," I murmured. "Only one to go."

I looked up at Karisto. "Thanks. You saved us."

The satyr had an odd look on his face. He staggered back a step, and then his hand went to his side. It came away covered in red.

"Karisto!"

He stumbled and fell to his knees.

"I guess that tail stung me," he grunted. "I'm . . . sorry." He flinched as we eased him to the ground. "I made a promise . . . to my brother. That I would come back. When you arrived, I thought . . . I thought I could save him. But I think . . . I always knew he was gone."

"Hey, don't talk," I said. "Get some rest."

He shook his head. "No. I feel the poison running through me." He gripped my arm, his eyes feverish. "I can pay you back now."

"What do you mean?"

"When I die, take me to the priests at Kragos. You'll have your passage to the underworld."

"No. Karisto, you can't give up."

But the satyr took one last breath and let it out, a faint smile on his lips.

I couldn't believe it. He was dead. This didn't feel real.

"I can't . . . he can't be . . ." I stuttered.

"Hey, Phoebes, it's okay," Damian said.

I looked at him in horror. "No, it's not okay. He's dead. D-E-A-D, dead. This isn't some made-up story in one of your books. What if this had happened to one of us?" I was breathing way too fast, and my heart was racing as if I'd just run a marathon.

Macario stepped close. "He is gone, but he can help us go on. You heard what he said."

"You want us to use his body to get to the underworld?" The thought made me want to throw up.

"Hey, Katzy, it's what he wanted," Angie said.

No one spoke as we loaded him onto the Argenta's back. I climbed in front of her wings, my limbs shaking. We took flight, soaring over the trees back to the sea cliffs. I kept replaying every snip, every sharp word he had ever said. Now I understood why pain had always lurked in his eyes.

The sun was setting when we landed in front of one of the open tombs. We chose it at random, not knowing how it worked.

We hadn't even had time to unload Karisto when a trio of necros appeared. They waved us away, motioning for us to step back. The twilight shadows highlighted the black x's that marred their sewn lids. They carefully lifted his body with pale hands and carried him inside without uttering a sound.

That was it. It was over.

We climbed on our pegasuses, flew up to the top of the cliffs, and waited. The winged horses were restless, pawing at the ground as though they were eager to take flight. The air had a chill to it. Macario and Zesto left briefly, returning with some thin blankets from the fishing boat we had left on the shore.

I wrapped mine around my shoulders, staring at the moon. It was a bright round disc in the sky. Mesmerizing. So much so that when a shadow crossed over it, I almost missed it. The creature had a pointed beak and webbed wings like that of a pterodactyl.

The animal landed on a ledge below, out of sight. We waited, ready to take flight. A keening cry echoed eerily in the night. Then the sound of wings flapping was followed by the outline of its shadow wheeling across the sky.

That was our cue.

The pegasuses ran swiftly across the ledge and jumped off the cliff into midair. There was a steep drop before their wings opened and we lifted into the night sky. The creature moved fast, but the pegasuses kept pace.

We rode for hours. At some point I slept, slumped forward, arms wrapped around Argenta's warm neck. When I awoke, the sun was rising, a slice of orange fire on the horizon. The weird creature circled above a cliff. A river ran over the top, spilling itself into the sea. With a flash of its wings, it disappeared into the curtain of water, parting it for a moment to reveal a dark opening.

The doorway to the underworld.

We set our mounts down on the sand, sending small crabs skittering away.

"So we going in now?" Angie asked, hiding a yawn.

She looked wiped. Damian's eyes drooped. Macario swayed where he stood.

"No. We're going to take a break," I decided. "We deserve one day where nothing's trying to kill us. We'll go in first thing tomorrow."

Their eyes brightened as though I had given them a golden ticket.

Chapter 33

Our day on the beach was the most fun we'd had since we'd arrived in this place. We floated on our backs in the aqua-green water, dove like seals, and exulted in having the last traces of gunk and grime washed away.

I stared up at the clear blue sky, trying to stay happy, but a creeping sense of doom sent a chill through me.

The underworld was up next. The underworld, people! You know, the place where dead souls go and hang out for millennia until they fade away into nothingness. It was one thing to face a man-eating lion, or even a multiheaded serpent, but to go *there*, to that place of darkness and death? I couldn't do it. I mean, *I* could, don't get me wrong. I just couldn't ask my friends to go. Not after losing Karisto. And there was no point in telling them that. They wouldn't listen. They would just say, "Yeah, yeah, Katzy, we know, but we're still going."

That's why I had to leave them behind.

The ends didn't always justify the means. Not at all. If there was one thing I had learned in this place, it was that. My parents thought protecting Olympus meant it was okay to ship me off. The ends justified their treatment of me, dumping their only daughter on a lousy bus bench with nothing to her name. *Wrong.*

Whether that swan was Zeus or some smart-alecky bird, he'd made me realize one thing. I had to stop acting as if things that happened around me weren't my fault. I was a demigod, like it or not, with a prophecy hanging over my head. I hadn't asked for it, but it was mine. Not Damian's. Not Angie's. Not even Macario's.

I was on my own.

Over a supper of broiled fish, Damian filled us in on what he knew about our final stop.

"To get to Hades's mansion, we have to find a ferryman named Charon and pay him to take us down the river."

Macario nodded. "And again when we want to leave. That's important." He pulled out the bag of coins he carried and counted. "Yes, we have exactly eight. Enough to get in and out."

"Great," I said, smiling. "Here, let me hang on to it." He hesitated.

"Unless you don't trust me," I said, arching an eyebrow.

He looked shamed. "Sure, I trust you. You've been a true friend since the day we met. You know, when we went to see the oracle, I wanted—" He stopped, his face flushing with shame. "I was going to let Python eat you. To prove my loyalty to my father. Rid Olympus of its destroyer. But I saw how you all stood up for each other, and I couldn't do it."

He thrust the bag of coins in my hand.

I was a complete fink, because I smiled at him and tucked that bag of coins in my pocket and didn't even blink. I waited until they were asleep, all curled up in the sand under their blankets. The stars were cold overhead as I folded back my cover and got to my feet, tucking the satchel my mother had given me over my shoulder. My friends were unmoving lumps.

I tiptoed away from the fire, taking the rocky path down the beach to the edge of the cliff. The river poured over the top, flowing down in a rushing torrent. I hiked around the edges of the rocks until I found a well-worn trail that led behind the curtain of water.

The opening was like a giant mouth waiting to swallow me whole. I couldn't make out a drop of light. Cold air wafted out, raising the hair on my arms.

"Let's do this, Katzy," I said aloud to give myself the courage to move my feet forward. The sand gave way to hard ground as I passed through the entrance. I had the smallest lightning bolt I could muster to give me light.

The air was freaky cold, as if the walls were made of ice. The stone was a deep crimson. I tried not to think about whether or not it was the color of blood.

The place was deserted—not a single guard in sight—which kind of made sense because who would be foolish enough to want to enter?

After several steps, a narrow set of stairs descended into blackness. Taking a deep breath, I walked down.

The coins jangled in my pocket, reminding me what a traitor I was. Angie would probably pound me when I saw her again. If I saw her.

"*Eeeeeee.*"

I froze at the noise. The hair rose on the back of my neck.

"*Eeeeee, oooo00, aaaaaahhh.*"

It sounded like multiple beings, maybe underworld zombies just ahead.

"Get back, zombies." I held the bolt in front of me. "Or I'll send you—" Where would I send someone who was already dead? "Back to your grave." *Ugh*! I was such an idiot. I couldn't even think of a proper insult for a dead zombie.

"*Feeeee-beeeee.*"

Oh, rats entrails. The zombies knew my name.

"*Feeee beeee isssssss aaaaaaa raaaaaaaat.*"

Phoebe is a rat?

Wait, that sounded like . . .

Angie stepped out into the circle of light, hands planted on her hips. Next to her stood Damian and Macario. All of them glared at me.

I bristled at their interference. Couldn't they just mind their own business for once? "What?"

"What? That's all you have to say?" Angie demanded.

"Fine. What are you doing here? I don't need you tagging along."

I pushed past them, but Angie spun me around.

"You do not get to walk away from us. You think we didn't know you were going to dump us? I knew it the moment you asked Macario for the coins."

"So why didn't you stay away? I can do this on my own."

Her glare deepened. "Of course you can't, you idiot. Even if you could, why would you want to? We came all this way to help you, because we're your friends, but as soon as things get too hard, you walk away. Look, there goes Phoebe Katz."

I flinched at the truth in her words, but it didn't change my decision.

"This is my problem, my prophecy, my fate. You guys should be back at Dexter worrying about the next history project, not fighting hydras or outsmarting a sphinx that wants to eat us. Karisto died because of my stupid quest.

I couldn't stand it if anything happened to you guys, even you, Macario."

"That may be, but I've never had so much fun in my entire life," Damian said.

I gawked at him. "Seriously? I've made you the bait, like, a dozen times. You could have been eaten by a lion, a hydra, or a fire-breathing goat. I mean, come on, Damian, how mental are you?"

He shrugged. "I've never been part of something that mattered. This—us four—we matter. I don't know if we're going to destroy Olympus or not. So far, things aren't looking good. But I do know we're trying to do the right thing. And I know that being with you guys is better than being safe back home. So no, Phoebe, you don't get to dump us. Not today."

I took out the mirror and studied it. Smoke streaks and cracks marred the face. It had been through a lot. Only one opening remained. The other five bulged with the power of the talismans we had collected. It felt heavy in my hands. Like it bore a great burden. Tingles of power ran up my spine, hinting at what I would be able to do once I completed it.

Feeling a weight lift off my shoulders, I tucked the mirror away and straightened. "Damian, ideas?"

He smiled. "If we keep going, we're bound to run into one of the rivers that leads to Hades's mansion. Cerberus guards the entrance. We don't have to actually go inside. With any luck, we can get a snip of his tail and be on our way."

I looked around at my circle of friends. "All right then, let's go raise some underworld chaos. Who knows, maybe I'll destroy this place too."

CHAPTER 34

The steps continued downward in an endless descent. We might as well have been heading to the center of the earth. The only sounds were the scrape of our boots over the stone and the rustle of fabric. Macario fell asleep on his feet, stumbling and nearly sending me tumbling headfirst down the steps. When we finally reached bottom, my legs were jelly. A gloomy cavern awaited us. In the dim light, I could just make out a stone bridge suspended over a pit of darkness. The bridge led to a massive wooden set of double doors. A large *H* was inlaid in bronzed metal in the center.

We scurried across the bridge in a tight knot, half expecting something creepy to leap out of that darkness and grab us. Macario shined his sun bolt at the bottom of the cavern, but the shadows swallowed the light, leaving only inky darkness.

"We should take a minute and think about this," I said, once we reached the other side. "Maybe one of us should wait here in case we get locked in."

"Don't look at me, I'm going," Damian said.

"Angie?"

"Nope. Always wanted to see this place."

"Sun-brain?"

He scowled. "You think the son of Apollo is a coward? That is not how I will earn my father's respect."

I punched him lightly on the arm. "Hey—you don't need to earn anyone's respect. Apollo is lucky to have you as his son."

He looked pleased but it didn't budge him. "I am still going with you."

I threw my hands up. "Fine, you're all certifiable. Do we knock or what?"

The pair of doors didn't have any handles or knobs.

"Maybe they're open." Angie walked to the door and held up two hands, palms forward, and thrust on them.

The top half of her disappeared through the door as if it wasn't there.

"Angie!"

I lunged to catch her, grabbing her ankle as she fell through the door, and found myself pulled through along with her. We tumbled onto a tiled floor, grunting as two more bodies came hurtling in atop us.

"Get offa me," Angie grunted, pushing us off.

We found ourselves in a small room with four windowless white walls. An abnormally pale woman with fuchsia pink lips and a beehive hairdo sat hunched behind a small desk stacked with piles of papers. She could have been twenty or eighty. Her eyes were hidden behind cat-eye glasses. She stamped each sheet vigorously and moved them to another pile.

"Welcome to the underworld," she said in a bored voice without looking up. "Hero, zero, or pure evil?"

"Excuse me?" I said.

She pointed to a sign on the back wall and continued working.

Damian read the sign. "All Heroes must submit proper documentation of Epic Deeds to be considered for entrance to Elysium. Those sentenced to eternity in Tartarus will be transferred directly to the Pit of Torment for processing. All others report to Asphodel Meadows to be assigned After-Life Duty according to Life Rankings."

"Um, excuse me, but we're not dead," I said.

Miss Paper Stamper's hand froze in midair. "Then why are you here?"

"We need to get to Hades's mansion."

She raised her eyes and I flinched. Pools of inky black looked back at me without a trace of white.

"You do know this is the underworld?"

"Yes." I gulped. Those eyes were like a living darkness.

"And that only the dead are allowed in?"

"Yup."

She drummed her fingers. "This is highly irregular."

"But we can go in, right?"

She shuffled through the papers on her desk until she found the one she wanted. "Sign here." She held out a fountain pen and pointed to a line at the bottom. "It waives Lord Hades from any and all liability should undue harm come to you, including death, dismemberment, and the odd maiming."

I scanned the page, but the words were scrawled in a cryptic language.

"Phoebes, let's think about this," Damian said.

"No signature, no entry," Miss Paper Stamper warned.

What was the point of thinking? Carl's life depended on me going in. I snatched the pen and scribbled my name. A sudden gust of wind blew across the desk, creating a cyclone of papers around Miss Paper Stamper. We ducked as the room became a hurricane.

"Knock it off, Phoebes!" Damian shouted

"It's not me!"

And then everything vanished. The walls dissolved around us, and we were in the underworld.

The place was massive. Rolling green hills blanketed with scarlet poppies stretched as far as the eye could see, broken only by a dark ribbon of river. The colors were muted as if a sepia filter had been applied. A distant iron mountain belched black smoke that left the sky a canopy of murky gray.

We were standing at some kind of crossroads. A blinking neon sign planted in the ground read ELYSIUM with an arrow pointing off to the right. A golden pathway led to a set of padlocked gates hung with a sign that read HEROES ONLY. Behind the gates, a brightly lit high-rise building glittered like a Vegas casino. A giant inflated pink flamingo on the roof bobbed from side to side. Throbbing music pulsed through the air. I could swear I heard laughter and splashing from a pool.

"Is that place for real?" Angie asked. "It sounds like there's a party going on over there."

"Elysium," Macario sighed, looking at the blinking lights. "A place where there is eternal fun and laughter. That is where I will reside when I have spent my life doing heroic deeds."

"Stick with me and you might end up in Tartar Sauce," I joked, eyeing a sign made of charred wood with TARTARUS burned into it. It pointed down a rocky path toward the smoking mountain.

Damian frowned. "That place is no joke, Phoebes. Tartarus houses the worst of the worst. The ones the gods want to punish for eternity."

"Yeah, the Erinyes have given me an open invitation, remember? How do we get to Hades's mansion?"

"Katzy, we have a problem." Angie turned me around to face the other direction. "Where are the doors we came through?"

Behind us, a field stretched as far as I could see, filled with rows of shuffling figures holding hoes. There were thousands of them, humans, satyrs, centaurs, all hacking away at dead stalks, kicking up clouds of dust.

WELCOME TO ASPHODEL MEADOWS a sign proclaimed. I counted four winged creatures circling overhead that looked an awful lot like the harpy lunch ladies. Every so often, they would fly down, cracking a whip over the heads of the workers.

I turned in a complete circle. Angie was right. There was no sign of the doors we had arrived through—which meant there was no way to get back to where we'd started.

"I don't know."

"You don't know? How are we supposed to get out of here?" Her voice rose with panic.

"We'll figure it out like we always do. Damian, where do we find this ferryman?"

"I'm guessing it's this way." He pointed at an unmarked trail that wound through the poppy fields toward the river. "With any luck, Cerberus will be sleeping, and we'll get the talisman and be gone before Hades even knows we're there."

I raised an eyebrow. "You really think we're that lucky?"

He shrugged. "I say the odds are five to one Hades tosses us into Tartar Sauce like a handful of fish sticks."

We all laughed a bit too loudly as we set off. I tried to count how many days we had been in this ancient world, but they were jumbled together. A week at least, maybe more. Carl must be so worried. I wondered if Ares was feeding him and taking care of him.

My jaw tightened. As soon as we had this three-headed mutt handled, the Eye of Zeus would be complete, and we'd be at the gates of Olympus by the end of the day. Then everything would magically get better.

We trudged single file along the path. The loud music of Elysium faded, replaced by a rumbling that steadily grew louder as we got closer to the river.

"What's that noise?" I asked.

"It's them." Damian pointed at the riverbank.

The bank was lined with green bullfrogs the size of cantaloupes. They turned to watch us and began croaking a chorus that sounded a lot like a funeral march.

"These are the Souls of the Forgotten," Macario said. "The ones so low on the Life Ranking scale they don't get assigned After-Life Duty."

The ground was thick with them, forcing us to step carefully. We reached the edge of the river. I accidentally stepped on one, and it leaped out of the way with a startled croak, splashing into the water. Instead of swimming off, it dissolved into a puddle of green sludge until only its eyes floated on the surface.

I took a healthy step back from the edge. "So now what?"

"Now we call the ferryman," Damian said.

Macario held out his hand. "Give me the coins." Taking the bag, he gave us each two. "Hide one in your cheek like this." He tucked a coin in his mouth. "Charon will demand all your money to take you. If he finds it, you won't get a ride back."

We each tucked a small coin in our cheek.

"Take the other coin and toss it into the water."

We lined up on the bank and tossed our coins in the air. They plonked into the water and sank.

We waited in silence, checking up and downstream.

Nothing. Zippo. No ferry and no ferryman.

"How long is this supposed to take?" I asked. The croaking chorus was really getting on my nerves.

A bubble of air popped, and the water turned frothy. The tip of a wooden pole appeared first, followed by the cloaked head of a man, then his shoulders rising out of the water. He must have been made of Teflon, because no water dripped from his black robe. A moment later, a sturdy raft made of knobby gray sticks lashed together bobbed on the surface.

"Who insults the ferryman with such a paltry fare?" He rolled the four coins around on his palms.

"We do," I said around the coin in my cheek. "Sorry, it's all the money we have."

The ferryman threw his hood back, revealing a thick head of white hair. His brows drew together as he sniffed the air. "Topsiders," he spat. "You don't belong here."

He began to sink again but I shouted at him. "Hey, we paid you for a ride."

His pale blue eyes filled with disdain. "I don't transport the living, only the dead."

"But I signed the paper," I said. "We have permission to be here."

"Did you now?" He scowled but beckoned us forward. "Hurry up then, haven't got all day. Places to be."

We jumped onto the raft, sending it tilting side to side before it steadied. On closer look, I realized the knobby sticks were actually bleached bones. Macario had gathered an armful of poppies along our walk. He sat down, plucking at them and tossing the red petals into the water.

"So I'm guessing you're Charon," I said.

"No, I'm Hades himself come to greet newcomers." He poled us into the center of the river, where the current began moving us swiftly downstream. "Of course I'm Charon. No one else would be foolish enough to be rafting about in this water. Where am I taking you?"

"We need to make a quick stop at Hades's mansion, and then we'll be leaving."

He laughed, a barking sound that echoed like a rifle shot in the stillness. "That's what all topsiders say. And then things happen and here they stay."

"Things happen—like what?"

His eyes slid to mine and then away. "There are creatures here who would love to sample the flesh of the living. They say it can restore life in them temporarily. Not sure if it's true. Very few topsiders are foolish enough to come down here."

"Orpheus did," Damian said. "To rescue Eurydice, the woman he loved."

Charon nodded. "Yes, I brought her down this very river. She sobbed the whole way."

"Orpheus almost saved her," Damian explained. "He came here and begged Hades to let her go. Hades was so taken by his story, he let Eurydice go on one condition. Orpheus couldn't look back at her as she followed him out."

"So did this Eurydice make it?" Angie asked.

Damian shook his head. "At the last second, Orpheus turned around to be certain she was there. He lost her back to the shadows."

"Hades does not easily give up what is his," Charon intoned. "A lesson you should have paid heed to. Here we are."

We were so taken by the story, we hadn't seen the imposing mansion come into view.

Hades's crib looked like a legit haunted house. I half expected to hear creepy music playing and see ghosts popping out of the trees. Thick shrubs and tall trees crowded around the two-story brick structure. Iron bars covered the windows—to keep people in or out, I couldn't be sure. The gabled roof was covered in dark shale. A wrought-iron fence surrounded the house and front lawn.

The raft bumped against the shore. We jumped off as Charon held the raft in place with his pole.

"Can you wait here?" I asked. "We won't be long."

He frowned. "You said you signed the release form."

"Yes."

"Then you're staying. You waived all rights to leave. You should have read the fine print." With that, his raft sank down in the water until his head and the tip of his pole disappeared.

"He didn't mean that, right, Katzy?" Angie said, spitting her extra coin out into her hand. "We're going to figure a way out of this dump."

"Sure, of course." Not that I had a clue how to do that, but there was no point in being pessimistic until we knew if we were going to survive against a three-headed dog. "Hey, Damian, you think I can use my powers down here?"

Damian chuckled in that nervous way of his, which meant he had bad news.

"What?" I said, facing him, hands on my hips. "Tell me."

"It's funny—did I mention? No—I don't think I did. The Erinyes—"

"What about them?"

He smiled weakly. "I'm not even sure it's true."

"I swear, Damian, if you don't spill it right now, I'm going to deck you one," Angie said.

"Fine. There are some mythologists who suggest Hades is their father. Funny, huh?"

It was about as funny as finding a wasp's nest in your gym locker.

"So they could already be here?" I asked. "Because they, like, live here?"

He shrugged. "It's possible. They guard the iron gates of Tartarus when they're not out seeking retribution."

"Lovely," I fumed. "We walked right into a trap. You should have said something, D. I can't believe you kept that to yourself."

"I'm not a walking encyclopedia, you know," he said, face flushed. "I saw Hades's mansion and wondered if he and his wife had kids and bingo—I remembered."

I blew out a lungful of air. "Sorry. I'm a little uptight. You've been a huge help."

We stared at the fence.

"So, any ideas?" I asked hopefully.

"I say we put Cerberus to sleep and take a snip of his tail."

The voice came from Macario.

"And how do you propose we do that?" I asked.

"With these." He held out a handful of yellow kernels. "The seeds of the poppy can be used to put a person to sleep. We just need to get Cerberus to eat them."

CHAPTER 35

As annoying as Macario could be, the kid jumped up to the top of my list with that idea.

"Brilliant! What does a three-headed dog like to eat?"

"Do you have any of your mom's cookies left?" Angie asked.

I gripped the satchel slung over my shoulder. "Maybe, why?"

"They're delicious, and I'm sure Cerberus will think so too. Come on, hand it over."

"Fine." I dug out the last cookie, unwrapping it from the cloth. It was sprinkled with raisins and nuts and smelled of cinnamon. "Here." I shoved it at Macario.

He pressed the poppy seeds into the cookie, smushing it into a tight little ball.

Angie put two fingers in her mouth and whistled shrilly.

I grabbed her arm. "Are you crazy?"

"What? I'm not going in there until beasty is asleep. Here, doggy, doggy," she called, cupping her hand over her mouth.

I'm not sure why I was so scared. There was a solid fence separating us from the mansion. We were perfectly safe.

The deep growl came from behind us.

We turned, taking in the snarling three-headed beast that stood not ten feet from us. It was a giant mastiff, crimson red except for black masks around its faces. Its trio of heads were square-shaped and massive. Thick strands of saliva hung from its jowls as all three heads growled menacingly at us.

"Way to go, Angie. Now we're dog meat."

"Go on, sun-brain. Feed it to him," Angie whispered.

Macario held the treat out. "Mmm, take a whiff of this. Pure manna from the gods. Who wants it?"

All three heads scented the air. Macario heaved it, tossing it high. Cerberus launched off its powerful hind legs, jumping higher than our heads. Each head battled, snapping at the other. In the end, the middle head won, lapping the treat into its throat with a satisfied gulp.

The other two were not happy, growling and snarling at the top dog. It might have been smiling, if dogs could smile, because its top lip curled upward, and there was a glint of satisfaction in its eye. Its bulky red body prowled forward.

"Uh, Katzy, I think it's still hungry."

"Yeah, Macario, how long does it take for it to work?"

"How would I know? I've never tried this before."

"Then we should run," I said.

"Where? We can't exactly swim away," Damian said.

"We could go inside the gate," I said.

"Bad idea. That's entering into Hades's reach," Macario said.

"I don't see any other choice," I said. "He's about to pounce on us, and Damian won't let me use my powers."

We were stuck between a man-eating dog with three heads and entering into the clutches of a powerful underworld god.

If it had been just me, I'd have taken my chances with mutt-face, but I couldn't guarantee we would all come out in one piece.

"I say we wear it down," Damian said. "Can't be any worse than the one we met in the park. Follow my lead." He started dancing around, waggling his hands over his head. "Hey, Cerberus, check out these moves." He clumsily dabbed left, then right, but he underestimated this mutant dog. Cerberus swiveled its three heads toward him, flinging a thick strand of drool at him.

Macario shouted a warning, but Damian got a faceful of dog spit. He screamed, clutching at his face.

"Get it off!" He swiped at his cheeks. Angie ripped off the hem of her tunic and wiped off the slobber. It helped a bit. He stopped screaming, but I could see welts on his skin, and worse, his eyes were swelling shut.

I grabbed his shoulders. "Damian, are you okay?"

"I can't see, Phoebes." His whole body shook. "I'm blind."

"It'll be okay," I said, trying frantically to think. Cerberus took another step toward us. Time to plant a lightning bolt in that slobber-face. My hand itched with the need.

Angie swatted my hand. "Don't make it worse. He's going to fall asleep."

"After he eats us!"

"I've got this," Macario said, wielding his sunbeam. They weren't as powerful as my lightning, but the mutt didn't like the flames. The three heads snarled and snapped, then simultaneously yawned widely.

The giant mastiff wobbled. Its legs trembled a bit.

I held my breath. It was working. Cerberus took another step and then, in slow motion, tipped over on its side. The first head hit the ground with a *thunk*. The second landed on top, and the third plopped next to it, sending up a chorus of loud snores.

Breathing a sigh of relief, I turned back to Damian. Red blisters marred his skin, and his eyes oozed a yellow fluid. "D, are you okay?"

He used Angie's scrap of fabric to tie a bandage around his eyes. "Just do what you need to do. I'll be fine."

Angie stood over the sleeping dog and drew her sword. "So, do I cut the whole tail off?"

"No, we just need a snip."

She moved the sword to the tip. "Here?"

"Yeah, sure, crud, I can't think. Just do it."

Angie raised the sword over her head and brought it down with a keening sound. The blade bit through the end of the tail, sending the tip sailing through the air. I dove after it, but it flipped through the bars of the gate to land on the grass on the other side.

This was not good. I reached my arm in, but the mangled tip lay just out of reach, oozing dark blood onto the green grass.

"Angie, use the sword to scrape it back."

She stuck the weapon through, reaching for the bit of flesh. The blade just touched it, but a sleepy-sounding growl had us turning our heads.

Why was nothing ever easy in this place? Cerberus had managed to get back on his feet, swaying a bit. And he was angry. Light-the-world-on-fire angry. He craned all three heads to study the stump of his tail, howling so loud we had to clamp our hands over our ears.

If that didn't raise the dead, nothing would.

"Inside the gate, now!" I ordered. "Angie, help Damian." The hinges groaned as I pushed it open. Macario took Damian's other arm, and they hurried him toward the gate as Cerberus shook off the last of the poppy effect. He lunged at us, stumbling once, giving us just enough time to get inside. I slammed the gate in its faces.

It gnashed the iron bars in a frenzy, howling in rage.

The still-moving snip of tail pulsated on the grass like a worm that had been cut in half. I pulled out the battered Eye of Zeus and held it over it. The tail flickered, trying to crawl away before it shot upward, sticking to the bottom of the mirror, then disappearing into the last opening. A shudder of raw power vibrated up my arm, sending a shock to my heart.

I let out the breath I'd been holding. I had done it! I had filled the Eye of Zeus. I could save Carl now, and maybe all of Olympus.

A shadow passed overhead.

I didn't even bother to look up. I closed my eyes, clenching my fists in frustration. The Erinyes were like flies on honey—the second they caught my scent, they swarmed all over.

The fury built in me. It had been days since I'd used my powers, and it was as if the charge had been building. As the Erinyes landed, the bossy Alekto out front, I was ready to explode.

"There is no use fighting us. Your powers are of little use here," Alekto said. "Surrender now that your friends might live." The other two drew their bows, aiming the flaming tips at my head.

In my hand I held the biggest, fattest, hottest lightning bolt I had ever called upon. It was as thick as a baseball bat and pulsated with power. My left palm itched, and before I knew it, I held two bolts.

"Yeah, well, first, have a taste of lighting." I raised my arms to launch them, hoping to take two of them out before they filled me with arrows, but the sound of a sharp whistle stopped my arm.

"Daughters, cease this," a voice boomed. "Let us welcome our guests properly."

A tall man with a long scraggly beard stood on the mansion porch. His eyes were like two burning coals that glowed with dark energy. In his long black robes, he looked like Death.

"Welcome to my home. I am Hades."

CHAPTER 36

"Father, please, do not interfere," Alekto said.

Hades's brows drew together like thunderclouds. "Alekto, remember to whom you speak."

She tilted her head. "Apologies, Father, but you tasked us with bringing justice."

"Is this her?" He nodded at me.

"Yes. She has completed the Eye of Zeus. She must not be allowed to—"

He cut her off with a sharp slice of his hand. "Give it to me," he commanded, holding one long arm out.

The lightning bolts in my hands evaporated into dust. My feet moved of their own power, as if I were a puppet on a string. I tried to fight it, but I had no control over my limbs. I dropped the mirror onto his outstretched palm.

He held it up, whistling softly. "Can you feel its power? Truly spectacular. And what else do we have?" His sharp eyes settled on Macario's sunbeam. "A child of Apollo? How interesting."

Cerberus howled through the bars, and Hades snapped his fingers. The gate flew open, and the monstrous hound bounded over to his side, rubbing up against him as it continued to moan its grievances.

"Yes, I know, very painful, but be grateful she didn't take one of your heads off," he said soothingly. "Besides, it will grow back. Go on now." Cerberus trotted off and plopped down under a tree to lick its stub. "Now, where were we? Yes, the Eye of Zeus. This shall prove very useful." He tucked it away in his pocket.

I wanted to scream in frustration. He had my prize. The thing I had worked so hard for was now going to be stolen from me.

"Father, there is the matter of her sentence," Alekto said firmly.

"Hush," he said, waving her off with one hand. "You grow tiresome. Let's think of something more interesting than an eternity spent in the bowels of Tartarus listening to Sisyphus cry about his fate."

"What would you have us do?" Alekto asked. "We have a sworn duty."

"Yes, duty. The curse of our kind. It is duty that keeps me here, you know," he said to me. "It's not as if the gates of my mansion can hold me. I can leave anytime I want."

"Then why don't you?" I asked.

He shrugged, splaying his hands out. "It is who I am. Shepherd of souls. Keeper of the dead. Punisher of the betrayers of the gods."

"But I haven't done anything," I protested. "I can't be punished for something I haven't done yet."

Hades laughed, a booming baritone. "Then you understand nothing of our world. What you have done is little compared to what others believe you will do. It is that belief in what you will do that leads to the action itself, wouldn't you agree?"

I wasn't sure what he meant, so I didn't answer.

"Consider, would you be here without the prophecy?"

"No, but only because Ares took my friend."

"Ares." He shook his head. "A pompous fool if I ever met one. Don't blame this on Ares. You're here by your own choices."

"Because he has my friend. Carl is . . ." The words clogged in my throat. "He's done nothing to deserve being in this mess."

"Then your motives are pure." He cast a glance at Alekto. "Are they not?"

"Her motives matter not if her actions lead to the end of Olympus," Alekto snapped. "It is our duty to punish her."

"Not if she intends no harm," Damian said, his eyes still bandaged. "There was a story about Orestes. He killed his own mother but was found innocent."

"Because she had killed his father," Hades agreed. "And these three wanted to hang him by his heels for eternity, but wisdom prevailed, did it not?"

Grudgingly, Alekto nodded. "His motive was deemed justified."

"And so, it would seem, is that of this young demigod. She must be allowed to continue her path. I have spoken," he added as Alekto argued.

A tsunami of relief washed over me. "Great, so we can go?"

"Go?" Hades laughed. "I never said that. You're here. Here you stay. You have no way home."

I tugged my coin out of my pocket. "We can pay your ferryman."

"He can't go upstream," Hades said with a satisfied shrug.

"But you can change the current," I reminded him. "You did it for that guy Orpheus."

His eyes flared in surprise at my knowledge. "So I did, but I was charmed by his story of love. And in the end, I kept what was mine, did I not? You have nothing to offer."

He turned to go, but Macario stepped forward. "Wait, there is something you want."

Hades paused.

"This place is dull and gray. There is no sunlight here."

"That is true, but it is the underworld, after all." Hades laughed bitterly.

"But you miss it, don't you?" Macario stepped closer. In his hand he clutched a sunbeam.

Hades's eyes flicked over it, but he gave a dismissive shrug. "Miss it? No, it's annoying, gets in your eyes, burns the skin."

"No, he's right, you miss it," I said, seeing the way his eyes were drawn hungrily to the glowing beam. "You crave the sun."

"I do enjoy the occasional day topside."

"Enough that you might let us go if we arranged a sunbeam for you?" I recalled how Macario had given a beam to Karisto's street urchins.

"A single sunbeam?" He chuckled. "It would burn out in minutes here. But if I had the power to create a sunbeam, that would be something worth bargaining for."

A creepy crawling feeling climbed my spine. "I don't think so," I began.

"I'll do it," Macario said. "I can get more from my father."

Hades whirled, pouncing on the boy. "So we have a deal?"

"We all leave," Macario said firmly, "all four of us with the Eye of Zeus, no strings attached."

Hades pulled the Eye of Zeus from his pocket, eyeing it longingly, then passed it back to me. My knees sagged in relief. "We have a deal," he said to Macario. "Now hand it over."

Macario extended the sunbeam, but Hades gripped it so both their hands were on it. Flames rippled along it between them. The sun energy moved like molten liquid across the beam from Macario to Hades. Light emanated from the underworld lord's eyes, his nose, his mouth, even his ears until the sunbeam sputtered out in Macario's hands.

The boy sagged.

Hades laughed, tossing his hands up and sending beams of light from his fingertips.

I had a terrible feeling about this. Macario had acted like it was no big deal, but something told me it was worse than cutting off a limb.

"Sun-brain, are you okay?" I took hold of his elbow. His whole body was shaking.

"I'm fine," he said. "Let's go, before he changes his mind."

We hurried to the river, leading Damian by the arms, and tossed our remaining coins into the water.

"You think he's coming?" Angie asked.

"He has to." We had no other choice.

We sagged in relief as first the tip of the pole appeared, then Charon bobbed to the surface, looking surprised to see us.

We hopped on his raft as sunbeams lit up the sky and the underworld took on a yellow tinge.

"Gods, what did you do?" Charon said, looking awe-struck at the glowing sky.

"It doesn't matter," I said. "Just go."

Charon stared at the golden beams a moment longer before the current tugged us upstream. He said nothing as he poled us along, and in minutes, we disembarked at the poppy field where we had begun. We ran all the way to the meeting center of the paths. Music still pulsed from Elysium. For a moment, I thought maybe Hades had double-crossed us, but a set of double doors shimmered into existence. We hurtled through them and tumbled into the cavern.

Safely on the other side, we picked ourselves up. Damian's eyes were still bandaged. Macario looked pale and shaky. But all in all, we had survived.

"Let's get out of here," I said. Angie put her arm under Damian's and I helped Macario as we crossed the bridge and began climbing the countless steps to the surface.

Outside, we collapsed onto the sand, gasping as we sucked in breaths of fresh air. Angie took Damian down to the sea and helped him splash saltwater on his face. Macario wandered over to the stand of trees that lined the edge of the shore.

I took a deep breath, feeling the thrumming in my pocket, wondering what on earth we were going to do next. *Take the pegasuses, ride to Olympus, and somehow defeat Ares and free Carl*, my mind listed.

Damian and Angie dropped into the sand next to me. Damian's eyes were still bandaged.

"That was something," Damian began.

"How're the eyes?" I asked, dribbling sand through my fingers.

"I can't see yet, but I think once the swelling goes down, it'll be okay."

"Where's the kid?" Angie asked, craning her head to search.

"Over there by those trees," I said. "I think he's looking for our pegasuses."

"Where?"

"Back there. I just saw him." I turned, staring at the stand of trees. They were tall and slender, waving in the ocean breeze. A smaller one grew off to the side. Had that been there a minute ago? And where was Macario?

A terrible feeling crept over me. I got to my feet, brushing the sand off. "Oh, crud," I said. "Crud, crud, crud."

"What is it?" Angie jumped to her feet, drawing her sword.

"Macario."

"What did he do now?"

"Look." I pointed at the slender tree.

"What about it?"

"I think it's Macario. Come on." We helped Damian up, guiding him over to the small tree.

Its trunk was no thicker than my arm. It stood about as tall as I was. Its leaves were a pale green that rattled in the breeze.

"Macario?"

"Uh, Katzy, you know you're talking to a tree," Angie said. "That's not sun-brain."

"I think it is. He gave his sun power to Hades. Remember—he said his mother was some kind of tree creature. Maybe it's part of him as well."

The bark shifted, swirling until a familiar face took shape.

A set of eyes blinked at us. Blue, the color of the sea.

"Oh no, sun-brain, you didn't." I reached a hand out to brush at his face.

"Hey, Phoebe." Wrinkled bark formed a grimace. "Sorry about this."

"Don't be sorry. Why did you do it? You gave up your sun powers for us."

"You're the only friends I've ever had," he whispered, his voice raspy. "And friends sacrifice for friends. Besides, I was never going to impress my father. That was just a dream. I belong with my mother's people. I'll be fine here."

Fine?

Nothing about this was fine.

Macario was a child of the sun, a fierce warrior with the bright light of energy in his eyes, not a tree stuck in the ground.

No.

I was not going to stand for this. But there was nothing I could do about it, because the rumble of thunder and rattle of hooves had us looking skyward. A carriage landed in the sand behind us.

"Sister, I hear there is good news. You have been triumphant in your journey."

I turned to find Ares jumping down from his carriage, arms flung wide with that hateful grin on his face. Phobos and Deimos slumped in the front seat, looking bored.

Behind them in the carriage sat Carl, his face haunted as he looked across the sand at me.

CHAPTER 37

"Hey, kid, you all right?" Carl called out.

I nodded, swallowing the lump in my throat. "You?"

He shrugged. "The food's terrible and the company's worse, but I'm doing okay."

"I promised no harm would come to him," Ares said. "Look at you!" He grasped my shoulders, dancing me around in a circle. "You did it. I had my doubts, but you showed us what you're made of, Princess of Argos. I am impressed."

"Don't be." I shrugged free of his grip. "Because I'm not going to help you destroy Olympus."

"Oh, it's too late for that." His lips turned up in that evil grin of his. "You've returned the talismans to the Eye of Zeus, where they belong. Can't you feel it pulsating in your pocket? The heart of the beast is waking up. All it needs now is a spark, and we will have our monster."

"Monster?" Blood drained from my head. "What monster? We destroyed all of them except for Cerberus and Agatha."

Angie helped Damian to my side. "She's right," he said. "There aren't any monsters alive that can destroy Olympus."

"Not yet there aren't. Let's remedy that, shall we?" Ares nodded to his sons.

Phobos and Deimos hopped down and dragged Carl to a spot in the sand, shoving him to his knees. They went back to the carriage and rummaged around in the back.

"You'll want a front row seat for this," Ares said, beckoning. "Come, come, children, don't be shy. The show is about to begin."

We looked warily at each other. What was he up to? We helped Damian over to sit beside Carl. I tried to sit down, but Ares swooped his arms around my shoulders. "Oh, not you, dear. You are the star of the show."

I hesitated, not liking where this was going.

"It wasn't a request, sister." He frog-marched me across the sand as the twins carried an altar over, setting it down with a *thump*. It looked heavy, made of aged bronze, and had serpentine monsters carved into the four legs. It stood about waist high.

"When this is over, you belong to us," Phobos hissed, bumping me hard as he passed by.

Deimos did the same from the other side, jarring my teeth. "Congratulations on being the destroyer of Olympus. Your friends will be the first to die."

I stood silent, uneasy, trying to puzzle out what came next.

"Put the Eye of Zeus on the altar." Ares indicated a round opening with his finger. "Place it with the mirror facing upward." His eyes were feverishly excited. Even his twin brats were keenly watching.

I looked at the mirror in my hands. I had gone through a lot of work to get all the talismans, but I had never figured out what I was meant to do with it. Was it a weapon? Was it going to wield some kind of magical power? I had placed all my faith in a scribbled prophecy, but now, a mountain of doubt landed on my shoulders, and my knees almost buckled.

Ares leaned in to whisper in my ear. "I won't ask again. Do it, now."

My palms were slick with sweat, but I forced my legs forward. I repeated the words of the prophecy silently to myself, "*When the Eye of Zeus is finally complete, only then this prophecy will she defeat.*" My arm shook as I placed the mirror on the altar. It fit perfectly into the round opening.

I stepped back. The sound of the sea breaking on the shore was the only thing that could be heard.

"Now, Phoebe, one last favor." Ares squeezed my shoulder. "I want you to call up one of Daddy's little light-ning bolts and place it in the mirror."

I looked up at him, seeing the madness in his eyes, and knew with certainty that was the worst idea in the whole world.

"No." I backed away.

Ares snapped his fingers, and the twins turned toward my friends, each casting a hand out. Immediately Carl, Damian, and Angie were dragged to their feet by invisible strings. They hovered in the air, clawing at their throats, eyes filled with terror.

My heart broke open. "Stop it! I'll do it."

Ares nodded, and my friends collapsed in the sand.

Carl looked up at me, clutching his throat. "It's okay, kid. Do what you gotta do. Remember what I told you— you got potential."

His words gave me enough courage to allow that familiar tingle in my palm.

I would do whatever Ares asked of me. And then I would find a way to shove a lightning bolt in his smarmy, smug mouth.

"Now, sister, raise the bolt up and bring it down into the Eye."

I raised the lightning over my head, grasping it with both hands. The Eye of Zeus winked at me in a glint of sunlight. I thought of all the times I had tossed it aside in my drawer and given it hardly a second thought. And now I was about to turn it into a powerful weapon that was going to destroy Olympus.

"Now, Phoebe," Ares gritted out.

I brought the bolt down as hard as I could, aiming straight for the piece of glass. Part of me hoped the lightning would shatter it into a million pieces, but that didn't happen.

The glowing bolt simply disappeared into the mirror, as if the mirror wasn't there. A burst of blinding light shot out. I threw my hands up over my face to protect my eyes. I squinted through my lashes, dreading what came next.

It was like something out of a nightmare.

As the mirror glowed and rattled in its slot, something began to climb out of it. First it was a single claw, yellowed and ancient looking. A scaly green toe followed, and another, until a foot clawed its way out of the mirror, growing larger as it freed itself. The foot extended into a reptilian leg that crashed down into the sand. The sharp pointed edge of a wing poked its way upward, stretching wide. Another wing emerged on the other side, lined with barbed tips. A second leg began to pry its way out. A curving tail with razor-sharp spines lashed the air.

"What's happening?" I asked through numb lips.

Ares eyes were riveted on the unfolding scene. "Have you ever heard of Echidna?"

What did Macario say, back when we were reading the prophecy? "Wasn't she the mother of monsters? She gave birth to all six of the creatures we were sent after. Is that right?"

"Yes, that hideous she-hag gave birth to the most awful creatures ever known. But the touching part is, she loved an even bigger monster. Typhon, the father of all monsters. The only monster to defeat Zeus. He cut out the sinews in my father's legs, stole his lightning bolts, and left him helpless. But Zeus had help from the other gods, and when he faced Typhon again, he tricked him. But even Zeus couldn't kill him, for Typhon is immortal, so he trapped him in this mirror, scattering his powers in Echidna's children, knowing none but he could bring them back together."

The Eye of Zeus held all the ingredients to bring Typhon back. Claws, tusks, wings, horns, fangs, tail, all the bits and pieces to form a perfectly terrible monster.

Great. I had just given Ares the key to a very bad jail cell.

A head emerged from the altar, reminding me of a crocodile with its pebbled snout filled with wicked-looking fangs. Its mouth was slightly open, revealing a pink tongue that salivated with hunger. Yellowed eyes with black slits for pupils blinked open as the head poked up higher, followed by broad shoulders. The wings snapped open, spreading wide.

I stepped back as the torso thickened, growing and swelling in size until it was as big as a locomotive. With a final *pop*, Typhon was freed of the mirror. The altar promptly exploded, vaporizing into metallic dust.

Typhon raised his head, drawing a rattling breath into his lungs, and gave an ear-piercing screech. He followed that with a belch of flame that shot across the sand, nearly scorching my friends, who scattered.

Maybe I could convince this he-monster to swallow Ares whole. Its head swiveled around, fixing a gaze on Ares, who waited with his shield in one hand and sword in the other. He didn't seem the slightest bit afraid.

Typhon crawled forward on scaly legs, stopping when he was directly in front of Ares. He brought his head down and flared his nostrils, taking in my half-brother's odious scent. The god of war stood grinning like the fool he was, and then he gave Typhon a pat on the nose. "Welcome home, old friend. Look, I provided you your first meal." Ares swept his arm toward my friends.

The monster sniffed the air, spying my helpless friends huddled together on the beach. A light came into his eyes, and he rumbled a satisfied growl.

"When you're done eating, you can have all the revenge you could ever imagine feasting on the gods of Olympus. Zeus will be the first course."

Typhon's eyes glinted even brighter.

Angie held her sword out, bravely standing in front of Carl and Damian. "Back off, you oversized green tank. I'm not afraid to stick this in your eye."

It was laughable. Angie's sword was no match for this monstrous beast. It towered over them, a sliver of drool hanging from its jaw as it ran a huge pink tongue over its scaly lips.

The lightning was in my hand before I even blinked, and I launched it in the air, aiming straight at one glowing eye socket. A spinning shield blocked the lightning, causing it to explode in a shower of sparks. Typhon whipped its head toward me, letting out a roar.

Ares held his hand up, staying the monster as he snarled at me, "Do that again, and I will serve you to Typhon myself. You have served your purpose well, sister. Do not make me regret leaving you alive."

"Fine. Tell it to back off, or you and I can have it out now. I will defeat you, you know. The prophecy made it clear if I collected the talismans—"

Phobos and Deimos snickered with laughter. Even Ares's face twitched with a smile.

"About that prophecy," he said.

The twins were literally rolling with laughter now, making fools of themselves in the sand. Even Typhon looked amused, the hunger dying in his eyes as Ares went on.

"It wasn't exactly written by the Oracle of Delphi."

"Then who wrote it?" I asked, dreading his answer.

He grinned, raising his hands in a helpless shrug. "Guilty. I thought it rather clever rhyming, don't you think? It's not easy to rhyme the tail of Cerberus with the chimera's horn."

The truth hit me over the head like a sledgehammer. Ares had faked the prophecy and placed it in the book, knowing I would find it and go on this fool's journey.

I stood in the sand, hands clenched as I fought to control my temper. Ares climbed into his carriage, followed by his twin progeny, as Typhon prowled closer to my friends.

This wasn't over. I had a pair of bolts in my hands ready to throw when Ares whistled.

"Leave those poor mortals be, Typhon. Olympus awaits!" His carriage raced across the sand, lifting off to circle overhead before making a beeline to the east.

The monster gave us one last hungry look and then launched into the air, soaring high into the sky to wheel after Ares.

I let the sizzling bolts drop in the sand. I had been duped. Ares had played me for a complete and total sap, and I had fallen hook, line, and sinker, thinking somehow, I could be the hero.

Right.

When was Phoebe Katz ever the hero?

CHAPTER 38

I might have gone on standing there all day if my sister hadn't arrived. Typical Athena, she flew the carriage we had stolen from Central Park over the treetops, landing in the sand with a crashing *thud*. Pepper tossed her head at me, pawing at the sand. There was an old man seated in the back.

"Where is he?" Athena asked, jumping down from the carriage, sword in hand. Her helmet gleamed in the sunlight. In her other hand, she clutched a golden shield. "Where is Ares?"

"He's gone," I said.

"Tell me you didn't complete the Eye of Zeus?" the old man said, climbing down from the back. Wild gray hair flowed behind him. His tunic was stained with age. He limped heavily on a cane. I could see the reason. His right leg bore terrible scars.

One look at my guilty face told them both that hope was foolish. "Oh, Phoebe, I warned you," Athena said.

"I'm sorry," I said as scalding tears fell. "I'm not exactly an expert on this stuff. Ares put a fake prophecy in the book that we found at the temple of Delphi. It said if I completed the tasks, I could stop him. How was I supposed to know it wasn't real?"

"You should have trusted me," Athena said. "I'm not your enemy."

"You haven't exactly been my friend!" I shouted as the tears continued to fall. "All you've done is kept me as far away from you as possible. Now I've gone and done the stupidest thing. Ares used the Eye of Zeus to bring Typhon back."

"That's impossible," the old man wailed. "It was guaranteed to cage that immortal beast forever. Only Zeus carries the power of lightning."

"No, Zeus gifted her with it," Athena said. "Phoebe, meet Hephaestus. Maker of the Eye."

Hephaestus wheeled away in shock, one hand going to his head. "Then this is terrible indeed."

"What do you mean 'immortal beast'?" Angie asked.

"It can't be killed by anyone or anything. Where is Typhon now?" Athena asked.

"Ares said he was riding on Olympus."

Athena's eyes grew wide as true fear crept into them. "By the gods, I must return immediately. Zeus is nearly alone. Every god and goddess is out searching the countryside for you."

"We'll come with you," I said, but her searing look made me step back.

"Demigods and mortals are not welcome in Olympus."

"Athena, we can help—"

She jabbed a finger in my chest. "We are the gods and goddesses of Olympus. We do not need the help of children. We will not bow so easily. Ares will find that we are ready for him."

She assisted the old man back into the carriage, then whipped the reins over Pepper's back. The horse gave me one last wild-eyed look before launching into the air, leaving me standing on the sand.

"Hey, kid."

Carl.

I had almost forgotten he was there.

He held his arms out, and I flung myself into them, inhaling the scent of his woolly sweater. I blubbered like a baby as he held me tight. When the tears finally slowed, I pulled back, hiccupping.

"I'm . . . I'm so sorry, I—"

He put a finger on my lips. "No. You do not get to apologize for this. You didn't ask to be left at a bus stop with barely a name to go with you. And you definitely didn't ask to be responsible for bringing that monster back. You can't cry over spilt milk, Phoebe. You have to find a way to make things right."

"But how? Damian's blind. Our friend Macario turned into a tree. And Angie's scared out of her mind."

"Not that scared, Katzy."

I turned around. Angie stood by Damian's side.

"And I'm not that blind," he added. He'd taken his bandage off. His eyes were raw and swollen but open. "I can almost see out of my left eye."

"Go," Carl said. "Get this guy and take him out. Don't listen to some prophecy. Just go be Phoebe Katz."

A wild thrill went through me at his words. Be Phoebe Katz? That I could do.

"What about Macario? We can't leave him here." What if someone turned him into firewood?

"I'll stay with him," Carl said. "I won't be much use in a fight anyway. But how will you get to Olympus?"

Angie put two fingers to her lips and whistled shrilly. "We have our own rides."

Carl grunted in surprise as our pegasuses appeared over the treetops.

We left Zesto behind with Carl. It was good to feel Argenta's silvery warm body underneath me. She gave me courage as she tossed her head at me over her shoulder. We flew over rolling hills, skimming the tops of trees. Mount Olympus stood out on the horizon. It had a flattish top, and snow clung to it like frosting. A rim of clouds encircled it.

"So where is this city of the gods?" I called to Damian. I couldn't see anything besides trees and snow.

"It's hidden behind the clouds," he said. "Each god has his own palace made of brass and gold. Zeus has the biggest one, of course. It's at the top of a hill."

We broke into the clouds. Swirls of mist and cold air surrounded us. The winged horses kept on, flying blindly. My clothes grew damp and clung to my skin. The mist thinned, and we burst out onto the other side. The gates of Olympus came into view.

The ornate solid gold gates might have been impressive at one time, but now they were a crumpled mess—as if some monster had torn them from their hinges, spitting out the pieces like broken bones in a graveyard. Smoke scarred the pylons that had held the gates in place. The fire had already burned out, leaving only charred remains of stumps. The road that led to the city was shrouded in smoke.

We walked the pegasuses through the gates. No one challenged us. In fact, there was no one around at all, as if the city had been abandoned.

"Where is everyone?" Damian asked.

"Don't know," I said. "Athena said they were scattered looking for me." *If only they had found me and stopped me*, I thought bitterly. Would have saved all this trouble.

"Ares wasn't kidding about destroying Olympus," Angie said. "It's like a nuclear bomb went off here."

Typhon had knocked down entire buildings, tumbled them to the ground. Chunks of rock and twisted metal littered the streets.

At the top of the hill, a temple stood unscarred. The sound of Typhon roaring echoed. That must be were the action was.

"Let's go on foot," I said. "I don't want Argenta and the others in the middle of this."

"Agreed," Damian said.

We walked past rubbled buildings. Partial names were legible on shattered stone. None of them made much sense until I saw ATHE- on a fallen piece of stone.

I stopped. "This must be Athena's palace."

"So? She was annoying," Angie said. "Way too bossy."

A groan floated out of the debris.

"There's someone in there!" I scrambled over crumbled metal and stone. A pair of legs wearing familiar golden sandals stuck out from under a fallen column. I peered over the top. "Athena!"

Her pale face was streaked in dust. "Phoebe, you shouldn't be here. I told you to stay away." Her voice was faint, weak.

"You should know by now I don't take orders well." I heaved up on the column pinning her, but it was too heavy. Even with all three of us, we couldn't budge it.

"Must you always be so stubborn?" A flicker of a smile crossed her face. "I do not wish to fight with you. You need to let the gods take care of this."

"Sorry, sis, there's no one else here. Where's Zeus?"

"In his palace. Ares stole his scepter, the source of his greatest power. He has Father in chains. I must get up there and help him." She struggled to sit up, but the column kept her pinned.

"We'll go," I said.

"No, it's too dangerous."

"I know." I grinned. "Wouldn't have it any other way." Before she could argue, we ducked out, leaving her to shout after us to come back.

We crept up the hill, keeping to the shadows of the buildings. At the top, a spectacular palace awaited. Massive pillars held a domed roof. An enormous set of metal doors hung half off their hinges, as if they had been ripped open.

We crept inside, darting behind a row of potted ferns, and crouched down. The room was lit by a trio of iron chandeliers. Twelve thrones sat arranged in a circle, and behind them was a small tiered seating area for observers.

The thrones were all empty save for one—the largest—made entirely of gold. Ares lounged on it, legs crossed. On his head he wore a flashy golden crown inset with glittering white diamonds shaped in jagged lightning bolts. In his right hand, he held a glowing scepter. It appeared made of radiant light with silver bands.

Behind him, Typhon lay sleeping, his massive head resting on his front claws. In the center of the room, a man knelt before Ares. He had thick white hair that fell to his broad shoulders and a snow-white beard that reached his chest. I couldn't see his face, just the side of it. His tunic was trimmed in fine gold, but his hands were chained in front of him, and both ankles were bound with loops of iron.

Zeus.

My father.

Angie gripped my elbow as I swayed on my feet.

"Isn't this a lovely sight," Ares said. "You kneeling before me. I've always wanted to see what you looked like from this angle."

The twins stood at either side of the throne, smirking alongside their father.

"Let us show him what fear is," Phobos said, his ice-blue eyes eager to cause pain.

"Yes, Father, we can break him and render him a drooling, puling, mindless thing," Deimos added in that lethal voice of his.

"Quiet!" Ares jammed the scepter into the ground. White lightning crackled around the top of it. "This isn't some demigod. This is Zeus, king of the gods. Your powers are useless on him. Save it for that offspring of his that is bound to follow."

They slunk back sullenly.

"Ares, it's not too late to stop this," Zeus said. "Send Typhon back from whence he came." His voice was deep, commanding, steady.

"It is too late. I rule this kingdom now. The son has overthrown the father, just as you overthrew yours and he overthrew his. History repeats itself."

"You'll never be able to hold on to the power, Ares. You're too angry and foolish. If your mother, Hera, were here, she'd be very disappointed."

"Would she? I thought it was you she was constantly disappointed in. Soon, every kingdom in this wretched place will bow down to me. You see, I made a deal with them up front. Nemea, freed from its lion, now kneels to me. Lerna, safe from its terrible hydra, is thankful to me. Argos, Thebes, Lycia. I arranged for all of them to be free of a wretched beast. Something you never did." Ares leaned back in the throne, kicking one leg over the other. "I'm the mighty god that saved them, and they'll show their thanks by swearing allegiance to me."

"The other Olympians will never stand for it," Zeus intoned.

Ares laughed. "The other Olympians are in chains. My army has imprisoned them. No one rides to your rescue. Only Athena, and I buried her in her palace. Soon my armies will spread across the waters, and history will be rewritten with me as the immortal leader."

Zeus laughed. "You've gotten too big for your britches, my son. I should have put you over my knee centuries ago. It is inevitable you will fail."

"What is inevitable is that you would give me a lecture," Ares shouted, leaping to his feet, "when I am the one on the throne wearing a crown, bearing your precious scepter."

Zeus cleared his throat. "You know, I never once wore that crown. I found it too showy." His chin tilted slightly in our direction, as if he knew we lurked in the shadows.

I frowned. *Zeus never wore the crown?*

My mind played back the original prophecy. *From the same womb as Perseus will she arise. To a mighty god she will be his demise, for she will bring the kingdom down in ruins round and round his crown.*

What had that retired oracle Phaea said? Prophecies aren't always straightforward. People hear what they want to hear. My heart raced. That was it! I was going to bring down a mighty god, all right. The one wearing the crown.

"Come on." I gripped Damian's arm. "I have an idea."

CHAPTER 39

We burst into Athena's ruined palace to find Hephaestus trying futilely to move the column.

"I know how to stop Ares," I announced.

Athena lifted her head, eyes glazed with pain. "What do you mean?"

I kneeled at her side. "The fate of Olympus rests on me saving it, not destroying it."

"How?"

I explained my theory.

"You think Ares read his prophecy wrong?" Athena's voice was loaded with skepticism.

"Yup. But I'll need your help."

She indicated the column pinning her legs. "How? I'm stuck here."

"Maybe I can help," a cheerful voice said. "Athena, I leave you alone for one day, and you let Olympus fall into ruins." A man with a thick sheaf of golden hair and sparkling blue eyes entered, crossing swiftly to Athena's side and lifting the column off her in one easy toss. He wore a golden tunic trimmed in white braid with a small sunburst on the shoulder. "And someone do please explain why the soldiers of Argos tried to throw me in prison."

"You're Apollo," I said, awestruck by the power that radiated from him.

His smile widened as he helped Athena up to sit on the fallen column. "So I am. And you're the one I've heard so much about. For the destroyer of Olympus, you look harmless enough."

"You have a son," I blurted out. "A really cool, amazing kid named Macario. He's done everything he can to impress you. He helped slay the Nemean lion and got us out of the underworld by trading his sun power to Hades."

Apollo blinked as the meaning hit home. "His mother was a tree nymph. Without his sun power—"

"He turns into a tree," I said.

Apollo looked guilt-stricken.

I turned to my sister. "Athena, I have to stop that monster."

Her eyes darkened. "Zeus wouldn't approve—"

"He would. He knows I'm here. I swear to you. Ares misread the prophecy. I am going to take him down. I just need a little help."

"How? Typhon is immortal. The only monster to ever defeat Zeus. What can you do to stop him?"

"I usually do something like this." I turned. "Damian, ideas?"

Everyone turned to stare at poor Damian. His face was red and raw, but his eyes were open.

He cleared his throat. "Right, you said this Typhon is immortal. That means we can't kill him. So we need to contain him."

Contain him. I liked the sound of that.

"There is no prison that can hold a monster like that," Athena scoffed. "And the Eye of Zeus is destroyed."

"No, wait." I had a thought. "Damian, remember what sun-brain said about the swamps where the hydra lived?"

"They're fed from Lake Lerna."

"Which he said was—"

"Bottomless." His eyes lit up. "Yes, that could work."

"What could work?" Athena asked.

"We lure Typhon to the lake, weigh him down, and sink him to the bottom," I said.

"There is no bottom," she said, confused.

"Exactly. Which means he would sink forever. Problem solved."

Hephaestus stepped forward. "The child has a good idea. I can make a snare if my lab isn't destroyed. I'll need Athena's help and Apollo's sun power to forge the metal quickly. Someone will have to lure Typhon there."

"We'll get him there," I said confidently.

"Phoebe, you can't do this alone," Athena said.

I smiled. "I won't be alone. I've got friends." I nodded at Damian and Angie. "You and Apollo go make the trap. After we take Ares down, we'll lead the monster to the lake. Meet us there at sunrise. Don't be late," I added. "I have a feeling we'll be short on time."

Athena looked slightly awestruck. "I never realized how much like Father you are. We won't be late, sister, I promise you." She lifted her bronzed helmet off and placed it on my head. "To help give you wisdom in battle." She unstrapped her chest armor and slipped it over Angie's shoulders. "This will protect you from the sharpest blade." To Damian, she gave her gleaming golden shield. "This is Aegis. It will defend you against many sorts of dangers."

This time, we led our pegasuses up the hill, leaving them outside the building for a quick exit.

"Ready?" I looked at Angie.

With her headband and Athena's armor, she looked like a warrior princess. She gripped the Nemean sword in one hand. "Oh, yeah. I'm ready to teach Typhon a lesson in manners."

"Ready for your job, D?"

Damian nodded, looking small behind the shield Athena had given him. "I'm ready. Just don't do anything too foolish."

"Foolish?" I flexed my fingers and called up a lightning bolt. "You know I can't promise that."

We huddled inside the entrance. Zeus lay facedown, his hands and legs splayed out, bound by the chains. Ares stood over him. In his hand he held the lightning scepter, the source of Zeus's great power according to Athena. It glowed like a living thing, as tall as Ares and tipped with a ball of energy. He jabbed the scepter in Zeus's back, causing the god to spasm as electrical current flowed through the staff.

The twins lounged feet up in a pair of thrones, looking bored. Typhon watched Zeus, his slitted eyes glowing with satisfaction.

Ares laughed. "Isn't this fun, Father? Typhon is enjoying watching you suffer. I've promised when I've finished, he can tear you limb from limb and scatter you across the world while I take your scepter and conquer every kingdom under me."

He raised the scepter again, prepared to jab Zeus with it, when we stepped through the pillars.

"Ares, your time is up."

I cocked my arm back and flung the lightning bolt forward, hoping to catch him off guard. He swung the end of the scepter up, batting my lightning away like a baseball. It exploded against the ceiling, sending sparks flying.

Typhon was on his feet, his tail crashing against a pillar. An ominous crack rang out.

"Angie, you and Damian—"

"On it," she said. "Here, monster, monster, come and eat me."

Typhon's tongue forked out at Angie as he crawled after her. She dodged between columns as Damian called out to the twins. "Hey, Phobos and Deimos, you don't scare me."

At Ares's nod, the pair stalked off toward Damian.

My odious half-brother paced in front of me, shaking his head. "Phoebe, you had your chance to let this go. Why don't you demigods ever learn? You're not the true heroes. It's the gods like me that live on forever."

"From now on, I'm pretty sure you're going to be living in Tartarus, or whatever dark hole Zeus sends you to."

He jumped forward, stabbing the scepter at me. Pure bolts of electricity shot out, aimed straight for my heart. I hit the ground, and the blast ricocheted off Athena's helmet, leaving me dazed but alive.

I rolled onto my feet, throwing another bolt at him. He swatted it away again and then blazed electric fire at the ceiling, knocking the iron chandelier down. I dove to the side, just missing being flattened. Before I could move, Ares stood over me, scepter pointed at my heart.

"Foolish child, you have no business trying to be a hero."

He thrust the scepter into my chest. It was as if I'd stuck my finger in the world's largest light socket. Pain radiated through every pore. I couldn't breathe. My heart rate slowed to a near stop. My strength faded. *This is it*, I thought. Ares wins.

His eyes were wild with anticipation as he thrust harder. But some part of me resisted. I had been fighting for the right to live since the day I was born. No way Ares was going to be the one to take that away.

With a stubborn force of will, I raised first my right hand and then my left from the stone floor. Slowly, I brought them toward the scepter.

Ares smirked. "Give it up, sister. Even now your life drains away. You are not immortal like I am. You can die."

Maybe so. But not today.

I clenched the scepter tight, taking in all the energy it put out. The shock arched me upward, but I refused to loosen my grip. Pulsating electricity ran through my veins. My teeth went numb as if I'd been dosed with Novocain. I had no feeling in my limbs. I felt my heart lock in my chest.

My head rolled to the side. My eyes met the blue eyes of Zeus across the room, where he lay in chains.

You are my daughter. Fight.

His lips didn't move, but it was as if he'd shouted them directly into my brain. Energy began to flow back into me. With a painful kick, my heart started to beat again.

I looked back up at Ares.

I was a child of Zeus.

My father had gifted me with the power to wield lightning.

Lightning couldn't kill me.

Ares caught on too late. He pulled back on the scepter, but it wouldn't budge.

He tugged harder, but I held it easily. I raised my knee and kicked him in the chest, shoving him backward and breaking his grip on the scepter.

I leaped to my feet and spun the scepter in a circle. "I may not be immortal, but I am gonna knock that silly crown off your head."

I swung the scepter, aiming for the fences. He grimaced

as the glowing tip made contact. His crown went flying, spinning across the floor.

Ares wasn't finished though. He drew his sword and brought it down on the scepter, splitting it in two, sending half of it head over tail across the room to embed in a column.

I held the broken end as we warily faced off.

"This can only end one way, Phoebe. With me victorious. You cannot kill me, so give it up. Your friends are about to be eaten by Typhon or destroyed by terror and fear. I have a date with my army. Are you going to chase me or save them?"

Angie's cries registered. I shot a quick glance her way. Typhon had her pinned down behind the thrones. I couldn't see Damian, but his moans were getting louder.

With my attention divided, Ares pounced. The tip of his sword pierced my rib cage and went in deep. The breath went out of me as pain blossomed.

I gasped, looking down in horror.

His eyes glinted as he drew the blade out, dragging agony through me. "See you later, sister." He whistled shrilly, and a black pegasus with a white diamond on its forehead landed with a clatter of hooves.

I stumbled. One hand went to the wound. My fingers felt slippery. A dizzy spell hit me as I looked at the crimson stain on them.

Ares leaped on his pegasus and took flight, circling overhead with a triumphant grin before winging into the sky.

I forced myself to move, picking up the broken scepter and searching for the other piece. There. Stuck in the pillar. I tugged it out, holding the pieces in each hand.

Damian first.

I followed the sound of his moans. Damian was crouched behind Athena's shield, using it to ward off the fear and terror sent his way by the twins. It had sounded like a good idea on our walk up here, but he was clearly losing. His face was sweaty and pale, his eyes unfocused as a keening moan escaped his lips.

I staggered behind the twins. They were so focused on destroying Damian's mind, they didn't hear me. I stuck the broken ends of the scepter into their backs, digging them in hard and firm. They jerked, trying to turn, but I kicked out the backs of their knees, taking them down to the ground, forcing the raw, blistering power deep into their sides.

As they writhed and twisted, Damian stood, taking an unsteady step forward. He smashed Athena's shield down on one head and then the other, knocking the twins out cold.

"Nice work," I said, fighting a wave of lightheadedness.

"A little help here, Katzy," Angie yelled.

I looked at the glowing broken pieces in my hands. I brought the ends together, holding tight as the two ends mended. A dazzling light flared, making me blink, and the scepter was whole again.

Typhon was wrecking columns left and right as he chased after Angie. She was like a mouse, avoiding capture because she was so small and fast, but she was running out of hiding spots. Cracks in the ceiling were spreading. The whole place might come down if Typhon took out any more columns.

I blinked away the black spots behind my eyes. "Hey!" I called out. "Come and get me, you butt-ugly dinosaur."

Typhon swiveled its scaly green head toward me, belching out a blazing trail of fire that burned straight for us. Damian knelt in front of me, holding up Athena's shield.

We crouched behind it, feeling the searing heat of the flames roll over us.

When it stopped, Angie raced to our side. "How do we lead this dinosaur to the bottomless lake?"

"We need it to follow us," I said. "And I know the perfect bait. Damian, get the pegasuses ready. Angie, distract Typhon. I'll get Zeus. On the count of three . . ."

Damian gave Angie his shield and made a run for the exit. Angie charged, holding the shield up to fend off the flames Typhon roared at her. She got close enough to stab Typhon in the foot. The beast roared in pain, sending her flying backward as he swept his paw at her.

My turn.

With a swing of the scepter, I cut the chains binding Zeus and put my arms underneath him, helping him to his feet.

"Leave me here," he groaned.

"Nope, sorry, you're the bait this time." I helped him outside, where Damian waited. Argenta lowered her head and he climbed on. I hauled myself up as Angie came running.

"Time to go," she said, leaping on Nero's back.

The temple exploded in a shower of crumbled rock as Typhon broke free from the palace, tearing down the last of the pillars so that the ceiling crumpled into dust. We took to the sky, winging away as Typhon gave pursuit.

I held on to Argenta's mane, wondering if I was crazy.

"Yes, probably," Zeus said, as if I had spoken aloud. "You just destroyed my palace. But then, you are my daughter."

I caught a sense of pride in his voice. It made me forget for a moment the cold spreading through my veins from the wound in my side.

Typhon screeched, belching fire. Warm flames rolled toward us. I searched for a flicker of my power, but it was spent. Zeus swung his leg over Argenta and turned around backward. With his powerful lungs, he blew the stream of fire backward so that it engulfed Typhon, making the monster scream in rage.

"You'll feel much worse before I'm through with you," Zeus taunted. He turned back around. "So, daughter, where are we headed?"

I quickly gasped out our plan—we had to give Athena time to get to Lerna with the chains that would bind Typhon, which meant we would have to fly all night and keep Typhon close. But not too close.

"Head south," Zeus said. "I don't have my full strength yet, but I'll keep him engaged."

Our agile pegasuses flew hard, staying just out of reach, leading Typhon on a merry chase over the dark countryside. Zeus guided me, sending bolts of lightning at Typhon when he got too close, taunting him with threats and jeers. It worked to keep Typhon enraged and furiously giving chase.

The moon was a beacon in the sky, casting a white glow over us. I passed out at one point, opening my eyes to see the pink edges of the sun begin to crawl over the horizon. A murky bog came into view below. We passed over the hulking carcass of the hydra. And then we zoomed over a wide body of blue water.

The bottomless lake.

I gripped the glowing scepter in hands that had grown cold.

We had to hope Athena was waiting. That she had the trap ready.

I pressed a hand to my side, looking down at the sticky blood on my fingers.

We needed a miracle.

CHAPTER 40

A mist clung to the surface of the lake as we flew over it. A small trail of smoke made its way up through the trees at the shore. Fingers crossed that was our signal.

"Stay clear," I shouted, waving Angie and Damian off. They peeled away as I urged Argenta lower. The moment I shifted course, Typhon followed. Argenta panted heavily, her body streaked with sweaty foam. "Just a few more minutes, girl," I whispered, rubbing her neck.

Athena stepped out of the trees. A strange weapon sat on the shore—some kind of giant crossbow mounted on a stand. Where were the chains to bind Typhon? Did Athena think a spear was going to bring this beast down?

She moved behind the weapon and drew back on the bow.

As we passed over, she let the bow loose. I twisted around to see. The spear whistled through the air aimed straight at the monster. Typhon saw the danger and rolled on his side. The spear flew harmlessly past him. But it made the beast angry enough to give up on Zeus.

He landed with a large splash on the lake's shore and bellowed his rage, blanketing the shore with scorching fire.

Athena!

I looked on in horror as flames engulfed the spot where she had been standing.

And then over the treetops, two massive griffins soared, carrying a net between their beaks made of metal mesh and barbed hooks. The oversized eagles dropped the net over Typhon. The beast launched itself in the air, but its wings were tangled, and it crashed on the shore.

Athena rose unscathed from behind the charred crossbow, shedding a heavy cloak. A battalion of men began dragging a thick chain from out of the trees. As Typhon thrashed, they hooked the chain to the net, cinching it tighter around him.

"Turn back," Zeus said. "We have to drag Typhon into the center of the lake."

Given that the monster must weigh two tons, I didn't see how we were going to manage that, but I turned Argenta. Athena stood on shore, swinging the chain. She let it loose and it soared into the air. Zeus snatched the end, wrapping it around his fist. It snapped tight, nearly unseating us both. Argenta struggled to fly forward but she didn't have the strength. The griffins landed on Typhon, gripping the netting with their claws, and flapped their broad wings.

Still not enough.

Angie flew past on Nero, reaching a hand out to grasp Athena's arm. She pulled her up behind her. Damian followed suit, and Apollo leaped onto the back of Albert. Each of them held a section of chain.

Typhon roared, fighting at the mesh binding him.

"Use your wind, child," Zeus commanded. "The scepter will give it a boost."

I gathered my powers, head dizzy as I conjured the word. What was it? My mind was fuzzy.

Then I remembered.

"*Anemos!*"

I thrust the scepter in the air. A massive gust of wind lifted the pegasuses' wings, sending us forward. Typhon roared and thrashed, knocking us every which way as we headed for the center of the lake. Wind roared in my ears. My hand grew numb holding the staff as its power throbbed through me.

The water was a deep blue below when Zeus gave the signal to drop the chain. The griffins peeled away, as did the other two pegasuses.

Typhon flailed, trying to free his wings, but the hooks dug deeper into his flesh as he struggled. He hit the water with an enormous splash that sent a wave of water into the air. He lunged upward, snatching at us with his jaws, but the weight of the chains pulled him back. He lunged again, belching out fire. I rolled Argenta to the side, narrowly avoiding the flames.

And then Typhon began to sink, lower and lower until only his snout remained. The water churned and frothed, and then the last bit of him disappeared from view.

Argenta soared high, banking over the churning water as cheers went up from the shore. I tried to raise my fist in a victory sign, but a curious weakness made me dizzy. I couldn't quite breathe. I blinked away the dark spots dancing behind my eyes. "I can't . . . it's just—"

"Phoebe?" My father's voice sounded concerned, as if he cared. As if the one who had sent me away, who had never wanted me, actually cared.

It sent a sliver of warmth through the cold that leached into every pore. I clung to that warmth as I drifted away into a deep black nothingness.

CHAPTER 41

"**P**hoebe, wake up. Phoebes, come on, stop playing dead."

Water splashed in my face and I sputtered. My limbs felt weak and detached from my body.

"Just let me die," I croaked.

"You're not going to die," Angie said, thrusting her face into mine.

I blinked. "But Ares stabbed me."

"Yeah, well, apparently being the demigod you are, all you needed was a taste of ambrosia. Luckily, Athena had some on her, so knock it off."

I sat up in a fog. I had been so sure I was dying. I blinked again, clearing my vision. The wound in my side throbbed. I put a hand to it. There was already a rough scab over it.

Zeus kneeled next to me, a twinkle in his eye.

"So, daughter, we officially meet at last."

I didn't know what to say. This was Zeus. The king of the gods.

Dad.

I flung my arms around his neck. "I'm so glad you're okay."

He patted my back. "And I am so glad that you saved me. Just as the oracle predicted."

I pulled back. "But I thought I was the destroyer of Olympus. That's why you sent me away."

"Things here are always more complicated than they appear. The oracle told me Ares was going to betray me one day and that I would lose. There was nothing to be done. I prepared for the inevitable. Then she returned to me in secret and told me of a new prophecy she had received, one that gave me hope. An unborn daughter would one day stop Ares. If Ares had discovered that, you would have been dead before your first birthday. I had to make him believe you were a threat to me, not him, which is why I sent you away. To protect you until you were old enough to handle the challenge."

"You could have protected me here."

He shrugged. "Possible. But I couldn't be certain. Secrets are hard to keep in a place like this. The oracle who gave me the prophecy left with you to safeguard Ares from ever discovering it."

I frowned. "She didn't stick around long. Why give me the Eye of Zeus? Was that part of the prophecy, for me to bring Typhon back?"

He barked with laughter. "No. I did it to keep it out of Ares's hands. I had no idea you would complete it on your own, but it all turned out splendid, did it not?"

"We let Ares escape," I reminded. "And Typhon still lives. Those chains won't hold him forever."

Zeus sighed. "That is the way things are here, child. A never-ending cycle of misery. Get used to it." He stood up. Damian and Angie helped me to my feet.

"May I?" He pointed at the scepter still clutched in my hand.

I loosened my grip and handed it to him. He planted it in the ground, sending out a bolt of light that split the air, opening a jagged crack in space. Through the crack, the Erinyes appeared, carrying Ares between them.

They threw him on the ground in front of us.

Zeus stood over him. "Ares, my worthless son, you have broken the laws of Olympus. For that you will be punished."

"Where are you sending me?" Ares asked.

"Someplace where you'll learn your lesson."

"Tartarus?" He paled, dropping to his knees and grasping Zeus's hands. "No, Father, I beg you. I am sorry. I was overcome with that stupid prophecy. I thought it was meant to be. The way of our world. But I can change."

"No. You can't." Zeus sighed. "And you will spend the next two millennia in the black depths of Tartarus thinking of what you have done. Perhaps then you will repent, and we can discuss a reprieve."

"Two millennia?" Ares's eyes darkened. "You can't be serious. My armies will rise against you. They will tear down the gates of Olympus again and again until I am freed."

"Your armies?" Zeus laughed. "Did you really think the king of Argos would take your side over mine? I still haven't let him forget he put a son of mine in a box and set him adrift. And the Nemean king is less than happy your champion burned his city down. I'm afraid, Ares, you're going to learn that war solves nothing. My sentence is that you will wake up each day and launch your battle, and each day you will lose, only to wake up the next day and fight the same battle until you learn the futility of war."

Ares looked stricken. "That is torment. I will not survive."

"You will," Zeus said. "Come, we cannot delay. I must deliver you to my brother myself. It's been an eternity since we caught up."

"Wait," I said. "We have business with Hades. Let us come."

"Phoebe, the underworld is no place for children."

"Hades has something that belongs to a friend, and I intend to get it back," I said firmly.

"If you are certain."

"We are," Angie said. "Macario is our friend."

"I'm coming too," Apollo said. "I wish to make things right with my son."

"Don't think I'm staying behind," Athena said with a grin.

Zeus thrust his scepter into the ground, and a massive crack opened up in the earth, forging a set of stairs that led down into darkness. No flying across the seas to a river for Zeus. He had his own private all-access pass.

Zeus led the way, carrying the glowing scepter. We stepped out onto the lawn in front of Hades's mansion. The river wended its way the same, but everything looked golden and rosy with the glowing sunbeams that hung in the sky.

Cerberus guarded the gates, growling at the sight of us. His tail was stubby, but I could see a new tip growing.

Zeus ignored the mutt and cupped a hand to his mouth. "Hades, I have a guest for you."

The front door to the mansion creaked open, and a familiar figure appeared.

"Brother, it has been an age," Hades said in that dusty voice of his. His face betrayed no emotion, but his eyes glinted with something like pleasure.

Alekto shoved Ares forward. "Father, he has broken the sacred laws of Olympus. He is to spend two millennia in Tartarus."

Hades tipped his head at her, and the Erinyes lifted Ares, dragging him away. I could still hear his screams after they'd disappeared into a dark hole that opened in the front lawn.

"What have you done with this place?" Zeus said. "All this light rather hurts the eyes, doesn't it?"

"I want my son's powers back," Apollo demanded. "You tricked him out of his sunbeams."

Hades flicked a piece of lint off the sleeve of his robe. "I did nothing of the sort. He traded it willingly."

Apollo's eyes blazed with rage as he took a step forward, getting up into Hades's face. "Thief."

Hades's eyes glowed an ominous shade of red. "Spoiled brat."

The air was thick with power, as if any moment one of them was going to explode with it.

"Enough!" Zeus chided. "Brother, tell me you don't really want all this sunshine. You look terrible, almost healthy with that tan."

Hades hesitated, then shrugged. "It does get a bit annoying at times. Too bright for my eyes. I suppose I could return it on one condition."

"What?" I said. "Anything."

Damian elbowed me. "Never say that to the dark lord of the underworld."

"Fine, anything within reason," I amended.

"My brother must agree to spend one day a year here. It gets lonely," Hades added.

Zeus tilted his head in agreement. "It is not something you should have to ask for. I will be happy to visit yearly— if not more."

Hades thrust his bony fist at the sky, closing his eyes. The sunbeams returned to his hand in golden slivers. The place went back to its gloomy visage. He held the glowing beam out to Apollo.

Apollo clasped it, tucking it into his belt, and bowed his head. "My thanks, Hades. I am in your debt."

We left then, quickly returning to the surface with the help of Zeus's scepter.

Our pegasuses were tired but happily flew us north again to where Carl waited on the beach watering the tree, which had grown an inch or two.

"Phoebe, is that you?" Macario's face appeared in the trunk.

I slipped off Athena's helmet, tucking it under my arm, and grinned. "Yeah, it's me."

"And me, sun-brain," Angie said.

"And me," Damian added. "You look good as a tree."

"Thanks," he said. "It's not so bad."

"So you don't want your sunbeam back?" Apollo said, stepping forward. "You've earned it, after all."

"Father?" Macario's eyes turned into round knots. "Is it really you?"

"Yes, and I've been a fool. I should have taken you under my wing long ago. Now, if you don't mind, I'm going to return this to you. That is, unless you want to continue being a tree. I would understand."

Macario's eyes blinked. "No. I mean, I loved my mother, but being a tree is boring. I would very much like to be a demigod again."

"Then hold on." Apollo took the sunbeam and sank it into the trunk. Light flared out in a golden blaze. When we blinked, Macario stood there, looking shocked as he took in his human limbs and feet, wiggling his toes in the sand.

"I'm a boy again. It worked!"

I hugged him, followed by Angie and Damian. When we stepped back, Macario looked at his father.

"I'm sorry," Apollo began, "I should have been a better father—"

But Macario rushed forward, throwing his arms around Apollo's waist.

"It's okay, Papa. You need to hear the stories. Did you hear I killed the hydra of Lerna? And the Nemean lion bowed down to me."

Apollo laughed, ruffling his hair. "I can't wait to hear all your tales."

"Hey, kid, we need to find a way home." Carl's brown eyes rested on me. His mustache ruffled in the breeze.

Behind him, Angie and Damian huddled together, saying nothing, but I could see the homesickness in their eyes.

"You can stay, child," Zeus said, "if that is what you wish. The prophecy has been fulfilled. There will always be more threats, but for now, this place holds no danger to you."

I hesitated, torn. I really wanted to return to Seriphos to talk to my mother and visit with Perseus. But Damian and Angie were looking at me as if I was tearing them apart. And Carl. They were my family too.

"I have to go back."

"I understand." Zeus squeezed my shoulder. "Do you know I named you Phoebe because it means a bright and shining light? You will always be that to me."

Athena stepped forward and clasped me in a hug. "Oh, sister, I'm sorry we didn't have more time together. Just know, I am always watching over you. There will be another time for us to meet, I promise you."

I hugged her back, deciding I liked this big sister of mine. "This belongs to you," I said, passing her golden helmet back. "Ares would have taken my head off without it, so thanks."

Angie lifted Athena's golden armor off and handed it back, along with the shield of Aegis. "Yeah, I'm pretty sure this saved my life, like, three different times. Sorry it's got some scratches on it. That Typhon really wanted a piece of me."

"My brain would have been turned to mush without your shield," Damian said. "It's strange how you gave us each exactly what we needed."

"Strange indeed," she said with a warm smile.

Macario stood off to the side, scuffing at the ground with his sandal. His eyes were bright with tears, but he blinked them away as we encircled him.

"Sun-brain, I'm going to miss you," I said, giving him a hug.

"Me too," Angie said, wrapping her arms around us. "You've kind of grown on me."

Damian joined in, so we were wrapped in a giant hug.

"I'll miss all of you too," he said, gulping. "I will count the days until we have another adventure."

"It is time, children."

Zeus stood waiting on the sand, lightning scepter in hand.

I swiped away my tears and ruffled Macario's hair. "Stay out of trouble."

"I'll try, but you know me."

We said goodbye to our pegasuses. I hated to leave Argenta, but I whispered in her ear I would be back to visit.

I climbed onto the battered carriage. Pepper pawed the ground excitedly, as if she knew what was coming. Carl and Damian piled into the back. Angie sat up front next to me.

"What now?" I said to my father.

"Now you go home." Zeus slapped his hand on Pepper's rear, and the horse took off. The last thing I saw was Macario waving goodbye. Pepper winged up into the sky as a bolt of lightning cut through the clouds, and we disappeared into a shimmering hole.

CHAPTER 42

The carriage rolled to a halt on a darkened street in the middle of Central Park. Pepper tossed her head in the air as her wings folded into her sides and disappeared. She whinnied sadly as she cocked an eye at her wingless self. We climbed down, all of us tired to the bone.

I rubbed Pepper's nose. "We had quite an adventure, didn't we?" She nudged me back before trotting off eagerly, no doubt looking for her owner and her bucket of oats. We waved goodbye and began walking out of the park.

Angie and Damian were arguing about what they wanted to do first—eat a whole pizza or take a hot shower.

I got quieter and quieter. I knew my fate. I was being shipped out of state. I didn't expect that had changed because the threat to Olympus was over. Paperwork was paperwork.

We got to the subway that would take Carl to Brooklyn. Damian lived two blocks away. He gave us hugs and headed off, breaking into a run. Angie hailed a cab. I hugged her one last time. "See you at school," she said before diving inside and slamming the door.

I stood alone, uncertain. Angie must have forgotten I wasn't going back to Dexter.

Carl stood at the entry to the subway. "What are you waiting for, kid?"

I shrugged. "I got nowhere to go."

"You live with me now, didn't you hear?"

My breath hitched. "Hear what?"

He walked toward me, hands thrust into his pockets. "I figured I should just adopt you, you know, save the state the trouble of finding a suitable family since there's no one lining up to take care of you."

A sliver of hope ran through me. "Do you mean it? Don't say it if you don't mean it."

He gave another shrug. "I figure we could give it a go. I've never raised a kid before. I'm not really sure how it works. And I've got two cats, Maxwell and Frank, that have to approve. If they say it's okay, I can work on the official paperwork."

His brown eyes were warm as they looked into mine.

I threw my arms around him, hugging him tight. "You're going to regret this, you know. I can't always control my powers. I could burn down your house if I'm not careful."

He sighed. "I know one thing, it's not going to be boring. Let's go over a couple of rules."

"Rules? I don't do well with rules." I hooked my arm in his as he led me down the stairs.

"First off, none of that fancy lightning stuff in the house. It scares the cats."

Carl nattered on, but I wasn't really listening.

I had a home of my own. After twelve long years of waiting, I had a family. I was a daughter of Zeus. I had brothers and sisters galore.

I wasn't some freak. I was a demigod. And it was awesome.

I almost called up a lightning bolt, thinking how cool it would be to fire it off into the dark subway tunnel, but one look from Carl and I let my hand relax, tucking it into his arm instead and resting my head on his shoulder.

Yeah, I could get used to this.

THE END

From the Author

Dear Reader:

I hope you enjoyed reading *The Eye of Zeus*! After so many years writing about Norse mythology with my *Witches of Orkney* and *Legends of Orkney*™ series, I was so excited to share a story set in Ancient Greece. I loved creating a strong female protagonist in the sassy Phoebe Katz and hope you enjoyed reading about her as much as I did writing her story.

As an author, I love to get feedback from my fans letting me know what you liked about the book, what you loved about the book, and even what you didn't like. You can write me at PO Box 1475, Orange, CA 92856, or e-mail me at author@alaneadams.com. Visit me on the web at www.alaneadams.com and learn about starting a book club with my free book club journals, or invite me to visit your school to talk about reading!

Look for more adventures with Phoebe, Damian and Angie as they face new challenges and monsters in the next installment coming April 2021.

Keep reading!

—Alane Adams

ABOUT THE AUTHOR

Alane Adams is an author, professor, and literacy advocate. She is the author of the award-winning Legends of Orkney and Witches of Orkney fantasy mythology series for tweens and award-winning *The Coal Thief*, *The Egg Thief*, *The Santa Thief*, and *The Circus Thief* picture books for early-grade readers. She lives in Southern California.

Author photo © Melissa Coulier/Bring Media

SELECTED TITLES FROM SPARKPRESS

SparkPress is an independent boutique publisher delivering high-quality, entertaining, and engaging content that enhances readers' lives, with a special focus on female-driven work. www.gosparkpress.com

The Blue Witch: The Witches of Orkney, Book One, Alane Adams. $12.95, 978-1-943006-77-9. Nine-year-old Abigail Tarkana has a problem: her witch magic has finally come in, but it's different—and being different is a problem at the Tarkana Witch Academy. Together with her scientist-friend Hugo, she face off against sneevils, shreeks, and vikens in a race to discover the secrets about her mysterious magic.

The Rubicus Prophecy: Witches of Orkney, Book 2, Alane Adams. $12.95, 978-1-943006-98-4. As Abigail enters her second year at the Tarkana Witch Academy, she is up to her ears studying for Horrid Hexes and Awful Alchemy. But when an Orkadian warship arrives carrying troubling news, Abigail and Hugo are swept into a puzzling mystery when they help a new friend go after a missing item—one that might spell the end of everything they know.

The House Children: A Novel, Heidi Daniele. $16.95, 978-1-943006-94-6. A young girl raised in an Irish industrial school accidentally learns that the woman she spends an annual summer holiday with is her birth mother.

The Circus Thief, Alane Adams. $15, 978-1-943006-75-5. The circus is in town and Papa has agreed to let Georgie go! Georgie and his friend Harley marvel at the elephants and clowns, as well as the best act of all—the amazing Roxie, a trained horse that can do all sorts of tricks—but when Georgie is allowed to ride on her back, he discovers Roxie is in trouble!

Reading is Fun! Imagine That!: Book One, Ruth A. Radmore. $19.95, 978-1-943006-38-0. The first installment in a new educational activities series designed to help children expand their creativity and improve their reading and language skills, *Reading is Fun! Imagine That!* is a collection of children's story-poems that encourage children to respond by creating artworks and writings using their own ideas.

ABOUT SPARKPRESS

SparkPress is an independent, hybrid imprint focused on merging the best of the traditional publishing model with new and innovative strategies. We deliver high-quality, entertaining, and engaging content that enhances readers' lives. We are proud to bring to market a list of *New York Times* best-selling, award-winning, and debut authors who represent a wide array of genres, as well as our established, industry-wide reputation for creative, results-driven success in working with authors. SparkPress, a BookSparks imprint, is a division of SparkPoint Studio LLC.

Learn more at GoSparkPress.com